Other Titles By
Dyanne Davis

Another Man's Baby

Dyanne Davis

Parker Publishing, LLC

Noire Passion is an imprint of Parker Publishing, LLC.

Copyright © 2008 by Dyanne Davis

Published by Parker Publishing, LLC
12523 Limonite Avenue, Suite #440-438
Mira Loma, California 91752
www.parker-publishing.com

ISBN 978-1-60043-026-8

First Edition

Manufactured in the United States of America

Another Man's Baby

Chapter One

Blood covered her as screams filled the air and explosions reverberated around her. Gabrielle Jackson was trembling, drenched in sweat. She shrieked and tears poured from her eyes. "No, no, no," she shouted, "please, God, no. Eric, watch out!"

She woke but the dream didn't stop. The pictures sped by in her mind's eye as though she were watching a movie.

Eric was going to die. Gabi saw the truck loaded with explosives barreling toward the soldiers and screamed out to God to send an angel to protect her husband. "Please, God," she prayed, "don't let him die, I'll do anything, just ask. Please, Father, put out Your hand, touch Eric, save him." Then she saw the truck hit the barricade, heard the explosion and she fell back on her bed.

Trembling fear claimed her. "Eric," she called, "it's okay, baby." She visualized him there with her, in her arms, and wrapped her arms around her own body, imagining the feel of him. She drew in a breath and felt the quake down to her soul. She wouldn't allow him to die, not without knowing how very much she loved him. She pressed her lips to the nothingness and could swear she felt Eric's lips against her own.

"Have faith."

Startled, Gabi turned. She looked around but no one was there. She wasn't going crazy, that much she knew. She'd heard a voice. *Have faith in what?* she thought. It wasn't like she'd ever had much. She'd never had a reason to have faith. Life had dealt her a bad hand. Orphaned at three, raised in several foster homes, why would there be miracles waiting for her?

"Why wouldn't there be?" the voice asked loud and clear, making her remember. This wasn't the first time Gabi had heard the voice in her

mind. It had just been so many years since she'd last heard it that it'd taken her by surprise.

She had to admit there was a time when, despite her circumstances, she'd had faith. One of her foster mothers had taken her to church, had convinced Gabi that she had a guardian angel, that she would never be alone no matter what the situation. For years Gabi had believed that. When she married Eric she'd sort of let the belief in her guardian angel fall by the wayside.

Now once again she found herself in need of an angel, an angel that she desperately wanted to watch over her husband.

A feeling of calm settled around her. "Eric." She said his name aloud. "Have faith, my guardian angel will protect you." She looked across the room at the framed wedding picture and went for it. "Have faith, baby," she said to Eric's image. "You're coming home to me, we're going to have everything we've always wanted, our family. Baby, we're going to have our family, just hold on. Be careful, Eric, be careful."

He was buried to the hilt inside Gabi's wet warmth. As she moaned her pleasure Eric allowed his hands to slowly trail over his wife's body. "Gabi, I love you," he whispered into her ear.

"Lieutenant!"

Blinking, Eric shook away the image of his wife. Their lovemaking had been yet another daydream. He wasn't home, he was in Iraq fighting a war. His gun raised, Eric hesitated for a tenth of a second. He looked to his left, then his right, and saw his men waiting for his orders. The truck was barreling toward them, loaded with explosives. Eric's skin crawled with the knowing. And just like that the world slowed down and everything happened in slow motion. *"Eric, baby, be careful, look out."* He thought for a moment he was dreaming. It was Gabi's voice in his head. Then he heard another voice. *"Have faith."*

"Gabi," he whispered, hesitating again, "Gabi, baby, I love you." Then he fired his rifle and kept firing, ordering his men to move, take cover.

"There are explosives in that truck," Eric yelled. "We've got to stop it, but be careful."

His weapon was still firing when he felt a hand on the base of his spine. He didn't have time to look behind him, he had to stop the truck. The hand on the base of his spine shoved him with what seemed to Eric to be superhuman strength and his last shot went wild. It was as though he'd been propelled by the explosives.

Eric could see the truck still coming. Then there was the flash of an explosion and he heard the screams. He tried to move under the sudden weight on top of him. He dared a quick glance and was repulsed by the blood and mangled bodies.

Panic welling in him, he pushed the bodies off him. Then he realized he felt a comforting touch. He felt Gabi's hand wrap around him, heard her whisper again in his ear to be careful, that she loved him. He shivered. He must be dying. He couldn't die, not now. What would happen to his wife, to the babies he'd promised to give her?

"*Have faith,*" he heard the other voice whisper to him for the second time. Then the scent of sugar cookies filled his nostrils, Gabi's scent. That was impossible. He was dying, he thought, he had to be, and Gabrielle was the last thought on his mind.

It was okay, he could die with that. "I love you, Gabi," he kept repeating. Then it occurred to him that he felt no pain. He'd never known how death would feel, but this wasn't so bad, nothing hurt. That surprised him, especially that with so much blood that there was no pain.

All at once he was aware of the pandemonium around him. Screams, soldiers running, shots.

"Lieutenant, Lieutenant Jackson, you okay?"

Eric blinked. "I don't know," he answered. He glanced at his blood-soaked uniform as two soldiers pulled him away from the debris. They began ripping at his clothes.

"I think you're okay, sir. The blast must have thrown you clear."

"But the blood…" Suddenly Eric knew. It was the blood of his men, his friends, saturating him. He could even taste the blood in the back of his throat. Whose hand had pushed him away?

For a second Eric stared at the soldier. "It wasn't the blast. I felt someone's hand. A soldier must have shoved me from behind."

"Sir, I was behind you, no one was there. You were firing at the truck. You got the driver but his foot had been tied to the gas pedal to make sure he couldn't stop, even if dead, but you got him, sir."

"How many of our men?"

"I'm not sure right now. Several men were injured. I think three or four died but you stopped it from being more."

Eric looked up into the face of the soldier talking to him, knowing he had to get himself together. He was a marine; he had to behave like an officer. "Thanks," he said, accepting the hand offered and standing. He glanced at his bloodied shirt lying on the ground, bent and picked it up and balled it in his hand.

Even now he could feel Gabrielle's arms around him. He could smell her. The touch of her lips pressed against him so strongly that he couldn't stop the shudder that claimed his body. *Gabi, you're going to get me and my men killed*, he thought. *Stop it.*

He took in a couple of deep breaths, his head bent over, his hands on his knees. When he could no longer feel his wife's arms around him, he moved. But the hand on the base of his spine remained where it was, only now the pressure was gentle, as though guiding him.

"*Have faith*," the voice whispered again as Eric went to survey the damage. Order existed amidst the chaos. They were marines and had been trained to take care of things like this.

He looked at each body laid out and dropped down beside his friend Bo. Eric angrily wiped the tears that filled his eyes. Damn it, he was a marine, he wouldn't cry. But more tears fell.

It was then that he wondered if any of them would make it home alive. What the hell were they doing so far away from home, dying. Were they doing any good? he wondered. Then he took a deep breath and barked orders. That was his job. Lieutenant Eric Jackson was a marine, an officer. Eric would not break down; that wasn't what his men needed. In order to keep them alive he had to do his job.

Someone handed him a clean shirt and he put it on, wondering if his moment's hesitation had caused this. He shuddered hard. His mind had been on his wife, on his making love to her. The world had slowed down as it always did when he thought of her. Thoughts of Gabi never failed to take him from the harsh reality of the war they were fighting. He only permitted himself that luxury when things were quiet, when it was safe to do so. Things had been quiet when he'd allowed his mind free rein to think of his wife. A couple of minutes were all he'd intended to take. He'd thought it safe to do so.

Another hard shudder ripped through him. Was he responsible for all of this? He looked down at his bloodied shirt on the ground, blinking. The blood of his men saturated that shirt. He wouldn't dishonor them by tossing the shirt aside. He picked the shirt up. "Take this to my quarters." He handed the shirt over to the private, still wondering if his thinking of Gabrielle had caused this. If his mind hadn't been on his wife, would things have been different?

Eric loaded his gear into the truck for the ride to the airstrip. He could hardly believe he was leaving, finally. He took a final look around the American base in the green zone. He'd never forget this place or this time in his life.

A little ways off he saw one of Saddam's palaces. There were more than enough riches in Iraq to share, but only the leaders lived in luxury. Most existed in abject poverty. Eric saw no need for such a division. But that was the way it was, even in America. The rich got richer and the poor, poorer.

He took another look around, his gaze staying for a moment on the soldiers dressed in PT gear instead of body armor. They were still heavily strapped, each man loaded to the nines, but this base was thought to be relatively secure. The green zone was one of the few places the men got to shed some of the gear. Between the arid heat and the heavy gear it was a wonder more men weren't falling from dehydration.

He sighed and pulled his gaze away. The soldiers manner of dress didn't matter. They were still in a war. Their weapons gave testimony to that. Sliding his hand upward Eric ran his hand over his own gear. In a war zone a soldier was never without his weapons. It could mean the difference between life and death. In a war zone a soldier always remained alert. A wave of guilt washed over him and settled heavily on his shoulders.

Eric glanced at the huge pool that had been built in front of the palace and almost wished he had time to take a swim. The oppressive heat made his clothes stick to him, and a fine sheen of dust coated his skin, never seeming to go away, no matter what. When he got home he would kiss his wife a thousand times for her never ending supply of wet wipes.

Home, he thought, Gabi. He'd missed her so much this past year, had yearned for her touch. Her voice was always bittersweet when he managed a call to her. Her emails were filled with news, things that didn't matter, that were passed on in order for him not to feel removed from her life. She'd done a good job with that. If only she'd found a way to package her scent, her touch. Eric smiled. He was going home.

Without warning another pang of guilt hit him. Eric did his best to push it away. He'd done the job he'd been ordered to do. He'd done his best. In the four months since the truck had crashed through their defenses, Eric had replayed and replayed the scene in his mind, second-guessing his actions. But no matter how much he replayed it, he couldn't change the outcome. The higher-ups had praised him for his quick thinking, and pinned another medal on him. Yet Eric wondered. There were times he could still feel the hand on his back which had propelled him away from the danger.

A tremor began and Eric shook his head, ordering it to go away. As much as he'd dreamed of this moment, he didn't want to leave any of his men behind. He hated looking into the eyes of those left behind. There was always a look of longing, of regret, of fear. He was sure he'd had that same look many times when others said goodbye to him and left for the safety of home, but now on this end of it, it was hard.

This was Eric's third tour of duty, the longest yet, an entire year. Now he would be stateside. Some of his men had been in Iraq for weeks, some for months. Still others were on their second tour. The duration of their time there hadn't mattered. The moment they landed on Iraqi soil an instant bonding took place, friendships that would last a lifetime, if the soldiers survived the war.

With a sigh Eric pasted a smile on his face. It was time to leave. He shook hands, joked, said the usual things and inside he thought, *'Take care of yourself, be safe, come home.'*

A terrific shudder passed through the plane. Eric blinked, wondering what the hell was going on. He attempted to speak, to call out for help, but his vocal cords felt as if they'd been severed.

Blood was splattered on him, wetting his clothes. He could taste it at the back of his throat, hot, rusty and thick. So much blood. He had to get away from it, but he couldn't move. Terror seized him. Damn, what about his wife? He'd promised her he was coming home.

Eric struggled to breathe. He would not succumb; he had something to live for. He was going home to Gabrielle. He'd made her a promise and he'd never broken a promise to her in the almost nine years they'd been married.

Gabi had wanted to start a family for the last three years, had practically begged him before he was sent to Iraq the first time. He'd known the reason. If he didn't make it she wanted his baby. Hell, he'd almost given in that time, almost told her to ditch the damn pills. But he knew how hard it would be for a single mother. If he didn't come back, Eric didn't want Gabi to raise their child alone.

"I'm coming home baby," he'd whispered to her.

"Eric, that wasn't what I was thinking," Gabi had lied.

He'd stopped her with a kiss. *"I've never lied to you baby. I'm coming home and when I do, we'll start our family. I promise."*

Even now, here, covered in blood, he could feel her arms wrapped around him, her lips on his. He could smell her scent. He gasped for air. Hell no, he wasn't going out like that. He had a wife, he had Gabi. *I'm coming home baby, I'm coming home.*

With a start Eric woke. A shiver traveled from the top of his head to his toes and back again. He took in several breaths, steadying himself. He was on a military plane heading home, away from the fighting, back to Gabi. He was keeping his promise. He was coming back, alive and whole. It had been four months since the incident with the truck but it seemed every time he closed his eyes, he relieved it.

Shame washed over him, the need to retch all encompassing. Eric pushed his way up the aisle of the plane. What right did he have to live? He thought again of his wife, but this time it didn't help. Even she couldn't erase the horrors of the past year.

The wheels of the plane bounced on the runway. It was over, done. Eric's eyes closed as a rush of emotions flooded him. He was torn. Never in his thirty-one years had he been filled with so many doubts.

"We made it."

Eric attempted to adjust his lips to answer the marine sitting next to him. Yes, they'd made it, they were the lucky ones. He glanced across the aisle and met the gaze of another marine before the man turned away. But not before Eric had seen it, the same look that he was sure was in his own eyes. They'd all seen way too much of man's inhumanity. None of them would ever be the same again.

Thou shall not kill. Eric swallowed away the thought; he was a soldier. He felt again the brush of a hand along his spine, the same touch that had saved him from being blown into tiny bits. The hand that had pushed him away. Eric shivered. He'd been miraculously spared by some force, but why?

The journey seemed to take forever. Eric took a breath as he stepped off the bus to cheers from the crowd. His heart swelled. People wanted to see them return home safely to loved ones. For a moment he could throw away the doubts as he searched frantically for his wife. Tears burned at the back of his eyes, but he wouldn't shed them. He was a soldier and he would not let his wife see him cry.

"Eric."

He heard her scream his name but she was lost in the sea of bodies. Damn it, she was barely over five feet. "Eric," she called again.

"Fall out." Eric roared. He was the highest ranking officer among the returning marines. Again he yelled for the men to break formation, seeing how hard it was for any of them to do what they were taught, to stand there regardless of what was going on around them and behave like soldiers.

The men had tried to do that, but it was Eric who couldn't. The sound of Gabi's voice rolled through him. He couldn't play soldier, not now. Now he was a husband who hadn't seen his wife in an entire year. He turned, looking for his wife.

One moment he was dismissing the men, the next his wife had magically appeared and was throwing herself at him, holding him so tightly that he thought she would break a rib. She was crying. He breathed in her essence, taking her sugar cookie scent, the scent he'd missed for an entire year, deep into his lungs. He couldn't believe it, he was home. "Thank you," he whispered to the unknown force that had saved him.

Minutes later Eric and Gabrielle, like lots of other couples, remained in each other's arms as though they were afraid to move, afraid it was a dream. It seemed words had failed them all. "Baby," Eric finally moaned. He pushed away, looked at her hard, then pulled her back again against his chest. "Thank you," he muttered softly. *Why me?* chased his words.

"My prayers were answered," Gabi whispered in his ear, crying softly now, her grip loosening just a bit.

"So were mine," Eric whispered back, not really believing it, because if they had truly been answered that bus would have held a lot more men. The war would be over and he could forget.

"Come on, baby, let's go home," Gabrielle urged. "We have one day to ourselves."

Eric sat beside his wife enjoying her chatter interspersed with questions and tears. "Gabi, either look where you're driving, or pull over and I'll do it," he warned.

"I can't help it. I've been waiting so long for you to come home. How am I not supposed to want to look at your sweet brown face and your gorgeous bald head and your full luscious lips? You have no idea of the dreams I've had." She shivered. "I'm sorry, we don't have to worry about any of that now, you're home. And thank God that you don't have to go back. What's the first thing you want to do?" She grinned, turning again to him and he reached for the wheel.

"I'm not kidding, Gabi, watch where you're going."

"Close your eyes and stop worrying. God didn't bring you home to take you from me in a car accident. Get real."

Eric grinned though an ache of loneliness filled him. Why? He shouldn't be feeling this way now. "What are we in such a rush for? Who's at the house waiting for us?"

"Are you kidding? There is no way that I'm sharing you with anyone tonight."

"My mom's going to kill you."

"Not this time. She understands, she just wants you to call her. So do it now, you won't have time later. I can't wait to get you home in our bed." Gabrielle laughed.

That was it. A cold breeze crept up Eric's spine. He'd dreamt day and night of making love to his wife but now he felt tainted, as though he'd soil her. He'd felt that way for over four months, since he'd daydreamed of making love to Gabi, right before the truck came barreling down on them. He squeezed her hand, not saying anything. How could he tell her that he feared making love to her? He couldn't, so he used Gabi's cell and called his parents.

For the remainder of the drive home Gabi did as he asked, though she glanced at him at stop signs. By the time she pulled into their drive, jerking to an abrupt stop, she had him laughing. She was the medicine his soul needed.

Before he could close the door to their home his wife was in his arms pulling on his clothes, panting. A surge of pure lust washed over Eric, allowing him to forget everything for the moment.

This was what he'd been saved for, he thought, as he lifted her into his arms and carried her toward their bedroom. This was what he'd prayed for.

"I missed you so damn much," he growled, ripping the clothing from her body, then literally tossing her on the bed and falling down beside her. He buried his lips in her sweet smelling brown skin and gasped at the wonder of it all. Suddenly a tremor rocked him to the depths, and he clutched Gabi tightly.

"Eric, what's wrong? Are you okay?"

He shook his head, knowing she'd felt the movement. But he was overcome with emotion, unable to speak, unable to do anything but make love to her over and over, touching her, kissing her, tasting every inch of her and yearning for more.

He didn't think he would ever be sated. As soon as his release came he was filled again and took her, sometimes gently, sometime roughly, and all without a word. In his wife's body he was attempting to forget, to wash away the terrible images, the memories. For several hours it worked. Gabi was his world and all that he needed.

"Baby, welcome home," Gabi whispered. "I'm so tired now I don't know if I can stay awake. Boy, you wore me out." She grinned sleepily, laid her head on his chest and before he could answer her, she was asleep.

"I thought you couldn't wait to get me home," he teased to no avail. She was done in. He stroked her skin, wanting to follow her into sleep, but he couldn't. His mind and his body were wired. He kissed Gabi's forehead, grateful that he could touch her, that she was lying next to him, his sweat a fine sheen on her body, their sex perfuming the air.

He listened to the sounds of her gentle snoring and smiled, knowing that it was with good reason that she'd fallen asleep exhausted. He thought to wake her; he still had a hard-on. He couldn't believe it. Eric laughed. This was the medicine he'd needed.

An hour later Eric was still awake. Unable to sleep, he reached for the remote control and began flipping through the channels, hoping for anything to take the edge off the feeling of doom that was trying so hard to claim him.

News footage from Iraq sent a chill through Eric. He shouldn't have turned on the television. Unable to turn it off, he watched and began to shiver. Wrapping his arms around Gabi, he pulled her close though his eyes remained focused on the screen. Every step the soldiers took, Eric took with them, wanting to warn the ones he didn't think were being cautious enough. "Stay alert, damn you," he shouted.

"Baby, you okay?" Blinking awake, Gabi saw the TV on and looked at her husband's face. He was staring transfixed at the news, much as she'd done the entire time he'd been gone. She reached over him for the remote and turned it off.

"That's not going to stop it, baby. It's not that easy," he said.

"I know that, but you're home now."

"Yes." He pulled her into his arms. *But a lot of my men aren't,* he thought and he wanted answers. He couldn't forget his brush with death, the mysterious push on the base of his spine. Who? Why?

Eric didn't believe in things he couldn't see or take apart. That was just a part of him. However, he'd never put anyone down for believing. Hell, he'd even sat in church a number of times himself. But when he looked at the world he wasn't sure if he believed in the wispy creation from man's mind, the all supreme God that his mother worshipped, that Gabi talked so freely about.

And that was what was kicking his ass: being saved by Someone he didn't believe in. Eric thought of all the things he'd done while in Iraq, the things he'd ordered his men to do because he'd been ordered to do it. He struggled against the pictures of men and children blown apart, bleeding, whether by their gunfire or their own people.

The truth was that it didn't matter who did it. Dead was dead and living with body parts blown off was a reality. Children left orphaned and families left homeless were also realities. The innocent suffered right along with the guilty.

There were a lot of things Eric wanted answers to, things for which he didn't have a data base to search. He worked on logic. The war to him was not logical. And logic didn't explain how he'd heard Gabi's voice, felt her lips on his and her arms around him. He had not imagined those things.

Suddenly he felt the same as when he'd been sitting in the car beside Gabi, lonely and dirty. He inhaled, and her scent filled him with awareness that she was everything good in his life, too good for him. Her hand reached between his legs and he caught her fingers. He'd soiled his wife enough for one night.

Chapter Two

Gabrielle Jackson glanced across the table at her husband. He was so different, so quiet. He'd lost a little weight, maybe ten pounds or so, but it looked good on his muscular frame. His shoulders were just as wide; it was his lean hips that showed the difference. On a man of his height no one but a wife would notice the weight loss. Well, maybe a mother, Gabrielle amended, knowing Ongela, her mother-in-law, would notice it.

His beautiful bald head gleamed and she smiled knowing he'd probably shaved it just before he left. She liked that he was making himself sexy for her the same way she'd done for him. For a long moment she watched his long fingers that brought her so much pleasure; his hands were large and strong, but oh so gentle when he was caressing her. All six foot, three of this intense cocoa brown male belonged to her.

He gazed at her and her skin tingled. She couldn't believe they'd been so insatiable. She stared into his brown eyes and smiled. "I missed you so much, baby," she said seductively. "This time was the worst. I'm glad you're home for good now."

"I missed you too. So much that I thought of you when I shouldn't have. Thinking of you did prove to be a distraction for me."

At first she thought he was teasing her but when the look in his eyes changed drastically and an expression of sadness worked its way into his features, she knew there was truth in his statement. She thought of the haunted look he'd had the night before, his screaming out, waking her. Gabi took a sip of her coffee, trying to determine the best way to proceed.

"Is it as bad as what we see on the news?"

Eric blinked, glanced at her as though she were a stranger. "What they show on the news is the PG version. What's happening there is rated Triple X."

"What is happening there? Are we abusing the civilians? Does anyone feel bad about bombing their religious buildings?" Gabi stopped suddenly, the look in Eric's eyes freezing her. She'd said the wrong thing; that wasn't how she'd meant it. She only wanted to get him to talk, to open up. Each time he'd returned from Iraq his silence had become a little more pronounced. She stared into her husband's pain-filled eyes. She'd only wanted to release him from that haunted expression. Instead it had worsened with each question she'd asked.

"I'm not…I didn't mean. I just wondered," she faltered.

"If you're asking if we deliberately chose their holy sites to bomb or destroy, the answer is no. If you're asking me if they had a band of snipers in there trying to take our heads off when we were trying to give food and water to the people, then yes."

"Did that happen to you?" Another wrong question. She watched as a transformation took place. Her husband's jaw stiffened, then his shoulders and his entire body. He was sitting ramrod straight, as though waiting to fend off an attacker, an enemy. A little shiver touched her. Did Eric think of her as the enemy?

"You don't have to answers those questions," Gabi said hurriedly, "not now anyway. We've got plenty of time for you to tell me what happened."

"Baby, you do know I wasn't on vacation, right?" He worked his teeth back and forth against his bottom lip. "You understand I was in a war?"

"I know that."

"It wasn't a game, Gabi. I didn't come home to be debriefed by my wife." He stared at her for a moment. "I haven't been home for a full day. The last thing I want to talk about is Iraq."

He held her gaze, knowing his own was fierce, and drew his features into the mask he used for civilians wanting to ply him with questions about the war. It wasn't as though he hadn't known his wife was curious, especially after he'd acted a fool shouting out at the television. Still, now wasn't the time for talk. Now he was looking at all that delicious brown skin she was taunting him with. It was barely hidden by the short, see-through material she had on.

"I don't want to talk about it, Gabi."

"Not now?"

"Maybe not ever. You need to respect that."

"I need to respect that?" Her head rolled to the side and she threw it back and stared at him, not liking the way he was talking to her. She closed her eyes. She wasn't going to fight with him, not after all she'd gone through wanting him home.

The sizzling from the stove was just what they both needed, a distraction from a conversation that didn't promise to be pleasant. Okay, she could respect the fact that Eric was just home, that he didn't want to talk about the war. As long as it didn't have an effect on them, what did she care?

She piled Eric's plate with cheese and eggs, grits, potatoes and onions and hot smoked sausage. Then she buttered several biscuits and liberally applied the honey, setting them on a saucer for him.

"I did eat while I was gone."

"Not like this. Didn't you miss my cooking?"

A smile curved his lips and Gabi felt her heart stop. She was thankful that her husband still had that effect on her. "What, you didn't miss my cooking?"

"You're a good cook," Eric admitted, biting into a buttered biscuit and swiping the honey that dripped onto his lips with his tongue. He chewed, making appreciative sounds. "Believe me, it wasn't your cooking that I missed the most, though I did want a little taste of sugar cookies."

They stared at each other for a long moment. Gabi had never thought she smelled like cookies, sugar or otherwise, but she didn't mind that her husband thought she did. "And the taste of cookies that you had last night, was it what you'd been dreaming of?"

"A thousand times better, baby." His look softened. "I didn't expect you to go to sleep and leave me hanging like that, though. You must not have missed me as much as I missed you."

"Oh, I missed you all right, but you did wear this sister out." She took a bite from her own biscuit. "I'm rested now."

Eric smiled across the table at his wife, wanting to tell her that he'd thought she was there with him when he'd thought he was dying, that he could smell her and even taste her lips. Remembering, he shivered. There was so much that happened there that he hoped the news never reported. America deserved to retain a more innocent picture of the war.

"I'm sorry I spoke to you like that," he said after a slight hesitation. "But it's all anyone seems to want to talk about. Strangers, reporters, they hug you, welcome you back, then they question you. I'm dreading going to see my folks. I know if my mom didn't insist I come last night it's only because the two of you have every single person I know waiting to grill me."

"It's a party, baby."

"I know."

"You're not going to back out, are you? Your mother will blame me if you don't go. Believe me, she's not too happy that I got to spend time with you first. We even had a little thing." Gabi laughed, popping a piece of sausage into her mouth. "I told her you were my husband, and she came back at me with, 'So what? He's my son, I gave birth to him.'"

Now Eric was smiling, imagining his wife and his mother going at it. Good thing they actually loved each other. "How did you top her?"

"I told her I was the one who was going to give birth to your babies, her grandkids, and unless she wanted us to move out of the country, she'd better give me a night to try and see what I could do to make her a grandmother." Gabi laughed. "I won hands down."

"But you fell asleep."

"I've heard that it's easier to make babies in the morning." Gabi watched as Eric laughed at her, then dug into his food with new vigor, as if he thought she was going to take it away. "Don't worry, I'm going to allow you time to finish your breakfast. As soon as you refuel, what do you say we check out that theory?"

Another Man's Baby

Eric cringed when he saw all of the cars. His family and friends were all waiting inside to welcome him home. It's funny, he thought, how you could want something so badly, then when you got it you only wanted to shrink into the woodwork. Besides longing for Gabi, he'd longed to spend time with his friends and family.

His gaze landed on Gabi. Her eyes held that worried look they'd had since she'd found him awake watching news coverage of the war last night.

"You going to be okay?" Gabi was eyeing him, glancing toward the door, then back at him. He tried to smile.

"They only want to hug you, make sure you're home safe and sound. They're all so happy that you…that you came back. They've prayed so hard for your safety, well, yours and that of all the troops. We have to do this."

He pushed back the worry and ordered the tension from his shoulders. "I know they've all been worried, but they want to hear stories of the war. It wasn't a game, Gabi, it's all too real. I don't want to talk about it."

"Then just say that, but be nice." She smiled up at him and gave his hand a quick squeeze. "Don't worry, baby, I've got your back. Just a few hours. I promise I'll make it worth your while when we get home."

Before he could answer her, his mother was flying out the door. He could swear her feet never touched down. "Mom," Eric said, choking up, catching her and spinning her around. The need to bawl like a baby had never been as strong as it was now with his mother's arms around him, but thankfully there were fathers.

He glanced over his mother's shoulder, his gaze connecting with his father. Instantly his father was there, patting him on the back, pulling him from his mother and saving him from bawling.

It didn't do a thing for his mother or for Gabi who grabbed on to each other, each bawling, until he pulled Gabi away and his father took charge of his mother. "Women," both men said at once and laughed to hide their own emotion.

Hero, that's what everyone was calling him, clapping him on the back hugging him and making him feel like a fraud. Only his father gave him a look of understanding, along with a casual shrug of his shoulders. His look said, It's going to happen, Son, and there's nothing you can do about it.

The only thing Eric wanted was to go home and spend more alone time with his wife but that wasn't going to happen. Gabi gave him a look from across the room that led to an instant arousal. He grinned at her. She was being bad, knowing that his mother was walking toward him, knowing what her look was doing.

"What are you and Gabi up to?"

"Nothing, Mom," Eric said hurriedly, trying to think of things other than his wife in order to control his arousal. Instead, her eyes twinkling, Gabi moved so that he was in line with her. He blinked and turned away. Looking at her was not the best way to get rid of an erection.

"Seems like you two need a couple more days together." His mother was staring at Gabi when she started laughing.

"What did she do?" Eric groaned, turning back.

"Oh, something that I think she wishes she hadn't." His mother kissed his cheek. "Go talk to your wife before she goes crazy."

As his mother walked away Gabi sidled up and entwined her arm with his. "What did you do?" Eric asked.

"Nothing."

"I don't believe you. It must have been something. My mom was too embarrassed to even talk about it." He wrapped his arms around Gabi, pulling her close, nibbling on her ear. "Ready to go home?" he asked.

"Not yet, you two."

Eric groaned deep in his throat and nipped Gabi.

"Come on, you have to tell us the truth about how things were. Did you find anything, bring home any souvenirs?"

Eric didn't answer Mr. Evans, his parents' next door neighbor. He just stared. Gabi was rubbing him in that soothing manner she had, asking with her touch for him to be patient.

"Hey everybody, I want all of you to know that Eric and I have started work on our family." She grinned at the group, then whispered to Eric, "I told you, baby, I've got your back."

Another Man's Baby

Eric couldn't believe how talk of having a baby immediately changed conversations. He also couldn't believe the personal nature of the questions. But if he had to field questions about making love to his wife or the war, he'd choose the first. After all, he could get away with smiling and saying not a word.

They lay in bed in each other's arms, Gabi's head on his chest. Eric reached out his hand for the remote but Gabi stopped him.

"Honey, nothing's on," she said softly.

"You mean nothing but news. Are you going to try and monitor what I watch now?" He rubbed his thumb across her forehead. "That's not going to work."

"No, but when you make love to me and ten minutes later turn on the news it makes me feel as if I didn't do my job properly."

"Your job?"

"Well," she grinned, "at least you're paying me some attention."

"You think I wasn't paying you attention a few minutes ago?"

"You were distracted."

"Oh really?" He trailed his hand along the side of her face. "You're going to make me show you how much you're on my mind, aren't you?"

Her breath, hot and warm, touched his cheek and lit his center. Lust pure and simple shot through his groin. He looked deep into her eyes and love took over. Eric swallowed. "I love you so much," he whispered. "I'm so glad…" His words halted and he took possession of her lips, intending to show her what he didn't want to say with words.

He felt her shudder as their tongues battled back and forth. Her loving him, wanting him was obvious. He pulled that knowledge into his soul, needing it to heal the scars embedded there. He kissed her hard, wanting everything she had to give. For a moment he wished that he could share the pain, the fear and the horrors he'd seen in the last year. He ran his hands down the side of her body, cupping her round bottom, loving the softness of her. She began to moan and he began to work in earnest.

His wife didn't need to ever know what he'd seen. He'd left home to fight to protect her and the country. He was also protecting her by not telling her the horrors she thought she wanted to hear.

With each moan Gabi issued, Eric was determined to show her just how much he desired her. So, she thought he'd been distracted, huh? Just let her find reason to complain when he was done. He was giving her all of himself, holding nothing back, determined to let go of the memories that were trying to tug him away. He wouldn't allow it. This one was for his baby.

It was a month before Eric was sated. Now as he stood near Gabi watching her dress to return to work, he realized a month was not enough. He didn't want Gabi to leave him home alone. He was aware they'd been darn lucky that she'd been given an entire month's vacation to stay home with him. Still, he didn't want to be alone. He'd have to return to the base soon and something was making him uneasy. He stared at Gabi, and like a little kid he wanted to beg her to stay home with him. She was also watching him, her eyes wary. She must have read his mind.

"What?" Gabi asked.

"Nothing."

"Then why are you looking at me like that?"

"Like what?"

"Like you want me," she said softly.

"I do."

"Baby, you know I have to work."

He walked slowly up to where she was standing. "I don't know what it is, but doing it with a nurse is almost every man's fantasy."

"Why?"

"Hell if I know, but it is," he said, unbuttoning her flowered top.

"Eric, I don't have time."

"Give me five minutes."

"Do you really think I want to go to all the trouble of undressing and having to take another shower for five minutes?"

She stared at him with such a strange expression on her face that he started laughing. "It's called a quickie," he responded, still laughing.

"A quickie? I think it's more of a drive by. Bang, bang, you're off and running and I'm left just breathing hard. Now stop that," Gabi fussed, moving his hand aside and rebuttoning her top.

"I hate being here alone," he finally admitted. "I don't really feel like visiting other people or even leaving the house." He shrugged. "I'm tired of watching the news. I just want to stay home, but I don't want to be alone," he said quietly and honestly.

Gabi stared at him for an intense moment, then went to the phone. "Listen, I'm really sorry but I have a family emergency. I don't think I'm going to be able to come in for a few more days." She glanced in Eric's direction and noted the five fingers he was holding up. "It's probably going to be five or six days I'm off. Call Tracie and Jamilla, they'll probably work the extra hours. Tell both of them I'll return the favor someday."

When the call was finished, Gabi turned toward him. "Now what do you want to do?"

"Nothing," he said and reached for her hand. "I just want to sit on the couch with you beside me and not talk about anything. I just want to drink you in."

"I thought you wanted five minutes?"

"I did," Eric grinned, "but now that you're staying home, what's the rush?"

Chapter Three

*S*ix weeks to unwind wasn't nearly enough, Eric thought as he stared at his reflection in the mirror. His uniform was perfect as always. It had been a long time since he'd served stateside and a longer time since he'd called Great Lakes Navel Base his duty station. He smiled at the sight of Gabi staring at him.

"I like your uniform, Nurse Jackson." He smiled, giving her a mock salute.

"And I like yours," she answered with a smile on her lips that didn't quite reach her eyes. "You okay?" she asked.

"I'm okay."

"The dreams, baby, they're happening more often. You want to tell me about last night, what it was about?"

"No, I don't want to burden you with my dreams. They're nothing I can't handle." He pointed two fingers at his uniform. "I'm a marine, an officer. I can handle anything the world throws at me, so you know I can handle a dream."

"Can you handle a wife who really and truly wants to have a baby?"

Okay, so there was something he couldn't handle. Gabi's words put it into focus for him. Eric was having doubts about giving her the one thing she'd wanted for the past six years. She'd only put it off because of his service career. First, he'd told her they needed to save; after that, it was the war. He glanced at her and saw the pain of want hidden beneath the glassy look of her eyes.

"Baby, I just got home."

"What does that mean? It's not as though we're newlyweds." Her voice softened, "Eric, the older a woman gets, the greater the risks for things to go wrong."

"Women are having babies in their sixties."

She rolled her eyes but didn't comment on that. She wasn't going to get drawn into a conversation about how she thought there was a reason God had engineered the female body to bear babies when they were young. That was a whole 'nother story, one that distracted her from her goal. "I'm not waiting until I'm sixty," she said at last.

"I didn't ask you to. But can't you take your pills for a couple more months, just give me a little time to breathe? I'm feeling crowded. I don't like being pushed. Gabi, you of all people know that."

"I know it, but I don't like being lied to. You of all people should know that. You promised me that when you returned home from this last tour we could begin our family. You even told me that when you were in Iraq, that you couldn't wait. What's up with you? This isn't something we haven't talked and planned for. We're at a good point in our careers and in our lives."

"Can't you just give me a little more time, keep taking the pills for a couple more months?"

"One month, Eric, that's it."

"What are you going to do then?"

"I'm going to have a baby."

"Gabi, are you giving me an ultimatum?"

"Call it what you will. I love you and you love me. I want a baby and I have a right to have one."

"Even if I don't want one?"

He saw the look of horror drain her blood from her body. Her eyes spoke the word *betrayal* and she wrapped her arms around her body. Fear skittered down Eric's spine as he wondered what would happen if he refused to give his wife the child she desperately wanted. He wondered if she'd leave him. Fear at that thought rushed through him; he couldn't live without her.

"Gabi, baby, I didn't say that I didn't want one ever. I'm not ready, okay? Just a couple more months."

"It's not as though the baby would be born the minute I become pregnant. We'd have nine months."

24

"Gabi, please, can't you just take the pills a couple more months? What's the rush?"

"A couple more months, Eric," she said softly, then glared at him. "That's it." She barely brushed her lips against his as she left for work.

Eric stood in the doorway watching her and a groan traveled upward until it filled him with dread. He'd thought he could do it, that he'd come home to Gabi and all would be well in their world. Most of the time while in Iraq he'd managed to keep the nightmares at bay. But it seemed being home, in Gabi's arms, they'd returned. He was aware that a lot of it had to do with all the talk about them having a baby. He sighed. God, he'd wanted to give his wife the babies they'd both wanted. He couldn't tell Gabi of the real nightmares that plagued his sleep and on occasion his waking hours. She'd probably seen some of the stories about infants being wired with explosive and used against the troops. What she probably hadn't heard was that in order to protect themselves they'd had to kill mothers with babies who were trying to come near them. True, they'd never made one mistake, none of the women had been innocent. And all of the babies had been booby trapped. Still, it was the hardest thing any of the men had had to go through. Yes. they were justified. Yes, they were protecting the lives of all the soldiers around them. And yes, if the women with the blanket wrapped bombs or wired babies had been allowed on the post a lot of marines would have died.

Eric groaned. The right and wrong of it didn't matter. They had been babies, innocent babies wired with explosives to kill them.

A shiver ran up and down Eric's spine. Right or wrong how could he be a father? With the sins he'd committed on his soul, what right did he have for something as pure as a baby? As much as Eric thought he was soiling Gabi when he made love to her, touched her, kissed her, he felt a million times worse about the thought of bringing a child into the world to be tainted by the things he'd done.

The sins of the father. He couldn't allow a child to pay for his sins. But what the hell was he going to do about Gabi? His excuses were lame and she wouldn't keep putting up with them for much longer. Damn!

25

Eric sighed and felt a hitch in his chest. He wanted to bawl. The feeling was coming more often. He shook his head and pushed the feeling aside. Crying wasn't the way he indulged his feelings, working was.

"Welcome home, Lieutenant Jackson."

Eric glanced up, his gaze landing on a young woman with a baby in her arms. He blinked, at first not knowing who she was. When Linda, his secretary, came forward to take the baby, Eric remembered the young woman was Linda's daughter.

"Thanks," Eric said, staring at the women and at the baby. His throat closed as he finally recognized what the infant was wearing. Fatigues.

"Too cute." Linda was laughing. "Oh, this is so adorable."

Eric's mind shut off, and he clenched his jaw to keep from shouting out. He'd seen the outfits before but until this moment it had never elicited such a response from him. *Babies shouldn't be dressed as soldiers. What are these women doing, practicing for the real thing?* He shuddered and walked away from the women, unable to be near the infant.

Gabi's face swam before him. He could see her now, proud of their son, putting him in the same type of clothing. Eric's heart lurched as he saw the yet-to-be conceived son of his wrapped in a blanket filled with explosives. He swallowed. That would never happen, they were in America. They would never use babies as booby traps. Eric swallowed again. But they would use them to go to war. Another image of his still yet-to-be conceived son came to him. This time he was a young man who looked like a younger version of Eric. He was dressed in fatigues, going off to a war somewhere.

Without warning, the image of the truck exploding flashed into his mind and nearly floored him. He reached out a hand to the file cabinet to steady himself. No way in hell did he want a baby, no way. His heart seized when he thought of Gabi. He loved her with his heart and soul, but this was one thing he couldn't give her. He could only imagine her heartbreak if one of their babies was lost fighting a war in a foreign land. No, he would protect Gabi from that. Whatever the cost, he would endure it alone. He would just have to find some better excuses.

What's the rush? The first time Eric had used those words to her in terms of their making love she'd laughed. Now it wasn't so cute. Eric had returned to duty and with it his sex drive appeared to have become non-existent. She didn't understand what was happening. From the beginning of their relationship he couldn't get enough. Now he was back at work and it had been almost a month since he'd touched her, always saying, 'What's the rush?'

For a moment Gabi stood with her hands on her hips and glared at the open drawer containing her sheerest lingerie. She fingered the black silk before lifting it, remembering that Eric's returning to work coincided with his reluctance to touch her. How could she forget that? They'd fought. They'd both issued ultimatums. Eric had asked her to take the birth control pills for a couple more months. She'd agreed to that, but now she wondered what was the use.

What's the rush? he'd asked. Well, the rush was that she was missing his touch. Gabi didn't want to beg, but if he kept turning her away, the only step left was going to be begging. She looked up, surprised to find Eric staring at her. She hadn't heard him come in the room.

"Gabi, why aren't you dressed?"

Gabi looked down at the black negligee she was wearing and wondered what the hell she was doing wrong. That should not have been her husband's question. It never would have been before. She glanced at him to see if he was kidding. His eyes didn't change. He was serious. And she was hurt.

"I wanted to model this for you." Gabrielle held his gaze, wanting to ask him to just kiss her as he would have done a month before.

"Why?"

Damn. That was cold. Now what should she do? Behave like a slut in order for her own husband to notice her? *Okay, if that's what it takes.* She forced herself to sashay toward him, stopping in front of him, pulling the sleeve of the gown from her shoulder. "You like?" she purred.

"Gabi, get dressed. We're going to my folks for dinner."

"No, we're not."

"Yes, we are. I talked to my mom and told her we'd be over."

Gabi backed up. "You didn't think to call me?"

"I didn't know you were going to pull this the moment I walked in the door."

"Pull this?" Now she was truly hurt and a bit puzzled. "Do you mean you had no idea I was going to try and make love to my husband?" A flicker of something unrecognizable shimmered in his deep brown eyes.

"We don't have time," he said, not looking at her.

"How many times did I say that to you when I had to go to work? And how many times did I give in?"

"I'm tired, Gabi."

"You've been tired for a month now. What's going on?"

Instead of answering her, Eric walked to the shower, stripped, stepped inside and ignored her, as if she had not been standing there.

"What's with you?" she asked, following him. "You're showering four or five times a day."

"Is there a law against my showering?"

"You're becoming fanatic about it, as though you're trying to cover up something, wash off something."

She heard his growl over the steady hum of the water. What the heck was going on with him? She'd heard of men behaving in the exact same manner her husband was doing—when they were cheating.

She snatched the shower curtain back. "Are you cheating on me?"

28

"Am I cheating on you? I'm in the middle of taking a shower. Why? Because I want to. I haven't made love to you in a couple of days and you think I'm cheating?"

"Not a couple of days, Eric, a month."

"Excuse me, a month. If you're that desperate, then I suppose we can take five minutes." He reached for a towel, but before he had it Gabi had slammed the bathroom door and gone to her closet to get dressed.

"Don't do me any damn favors," she said aloud, though Eric wasn't there to hear her.

The hot water scalded his skin but Eric wanted it hotter. He needed something to focus on in order not to focus on how he was hurting his wife. Not making love to her, protecting her from future unhappiness, was killing him. He didn't know what to do. He'd thought of getting a vasectomy without telling her. Then when she found he couldn't give her a baby, maybe she wouldn't blame him. Maybe she wouldn't even check it out. But Gabi was a nurse, she would know. Besides that, she was his wife and he'd have to tell her eventually, just like he'd have to tell her the reason he wasn't making love to her.

Little did she know that the sting of the water as it seared his body was the only thing that had kept him sane this past month, the only way he'd found that would give him the needed strength to not touch Gabi. He'd tried cold water; it hadn't worked.

Eric shivered under the hot spray, wondering that something so hot could produce a shiver. But it wasn't the water; it was the thought of Gabi, of his lying next to her, smelling her, touching her soft brown skin when she was asleep, not giving in to the urge to have her, to make love to her, to taste her.

Damn. His ill-conceived plan was killing him and making him ornery as hell. It was making him take out his frustrations on her as though it were her fault that he was not sheathed at this very moment in her warmth.

He shivered again and fell back against the wall of the shower, the hot tiles making him flinch, but he didn't move away.

He could picture Gabi flinging things around the room. He didn't have to imagine her pain. He'd hurt her. Sure, he knew why she was wearing that negligee. If she'd bothered to look down at his erection she would have known he'd had the intended reaction. He groaned, wondering how wearing a condom would go over with his wife.

There was no way in the world even a psychic could have convinced Gabi that two months after Eric returned home they would be fighting. She would have sworn that she would have given in on anything. He'd earned that much from her. She respected what he'd had to do, and she was the first one to have his back this entire time. But this was the one thing she hadn't counted on, Eric treating her like crap. That would have never happened before Iraq. And to top it off, he had not even attempted to apologize.

When Eric pulled into his parents' drive, Gabi was out the car in an instant and ringing the bell before Eric could even stop the engine.

She gave Ongela and Terry Jackson a hurried hug and went to plop in front of the television.

"Trouble in paradise?" she heard his mother ask a moment later and Eric growled. Gabi didn't care that they knew they were fighting. He should have never accepted a dinner invitation without checking with her to see if she had plans. But that was the way it had been for the past month. The first month he was home she'd had to practically beg him to leave the house. Now it was as though he didn't want to spend time alone with her.

As Gabi fumed on the couch, she saw Eric walk into the den with his father, probably to discuss her, she thought, how demanding she was, how she couldn't keep her hands off him. She wanted to scream.

"You two having a fight?" Eric's mom asked.

"Is it that obvious?" Gabi asked and laughed, knowing that it was, that she'd done everything in her power to ensure the world knew they were fighting. "We don't fight," Gabi said sadly, "this isn't us."

"What's the fight about?"

"Personal."

"Ahh, you or him?"

"Him."

When the older woman's arm came around her, Gabi gave in and leaned on the woman's shoulder. For the last nine years Eric's mother had been her surrogate mother and she liked the feeling. "Be patient with him," the woman crooned softly, whispering to keep the men from overhearing. "I'm sure he's had a rough time. You two will adjust in time. You love and respect each other, and that will carry you though the rough patches."

"But he...he...he...he's not the same."

"Who would be, Gabi? Give him time, baby he'll come back."

"What if he doesn't?"

"You know better than that, Gabi. Eric's just going through some things right now. He's not going to do anything to lose you. You're his life, baby."

"Don't worry, he's not in danger of losing me but if he keeps talking to me the way he's been doing for the last few weeks I'll going to have to kick your son's behind."

The women high-fived and hugged, laughing together. Talking to the older woman made Gabi feel better. She was aware her husband had had a hard time the past year. That third tour of duty had taken something out of both of them. She'd thought it was way too much for the military to ask of any soldiers but Eric was the consummate marine. It was his duty. But what was she? She was his wife and needed him much more than the service. She sighed and burrowed her head against

Ongela's shoulder. She just needed to hear someone else tell her that he still loved her, that she had nothing to worry about, that in time Eric would return to his normal behavior.

"Gabi looks like she's about ready to blow." Eric's father sat down in his recliner and looked at him. "What did you do?"

"Why do you think it's something I did? You always go straight to Gabi's side." Eric shook his head. "That's not fair. You know Mom's in there being swayed by Gabi."

Eric sat down, feeling some of the tension ease out of him. The one thing in their favor was the relationship between his parents and Gabi. They had fallen in love with her the first time he'd brought her home, and had berated him when learning he'd been in love with her for three years without telling her.

"Gabi's our daughter," his father laughed, answering Eric's question.

"But you don't always have to take her side." Eric pretended to huff, then smiled at his father. He shook his head. "I don't know what's going on. I just don't feel normal. I'm trying and Gabi is trying. She's being understanding, loving, everything Gabi is and it's…" He sighed.

"Her being wonderful is ticking you off." Terry finished his son's words.

"How did you know?" Eric looked at his father in amazement.

"Did you forget I served in Vietnam?"

"You've never talked about it."

"I've never wanted to, same as you."

"Then why can't people understand that? Why is everyone always bringing it up in the conversation?"

"Is that why you're angry with Gabi?"

Eric scratched at his right eye nervously, then rubbed his hand across his forehead.

"You know, when I was gone I had to sometimes force myself not to think of Gabi, especially this last time. I kept thinking I was going to get my men killed if I couldn't keep my mind off her." He shook his head and sucked in a deep breath, unable to stop the emotion filling his body and soul. "I don't know how to be me anymore."

"It takes time, Son, you'll get the hang of it. You could talk to Gabi. She's a sweet girl, she'll understand."

"I'm not sure."

"Are you two…"

Seeing his father staring at him, Eric flushed with embarrassment. "She keeps talking about getting pregnant. I don't know for sure if I want kids."

"You did before."

"I know, but I'm not sure now." Eric shuddered. "I don't know if I could see my son go into war." He worried his top lip with the tip of his tongue. "Was it hard for you, Pop?"

"Of course it was hard for me to see you leave to fight a war same as I had. But you're an officer. I expected this to happen some day."

"I don't know if I want to worry about what could happen to babies if we have them. I don't think I'd be able to see a son of mine go off to war."

"And I presume you haven't told your wife?"

Eric toyed with the afghan that lay across the sofa. "No, I haven't told her."

"And you think it's easier not to be with her?"

"Until I get up the nerve to tell her." He closed his eyes for a moment before heaving a groan of relief. "Do you think a man can love a woman too much?"

He couldn't help seeing the surprise in his father's eyes. Eric watched as his father puttered around the room for a few seconds, opening and closing his hands, trying to think of a way to answer that question.

"I think I may love Gabi too much." Eric eyed his father, taking away the need for his father to answer. "I think I love my wife to the point where it's dangerous. She's an addiction for me. I swear she is, and sometimes I don't know if I like it. It's bad when a man knows that his nose is so wide open that he could endanger someone's life. I need to find a way to get my addiction to her under control."

"If you're addicted, Eric, your wife is just as addicted. I've never seen a couple more in love than the two of you. You've been like that since I first saw the two of you together. If I were you I wouldn't mess with that. It just might backfire on you and you're going to wish you'd listened to me."

"I hear you, Pop." Eric suddenly felt tired. He wanted to strike a balance between his love for Gabi and allowing her love to interfere with his job. That was a must.

"No, Eric, I don't think you do hear me."

"I'm just trying to protect Gabi from future pain. She could barely take my going to war. How do you think she'd survive having a child and have something happen to that child? I don't want her to ever experience that."

"You can't make that decision alone." His father glared at him, making Eric blink. "Gabi has a right to know what you're thinking. She's a grown woman. She doesn't need you protecting her from what ifs. What if you have a son and he grows up to be president? What if he finds a way to bring an end to all wars? Did you ever think about that, Son?"

"Don't tell Mom about my change of heart on having kids, okay? She'll tell Gabi and I want to be the one to tell her. Besides, nothing is set in stone. I might change my mind again."

"I wasn't planning on telling your mother."

"Thanks for listening to me. I heard all the things you said, but I'm still going to protect Gabi." Eric smiled. "It's my job to protect those I love."

He held his father's gaze. When his mother yelled for them, 'to come out of there,' they both stood, knowing the time for male bonding had passed.

The press of his father's hand on his shoulder stopped Eric from opening the door.

"Are you being completely honest with me, Son?"

When Eric failed to answer his father put his arm around him. "When I was in Vietnam a lot of horrible things happened that to this day I have to fight to forget."

"They used babies, Pop." Eric swallowed hard and held on to his father.

"I know. When I was in Nam, the same things happened."

For a moment both father and son pulled back and stared at each other.

"I feel so dirty, so unworthy to have a baby. I'm scared. Whenever anyone brings a baby near me, my hands shake and I have to make an excuse to leave. It's all I can do to make it to a bathroom and puke. I can't tell all of that to Gabi. I never want her to know. You know how she is, Pop. She loves babies. Knowing the things that happened would kill her. Who knows, it might even kill her love for me. I can't take that chance. I love my wife and I love making love to her. But she's determined to have a baby. She's getting sick of me with one excuse after the other. I know it, but right now I don't know what to do. My thoughts are muddled. Sometimes I'm not even sure what's going on with me. There's just so much going on in my head. I just need some time to figure it all out."

"Don't wait too long, Son," his father advised. "Either you tell your wife what's going on, or she's going to make up all sort of things in her head. The truth is never as bad as what a woman can imagine."

The ride home was just as quiet as it had been on the drive down. An almost three hour drive was much too long to not talk. The tension had eased a bit and the anger was in the background. Eric glanced at Gabi. Her shoulders sagged and she was looking out the window. He thought over what his father had said but he also thought about what he'd been doing during the most crucial moment of his life.

"Gabi." He called her name softly, allowing all of the love he had for her to seep into his voice. Yes, he was addicted, but right now his trying to give up the habit was hurting the woman he loved.

"Gabi, I'm sorry."

He could see a tiny tremor around her shoulders and suspected she was trying not to cry. "It's not you, baby," he said. "It's not your fault at all. I love you. I'm just so tired. At the base we're swamped, there's not enough people to do the jobs and it's causing stress."

"You made it sound like I was a nymph or something."

"I didn't mean it like that," Eric said softly, surprised and relieved that she was talking to him. That was more than she'd done the entire time they'd been at his parents.' She'd directed all of her conversation to the two of them, ignoring him, refusing to even look at him. His parents had laughed at the both of them.

"Are you really just tired?" Gabrielle asked.

"Yes."

"And it has nothing to do with me?"

"No, babe, nothing," Eric lied.

"Good. I was beginning to think I was funky or had bad breath or something."

He laughed, as she'd meant for him to do. The ice was broken. He moved his right hand from the steering wheel and slid it in her direction. When she took it he felt the relief rip through him. *Yeah, I'm whipped.*

"Gabi, I want to make love to you, baby." He squeezed her fingers. "But in order to do that I need to stop at the drugstore."

He waited.

"I can't take any chances on your getting pregnant right now. Can you go with me on that?"

Her nerves were frayed, her body was in knots, her womb was empty and her husband hadn't made love to her in a month. She needed him to hold her to let her know that he loved her, that she still turned him on. Short of begging him, at the moment she was willing to do nearly anything. Her eyes closed and she shook her head. She'd never thought

36

this desperation to have her husband make love to her would be part of their life. She felt him squeezing her fingers.

"Eric, I'm still taking the pills."

"I need more assurance that you're not going to get pregnant right now. The pills are not one hundred percent." He licked his lips and breathed deeply, glad that he was in the car and couldn't see her face. It was bad enough that he could feel her pain like a living entity wrapping around him, suffocating him, making him want to forget the need to protect his wife. "Are you going to be okay with this, Gabi?"

"Yes, she murmured. "I'm on board."

Chapter Four

Gabrielle pursed her lips and narrowed her gaze, determined not to glare. *"Have faith."* She'd heard those words now for months and hadn't known exactly what they meant, but it seemed she was learning fast.

Eric had been home for months now and with the exception of the first month he seemed to be going out of his way to avoid her. But why? she wondered.

She moved closer to Eric, reaching out to stroke his shoulder as he reached for the remote control. She was preparing to hear the worst, hoping to hear the best. She sighed softly as she observed her husband, wishing that for once when he turned on the cable channel there would be no news of Iraq. What a silly thing to wish for. Iraq was forever on the news and it was taking her husband slowly into a deeper depression. Something had to give.

"Eric, honey, are you okay?"

"Yeah, why?"

"I'm not trying to pressure you but I miss you. I miss our making love. You asked me a couple of months ago to keep taking the pills." She shrugged her shoulders. "There really hasn't been much need for the pills. Are you ever planning on making love to me again the way you use to?" She held her breath. She needed to know the answer.

"But I've been…"

"That's not making love." *And definitely not the way for me to have a baby*, she thought.

"Is there a reason we're not making love more often and when you do, that you're using a condom? Do you have a disease?" She wanted to try for lightness. "I'm not saying I haven't enjoyed what you've been doing but that's like an appetizer." She shrugged her shoulders. "I'm still waiting for the main course."

"You didn't complain last night."

Gabi rubbed her forefinger up and down against her chin. So it was going to be like that. Okay, she hadn't complained last night, just like she hadn't complained for the past two months after they'd talked and he'd told her how much he loved her.

When they'd gone home from his parents' and he'd begun undressing her, caressing her, making sweet love to her, Gabi had agreed to the use of condoms. But more and more lately they were engaging in oral sex. If it was what he needed, she didn't really mind, but she kept waiting, each time thinking he was going to completely consummate the act. Yes, she'd had release, that was the thing. And she hadn't minded on occasion. But it wasn't what she wanted for the rest of her marriage. More important things were at stake now. Now she wanted to broach the subject of their having a baby. He'd promised.

"Do you remember the promise you made?" Gabi watched Eric pull his lips tightly together. His jaw was hard, as though it wouldn't break if she decided to take a sledge hammer to it.

"Eric?"

"Listen, we have time."

"You promised," she answered softly.

"I didn't tell you the moment I got home. Is that the reason you wanted me home? What am I to you, a sperm donor?"

Gabi licked her lips and bit back her retort. She was trying her best to be understanding. True, she didn't know how rough it had been fighting a war. She'd only had a dream. Eric had experienced the real thing.

"I have to go to work." She looked at him expecting an apology, getting none. Something inside her snapped. "If I were looking for a sperm donor, I guess I looked in the wrong place. You haven't touched me in weeks, not the way that I want you to. What we've been doing is definitely not the way to make a baby, or to keep your wife. I don't know what your problem is but I know I'm much too young to give up making love. I'm sure there are plenty of men who aren't repulsed by me."

Another Man's Baby

She walked out the house, anger fueling her. She shouldn't have said what she had, but it was done. As she passed the trash she dumped her birth control pills into the can. She'd kept her word; in fact, she'd stayed on the things an extra month. Now she was done with them. She'd leave it up to God. If He wanted them to have a baby, then they'd have it. Given the fact that Eric's recent aversion to her would make it hard to reproduce, it would take a power greater than theirs to conceive. But her womb would be ready just in case.

Gabi stretched as the last patient left the office. For once she was glad the receptionist had overbooked. It had kept her mind occupied.

"What's up? Are you and your hubby fighting?"

Gabi looked in shock at Tracie, the other nurse on duty, but refused to respond.

"What?" Tracie laughed, "you didn't think you'd ever fight?"

"What makes you think Eric and I are fighting?" Gabi took a step back and peered at her coworker waiting patiently for an answer.

"Because since the moment you began dating him there has not been one day you haven't come in here and told us something cute he said, did, or how cute he looked in general. Now all of a sudden you're not talking. Something must be wrong."

"Maybe I finally realized after all of these years of everyone hearing me rattle on that you were all probably tired of it. Maybe I got a clue."

Laughter met Gabi's answer and she felt heat rise to her face. She was embarrassed, but she wasn't going to discuss her problems with Traci.

"Listen, Gabi, you're not the first wife who had a fight with her husband and especially not the first to find readjusting to a husband that's been in a war hard. When my husband returned from Desert Storm we tried hard to make it work, but it didn't. We ended up getting divorced. He died before I ever found out what the problem was. For years I thought it was me, but so many of our friends' marriages dissolved also. Your husband's been to Iraq three times. That has to be very hard."

A sigh escaped and Gabrielle sank into a chair. "I know it was hard on Eric, but he keeps watching CNN. What does he expect to happen? It's not like the war ended because he came home."

"And therein lies your problem."

For a second all Gabi could do was stare at the older woman before her eyes closed and she sighed again, louder. "I hadn't thought about that. We haven't talked a lot about what happened. I've asked and he keeps saying he doesn't want me to know. I told him I see it every day on the news and he gives me this look, like I'm crazy."

She hunched her shoulder. "I know some of his men died and several of his friends. If he talked to me I could help him through this."

"Have you ever been in a war?"

"No, but I'm sure I can help him…I love him."

"It's not your love that's the problem, Gabi, and this isn't your particular battle. More men than people know come back from wars all screwed up. But it's swept under the carpet so there will be no objection to the next war. This one your husband will have to handle on his own."

For several seconds Gabi thought over Tracie's remarks. This was not a battle Eric would have to fight alone, she'd help him. She'd make him remember how it was for them before all of this craziness started.

"Have faith."

Damn it. There it was again, the voice that had whispered to her. She hoped it didn't mean she was fighting a losing battle. Gabi shivered thinking of Iraq. The things Tracie spoke of would never happen to her and Eric. They would get through this. Divorce wasn't even in their vocabulary; that would never happen.

Eric was pissed. Had rational thinking prevailed, he would have addressed the real issue, which wasn't the fight he'd had with his wife or the fact that she'd practically called him a eunuch, had threatened to take a lover. Eric glared at no one in particular. Maybe those hadn't been the words Gabi used but that had been the sentiment behind them.

"Lieutenant, is there anything else I can do before I take off?"

Eric glared at the civilian secretary, wondering what the hell she was rambling about. When his eyes lit on the papers in Linda's hands he was jerked back to the business at hand. He was still a soldier, albeit a soldier who got to go home off base at night and travel an hour and a half to make it back each day. Gabi was giving him shit about being tired, but neither of them had time for a baby; they barely had time for each other.

And when that excuse wears off, what are you going to use?

"Lieutenant, will there be anything else?"

"No, thank you, Linda. We're done for the night." Eric shuffled papers on his desk until the woman left the office. Then he turned and looked out the window. He blew out the last of his frustration knowing it was time to go home and fight it out with his wife.

Two steps from his car he turned to answer the voice that called him. Mike had a huge grin. He'd returned from Iraq about a day or so before Eric left. Since Eric's return he had become closer with Mike.

"See you tomorrow," Mike waved.

"Hey, man, aren't you going to ask me to go clubbing with you tonight?"

"Why should I? I've done that for the last two weeks and every night it's the same answer. No. Let me know when your wife has gotten enough of looking at your tired behind and then I'll ask."

Eric looked Mike squarely in the eye. "Then I would suggest you ask me tonight."

"Problems?"

"A few," Eric answered.

"Welcome home."

"Come on, man, let off a little steam. It's just what you need."

"How would you know what I need?" Eric asked, narrowing his eyes at Mike, twirling his glass in his fingers. "I have a wife at home. I've never cheated on her and I'm not about to start now."

"Don't get bent out of shape. I know you have a wife at home, same as I do, a wife who keeps wanting to fix things, who wants you to tell her everything that happened, without leaving out one single gory detail. And all so she can kiss your boo boo and make it all better."

Eric squinted, taking a look at the women who were eyeballing them, the ones Mike was trying to coax him into leaving the club with. He took in several breaths, exhaled noisily and took a drink. "You think that will make it better?"

"It does make it better. One night of holding a woman in your arms, a woman who doesn't give a damn about you, doesn't want to fix things for you? Hell yes, I'd say it makes it better. All you have to do is get your rocks off. You don't have to worry about cuddling with her, you don't have to worry about soiling her with the things we were ordered to do."

"How did you…"

"How did I know?" Mike shrugged his shoulder. "Hell, Eric, you shouldn't have gone an entire year without. If you had eased your ache while you were there it wouldn't be half as hard on you now."

"I suppose you did." Eric worried his top lip with his tongue. He glared at Mike as he remembered the stories of the rapes, the tortures.

"Don't look at me like that," Mike snapped back. "I had a willing partner."

"Look, I went to fight a war, not to screw around on my wife. No, thank you. You think I feel dirty now, what the hell you think I'm going to feel like if I cheat on her?"

"A hell of a lot better than you do now. Do what you need to do, take the edge off, then maybe when you go home you can handle it, mellow out." Mike smiled. "I'll see you tomorrow," he said and sauntered off, motioning for the woman in the tight gray dress to come with him.

Eric watched him walk away with his arms around the woman. He watched until they were out the door and still he could not turn around.

For a moment he wondered if it would help. He had a boner the size of Texas and it hurt like hell. Mike was right about one thing, Eric was having a hard time connecting with his wife. He shook his head. Gabi would kick his behind if he screwed around on her.

Picking up his drink, he sipped and turned to look at the other side of the bar. He jerked back as a full pouty mouth pressed against his. *What the hell?*

"If you're lonely we could help each other out, no strings attached." The woman looked down, saw the ring on his finger and continued. "Your wife need never know."

She pressed her body against his. Eric didn't move. He felt frozen in time. The woman rubbed against him, running her finger down the front of his pants, finding the zipper and slipping her hand inside. Damn, it felt good.

Then she leaned into him and he took a whiff. She smelled like stale cigarettes and booze mixed with sweat and cheap perfume. She didn't smell like sugar cookies. A chill traveled over him, bringing him back to reality. He pulled the woman's hand from his pants. His penis jerked at the loss of the warmth.

"I'm not that lonely," he said softly.

"Don't you want to?"

"Yeah, I want to."

"Then why don't you?"

"Because I have a wife I love and if I want to keep her I can't diddle around with you."

"She'd never know."

"She'd know because I'd tell her." Eric smiled. "Thanks just the same, and hey, you were good for my ego. I needed what you offered, even if I can't accept." He plunked down several bills on the bar and beckoned for the bartender.

"Have a good time," he told the woman. "Your next few drinks are paid for."

With that, Eric walked out of the club, wanting to go back and take the woman to a cheap hotel someplace and drive hard into her body. But that wouldn't erase his pain and would only create more problems.

"Where you been?"

"I needed some time alone to just think about things so I went to a club with Mike."

"You mean you needed time away from me?"

"I guess I did."

"Tell me why."

"There isn't always an answer for everything."

"But in this case I think there is. I don't understand what's happening to us. You've been home for a little over three months and we're living like strangers." Gabi put her hand up to silence her husband's rebuttal. "I'm not trying to start a fight with you." She closed her eyes slowly, trying to continue breathing, trying not to cry. "If you found someone while you were gone…"

She stopped a lump pushing its way from her chest to her throat. She pressed past it and ignored the welling tears. She would get through this. She loved Eric, but she would get through this.

"If you have someone else, just tell me. Let's make a clean break."

Eric blinked. *Make a clean break?* What the hell was Gabi talking about? "I don't have anyone else."

"I don't know if I believe you."

"Have I ever given you a reason to think I was cheating on you?"

"Yes," she answered, almost whispering, her voice getting lost in the vastness of the room. "You use a condom to make love to me when you do, but most time you won't enter me and you ask if you've ever given me a reason to doubt you. Try right now." She lifted her eyes to his. "The smell you're reeking of…it's perfume and it's not mine."

Gabi stood firm, determined not to cry. If it was true, if they were over, she wanted him gone right now, like ripping away a bandage. She wouldn't let him see her cry. She watched as he sniffled his body. Then a smile broke out on his face.

"You think this is funny, you come home smelling like…" Her hand shot out.

"Baby, I'd never cheat on you," Eric whispered, holding the hand she'd intended to slap him with. "Don't you know how much I love you?"

"I thought I did. Now I'm not so sure."

"The one thing you never have to doubt is my love for you."

"Then where did you pick up this smell?"

"I was offered." Eric held Gabi to keep her from backing away.

"And?"

"And I was tempted."

"Why?"

"I don't know. I needed to be with someone who didn't give a damn about me, someone I couldn't hurt." He stared into Gabi's eyes, holding her angry, hurt-filled gaze, not breathing for the space of a heartbeat. "Gabi, baby, I'm sorry. I'm all screwed up and I can't seem to shake it."

"You thought making love to another woman would help you shake it?"

He hunched his shoulder. "I was told it would."

"What did you do?" Gabi's voice was laced with steel as she glared up at Eric. Her eyes narrowed as she readied her knee. "Tell me now, Eric, what did you do?"

"I thanked her for the offer and bought her a couple of drinks."

"Let me go." Gabi shoved against her husband's chest. She was so angry she was shaking. For two months she'd put up with his nonsense, trying to be sensitive, trying not to upset him, to give him time to adjust. What she should have given him was a good swift kick in the behind. She didn't play that, she didn't care what the reason was. She'd not stepped out on him while he was gone and she expected the same loyalty from him.

"Nothing happened."

"That's a lie, something happened."

"Nothing."

"Think again, you wanted to. Why would you even want to? I don't understand that. It's not as if I'm not here for you." She couldn't help it, the tears fell. "It's not as though I haven't been practically begging you. Is that it, you no longer respect me? I don't blame you because it's getting hard for me to respect myself."

"Gabi, it had nothing to do with us. It was just…she just…" He saw the fire in her eyes and changed his mind. Honesty was cool but at the moment she wasn't in the mood for total honesty. He'd best keep what she'd done to himself, for the moment. "I didn't do anything with her, not even dance. I never touched her."

"She was close enough to you to leave her scent." Gabi glanced downward at her husband's crotch. "For the moment let's say I believe you, that you didn't touch her. What did you have her do?"

She ignored the glare her husband was now sending her. He was in the wrong. How dare he act so indignant.

"Are you asking me if I had sex with her?"

"Since you men have a way of thinking that someone giving you oral sex is not having sex or cheating, let me be straight about this. I do consider it sex. Now back to my question. Did she do you?"

"We were in a bar, for God's sake."

"And I repeat, did she do you? Don't play with me, Eric, I'm not in the mood." And she wasn't. The long dry months were all that she could think about. The times her husband had flatly refused her advances, making her think there was something wrong with her, that she was over-sexed or some such nonsense. Sure, they'd made love a dozen times the night he'd returned, and almost that many every day for the next month. But if she had known he was shooting his entire load and they would be doing without for a month, then nothing but a hit or miss thereafter, she would have called a halt to that glorious month of passion.

And to look at him standing before her, telling her calmly that he'd thought of having sex with another woman. Un-unh, that wasn't going to happen. She wasn't going down like that. She prepared herself, gritting her teeth and taking a stance that meant business. "I asked you a question, Eric. Stop wasting time trying to think of a lie. You'd best answer me."

"You're giving me orders? Woman, have you lost your damn mind? Who do you think you're talking to, some little kid? *I'd best answer you?*" She was ticking him off royally. Eric had done nothing to make her act so crazy. Hell, he was telling her the truth. Women. "It sounds like there's a threat in your words. Is there?"

"No threat." Gabi stood wide-legged, her hands on her hips. "Just a promise. Don't ever screw around on me or…"

"Or what?"

"Do I need to spell it out?"

"Yeah, I think you do." Eric moved toward her. "Handle your business, baby."

"In that case if I ever even think you're screwing around on me it's over." She gritted her teeth. "But it won't be over before I do the same. Tit for tat, baby. You play me and I will make you regret having ever thought about it."

Eric's eyes narrowed dangerously as he moved even closer to Gabi. "Are you threatening me with having an affair?"

"Again, not a threat," Gabi said with not a sign of worry. "You hurt me, I'll hurt you. Simple as that."

This was nuts. They were fighting and he'd done nothing. Then Eric thought again of the woman's hand in his pants. Well, at least he hadn't done what Gabi thought. He rested his gaze on her, saw the hurt mixed with the anger and decided to give in. He was wrong in the way he'd been treating her and he was wrong to have allowed a woman to get close enough to him that her scent would be carried home to his wife. He sighed, hoping Gabi would accept his letting the matter go. "And if I love you?" he asked.

"Then I'll love you."

He noticed that her voice caught on the words, that her eyes became glassy with unshed tears, and he winced inside. Hurting Gabi was the last thing in the world he wanted to do. "I'm sorry. No, she didn't do me. It was a thirty-second conversation. She touched me, I will admit to that, and she leaned into me. Hell, that I couldn't stop because when I turned around she was there. She offered, said you never had to know, but I told her I would have to tell you. I told her that I love you and no thanks. Then I paid for a couple of drinks for her, thanked her for the offer and I left. I swear that's all it was."

"She touched you?"

"And I removed her hand."

"And you gave a woman that touched you our money and you thanked her?"

"Baby, I didn't want to be rude."

"Are you crazy or just drunk? Which one?"

Eric grinned. Gabi was no longer in her battle stance. "Maybe a little of both, baby, but not enough of either to actually allow anything to happen. It just kind of took me by surprise. I've never had a woman so boldly come up to me."

"Was she pretty?"

"I'd be damn if I know."

"Didn't you look at her?"

"To tell you the truth, not really. Like I said, it was thirty seconds or less. The woman didn't even tell me her name or ask for mine. The moment I realized what was happening I removed her hand. I walked out of there and never looked back, so I can't tell you if she was pretty."

Eric took a tentative step toward his wife. "Besides, no one is as beautiful as you are."

"But you were tempted."

"For a minute, and not because of her. It's been a long time since I've really made love to you."

"That's not my fault."

"I know, baby, it's my fault." Eric looked at her, reaching out his arms for her. "Baby, I've been having a hell of a time feeling normal. A lot happened while I was gone. I missed you so damn much that I ached every night. Now I'm home and I can't get the war out of my head. So much happened there, so much I don't want you to know about." He held her tight.

Gabi took a deep breath, wanting to tell her husband that he needed a shower, that she didn't want to rest her head on the spot where another woman's head had been. She didn't want to breathe in another woman's scent, but she didn't say it. What Eric needed now more than her complaints was her love. She wrapped her arms around him.

"I'm here, baby, I can handle it. If you need to talk, talk to me. We've been through so much together. I may not know what things you went through but you also have no idea of the things that went through my mind while you were gone, how much I worried about you or the dreams that seemed so real."

She laughed a little. "At one time I even thought I could feel you holding me, kissing me, but I knew I had to be going crazy."

"You could feel me kissing you?" Eric was looking at her strangely.

"That's not important now. What is important is that when you feel a need to talk, talk to me. You never ever have to go out looking for another woman to take away your pain. That's what I'm here for. I'm your wife."

"Don't you think I know that? Hell, no matter how bad I was feeling I knew you'd kick my ass to the curb if I screwed around." He felt her loosening her grip. "Besides, you're the only woman I want in my arms. No matter how tempting the offer I would never jeopardize us."

"Then why?"

It wasn't necessary to voice what Gabi meant. Eric had always known if he screwed up he was history. Reggie, her boyfriend before Eric, had screwed up. Reggie's bad luck had become Eric's lucky day.

"Sometimes I look at you and I thank the universe for every good thing in my life that begins and ends with you. Then I can't help but think how much I want you in my arms, to make love to you. And I wonder if the blackness of my soul will rub off on you."

"What are you talking about?"

"Sometimes I feel too dirty to touch you. That's why I was tempted."

Gabi's eyes widened at his comment. "Then let me do the touching." She walked toward the stairs holding out her hand for his. He clasped it tightly and she pulled while he remained where he was standing. "Baby, please," she pleaded, griping him tighter. "We can fight your memories together. Tell me what's bothering you."

He sawed his bottom lip with his teeth. Why was he fighting her? Eric wanted her so badly. He looked at her, shook his head and closed his eyes for a moment. "I think I'd like you to help me to forget, not help me remember. Is that okay with you? Can we stop the questions?" He didn't want to tell her about the horrors of war and he definitely didn't want to tell her about the booby-trapped babies.

He saw the slight tightening of her lips and knew she was hurt. He didn't want her to be. "Don't go there, baby. I didn't cheat on you in Iraq. I wasn't even tempted. I was too busy trying to stay alive, to come home to you, to keep my men alive. This has nothing to do with us."

"Can't you forget about what happened there?"

"Not until this war is over, baby, but I'll try." She smiled and her dimples showed. Her anger and hurt had subsided. So had his.

"I thought you wanted to make love." Eric asked as Gabrielle held his hand tightly and pulled him through their bedroom to the master bath.

"I do," Gabi answered, turning on the shower, adjusting it and undressing her husband, then herself. She stepped into the shower and held her hand out for him. Then she smiled at him. "But there are some things that we need to do first. Getting rid of that woman's perfume is one of them." Pouring the scented body wash in her hands and spreading it across her husband's chest she rubbed it in a little harder than necessary.

"And the other?"

She grinned. "I guess that is the only thing." She pressed her body against her husband's. The slickness of the soap made her hands slid downward. He caught her hand and looked at her, fire in his eyes. She knew what he wanted and she was more than willing to oblige.

She curled her hand around him, feeling him throb, feeling his heat as he thickened in her hand. A moan escaped her at the same instant as he exhaled.

"How could you ever put such a silly thought in your head that I would want someone else?" Eric whispered into Gabi's ear.

Eric moaned as he covered her mouth with his own and sucked gently on her tongue, pulling her even closer with the action. His hands slid to her hips. She was deliciously wet from the soap, the water, and from him.

He smiled at the thought, not breaking the contact, wondering how on earth he'd slept in a bed with her for over a month and entered her body covered in latex, had not made love to her completely, the way they both wanted. What a moron. One promise he was keeping to her was that he was going to try and strike a balance.

He'd already decided that he couldn't continue to watch CNN day and night. They had to have a life. He was desperate to reclaim the things they'd lost. They had an entire year to make up for and he'd been fool enough to almost blow it. He shuddered hard, thinking how easily all of this could have been taken away.

"What's wrong?" Gabi asked.

"You stopped my kissing you to ask me that?" A smile lit up her face and lust lit up her eyes.

"Everything okay?" she asked again, this time lowering her hand and wrapping it around him.

"It was," he answered, drawing her back into his embrace, ignoring her smirk. "Now if you think I'm clean enough-"

Gabi stood on tiptoe to sniff her husband, taking her time going down his body as though she were an inspector. "All clear," she announced at last. She laughed as he lifted her into his arms.

"We're wet."

"So what? We're going to get wet anyway. Besides they're just sheets. I'll throw them in the washer when we're done if you want. But I don't want to waste another moment, do you?"

Eric kicked himself mentally for the hell he'd put them both through in the past weeks. Gabi was right about one thing. For him the war was over, or it should be. He was going to have to do a better job of putting it behind him. After all, Gabi had been his focal point the entire time he was gone, his reason for coming home.

Eric thought of all the reasons for his coming home and he buried himself in his wife's flesh. With every shudder he wondered how he'd made them wait. He knew what to do to satisfy them both, to feel her heat with nothing between them. He could have hit himself for having not thought of this sooner. Gabi's body tensed and she screamed his name, giving her orgasm control. With her last shudder Eric, too, allowed his orgasm free rein, but not before he pulled out.

Chapter Five

Three test strips laid out in a row mocked her. Of course Gabi wasn't pregnant, and she was aware of that but still she was trying to get there. A little more help from her husband in that department would make getting pregnant a lot easier. She was trying to be patient; their loving had improved but it remained unpredictable at best.

The nerve of him pulling out. Did he really think she was too stupid to notice?

Gabi remained determined to keep her promise to her husband. She allowed her unasked questions to remain just that, unasked. If what Eric needed was for her to help him forget, then she would give that to him.

She tossed the negative test strips into the trash, trying to thank God for allowing her husband to come home alive. She'd heard the news reports, same as Eric. He had said nothing about it and neither had she, but the knowledge that every day his friends and fellow soldiers were dying was still driving a wedge between them. With every news report, every killing, they took two steps back, all their progress gone. It was maddening to continually have to start over.

She understood that her words gave him little comfort and she regretted having asked him to get over it. She was aware that he couldn't. At the same time she knew if he didn't at least try she didn't know what would happen to them. He had another year in the marines and she was praying for the months to fly by. She wished he had a regular job that he could quit, just walk out on.

Enough of being patriotic. Gabrielle wanted her husband back. Selfish or not, those were her feelings. She suspected it was the feelings of a lot of people but everyone was too afraid to say anything. She'd never tell him how she truly felt. But the one thing she refused to do was censure her thoughts.

Gabi had been too caught up in her thoughts to notice that Eric was in the room. He was staring at her, a worried look on his face.

"What's that you're doing," he asked.

Her eyes slid to the wastebasket and she hesitated. "Nothing," she said finally, knowing he would come over and peer inside.

"I was just checking," she sighed. "Don't worry, I'm not pregnant."

"Aren't you still taking the pills?"

For a moment she started to tell him the truth, that no, she wasn't taking them, and no, she had no plans on taking them.

Gabi thought of the long dry month and dread filled her. She didn't want her husband to stop making love to her; she didn't think she could handle it. Then she thought of his pulling out of her each and every time and felt justified. If he thought he could control their having a baby, then what was wrong with her doing the same?

"I'm still taking them," she lied.

"Let me see them."

"Excuse me?"

"Let me see the pills, I want to see them."

"Go to hell, Eric," Gabi snapped, racing for her purse and walking from the room. Who did he think he was? she wondered. No way was he going to intimidate her into being frisked or searched by him. She was not the enemy insurgent, she was his wife.

The moment she arrived at work Gabi made her way to the medication sample room. She threw her things carelessly on the countertop and rummaged in the cabinets she'd recently filled. Finding what she needed, she took three of the sample packs of pills that she doled out to the patients.

That was one side benefit from working in the office; they were able to have many of their scripts comped. She opened one of the pill containers and popped out half of the pills, throwing them in the sink and flushing them with water. When she was done, she looked up into Tracie's face. A flush of shame stole over Gabi and she cringed.

Her actions were obvious, the look on Tracie's face told her that. Gabi couldn't force words of explanation past the lie that was sticking in her throat.

It was obvious to anyone what she was up to. She was fooling her husband into thinking she was taking birth control pills while she was deliberately trying to get pregnant. A despicable underhanded trick. Gabi cringed. She wanted a baby. Eric had promised and she was determined that he would keep his promise.

For the remainder of the afternoon Gabi avoided Tracie. She couldn't force herself to say the words out loud. What she was doing was wrong; deceiving her husband was rotten. There was no other way to put it. Just because he was deceiving her didn't make it right. Tit for tat, she thought, but the sound of the words in her head produced the taste of bile in her throat. Who were they? In the past months she and Eric had changed into people she no longer knew or liked.

Nurses were too damn nosey. Eric glared at the woman taking his blood pressure, trying to remain somewhat civil, but there was no way in the world he was divulging his reason for coming to see the urologist. His own wife didn't know and he sure as hell wasn't going to tell this strange woman with the sour look.

"Are you done yet," Eric asked. Seeing the nurse frown, he asked again. Hell, he was used to ordering men about. A nurse was not about to intimidate him.

"I'm done."

"Then tell the doctor I'm ready." He reached for a magazine from the wall rack. There was no need to be rude but he wanted the woman gone. The moment the door closed he allowed his body to give in to the shudder he'd held in check from the moment he'd entered the door.

There was something wrong with his plumbing and he needed to take care of it. In the beginning when he'd first started depriving both himself and Gabi of satisfaction, it had been his choice not to make love to her. Lately he'd found that his body was taking longer to respond.

"Lieutenant Jackson, I'm Dr. Samson. My nurse is a bit irritated with you. Seems as if you wouldn't give her much information."

"Can she prescribe medication?"

"No."

"Then I didn't see a need to tell her all of my personal business." Eric waited for the doctor to protest but he didn't.

"Lieutenant, can you tell me a little about yourself? Are you stationed at Great Lakes Naval Base?"

For a split second Eric started not to answer. What did where he was stationed have to do with anything? "Yes," he finally admitted and waited.

"I heard on the news that lots of marines from Indiana and Great Lakes and the reserve facility in Chicago had been deployed to Iraq. Were you?"

Eric glared and his jaw clenched as he waited to be accused of being a killer. He'd heard it enough from the protesters.

"Were you in Iraq?" the doctor repeated.

"Yes."

"Thank you."

Thank you. This Eric hadn't expected. "What are you thanking me for?"

"For protecting our country."

"I don't know that I was." Eric looked away for a moment. He'd never once said out loud that he had doubts, that he wondered what the hell America was doing in Iraq. Yes, he wanted freedom for the Iraqi people but he didn't know if that was the real reason they were there. He wondered who the hell would come to America and fight for blacks. They weren't yet free.

"No one is ever sure of the cause in a war," the doctor continued.

57

Eric didn't answer, just sat there while the doctor wrapped the blood pressure cuff around his arm and proceeded to retake his pressure.

"Your nurse just did that."

"I know."

"Then why are you doing it again?"

""I'm just giving you a chance to make up your mind to tell me why you're here."

A small smile eased across Eric's face. "Are you a urologist or a shrink?"

"I'm a urologist, but my wife just happens to be a psychologist and she's rubbed off on me. Besides, in the last year and a half I've treated a lot of soldiers home from the war. I'm in my fifties but I remember how it was when I came home."

"Which war?"

"Vietnam, what else?"

"Were you married when you went over?" Eric couldn't help asking.

"Yeah."

Eric scooted back on the table, aware of the paper crinkling beneath him. This was the most unusual doctor appointment he'd ever been to. And the doctor was the most unusual doctor he'd ever known. His heart was pounding in his chest. He wondered if Mike had talked to the man. He studied him. Eric had not told Mike what problems he was having, just that he thought he needed to see someone before he and Gabi started trying for a baby. Mike had suggested a urologist, which made a lot of sense. When he'd given Eric the name of one in Indiana, along with a look of pity, Eric had looked away but had taken the number. Neither man had spoken of Eric's reasons for going since.

"A friend of mine recommended you, Mike, another marine from Great Lakes," Eric said slowly, baiting a trap just in case. "Have you had a lot of luck with soldiers?"

"I've seen a lot of soldiers, marine, air force, navy and army, but I can't discuss any patient's complaints or treatments with you. That wouldn't be ethical."

Good, Eric thought, the doctor had passed the first hurdle. Let's see how he does with the next one, he thought, going in for the kill. "Mind if I ask you a personal question about your return to the States?"

Eric was watching the man's eyes, looking for a change. But his eyes remained open and friendly as he folded his arms across his chest, pushed back in the chair as though he had all day to talk and wasn't worried about any other patient.

"Go ahead, Lieutenant, ask away."

"When you returned home did you have problems making love to your wife?"

"No, but I also didn't have any problems making love to hookers and every other woman who would let me."

"You said your wife's a psychologist. She forgave you?"

"No, she divorced me. She should have but it wasn't like we were soul mates or anything. I got her pregnant while we were in high school and married her. I've been married twice since then. My last marriage was the magical number. We've been married almost fifteen years."

This couldn't be happening. He'd come to the doctor for a quick fix. Eric couldn't believe the man was just opening up, sharing his life with a stranger.

"Why are you looking at me like that? You think I'm nuts, right, Lieutenant? You're still a soldier. It's been a long time since I was one. Having been married to a psychologist, I keep nothing inside, especially when I figure my talking can help my patient."

"You think there's nothing physically wrong with me?" Eric asked suspiciously. "You haven't even examined me."

"Don't worry, I'm going to."

While he did his exam Eric noticed the man couldn't stop talking.

"Any problem getting an arousal around your wife?" he asked.

"No," Eric muttered between clenched teeth. "My wife is beautiful."

"I'm not prying."

"It felt like it."

"You wanted an exam."

"That's a question."

"Part of examining is asking questions. Have you been able to make love to your wife since you returned home?"

"Not as much as I'd like," Eric sighed, "and definitely not as much as she'd like."

"So you're not having a problem achieving an erection?"

"No."

"How about maintaining it during the act?"

"I'm maintaining it." Eric swallowed, not wanting to admit to his difficulties. "Sometimes I find myself putting more thought into making sure I maintain it. I've never had to worry about that before."

"Why are you worrying about it now? Why are you here?"

Eric sucked in a deep breath, then another, and exhaled before answering. "My wife wants a baby."

"You don't."

"I promised her before I went over there the first time that we'd have a baby when I came home for good."

"You're feeling pressured?" the doctor asked, then put his hands under Eric's testicles and ordered him to cough.

Damn, how Eric hated this, having a man touch him, especially while asking him such personal questions. Eric could barely stand still. He wanted to yank the doctor's gloved hand from between his thighs. He gritted his teeth, not answering, waiting until the man was finished with his prodding.

"There, all done. I'm going to order a few tests just to make sure you're in good health. In the meantime I'd like to start you on a lose dosage antidepressant, just enough to take the edge off."

"I'm not depressed." Eric narrowed his eyes. "I didn't come here for you to screw around with my head. I came because I'm having a problem making love to my wife. What I mean is, it's taking me longer to get there, both before and after."

"I know that."

"Then why are you ordering me pills for depression? I'm neither depressed nor crazy."

"And you're not having a problem achieving or maintaining an erection so the odds are it's nothing physical. You tell me, Lieutenant, what else can it be?"

He wrote the prescription, then handed it over to Eric. "Look, it's your decision; fill the prescription and either take it or don't take it. It's your choice, but what will it hurt? You can come back and tell me it didn't work."

Eric grunted his thanks, folded the script and put it in his shirt pocket.

"Now that that's done, I want to ask you a question. Aren't there any urologists in Chicago?"

Eric remained silent, knowing the doctor was on another fishing expedition.

"I would think there would have to be a few. After all, Chicago is a huge city and there are a dozen large suburbs surrounding it that have more than competent doctors."

"I don't know, I didn't check. Like I said, a friend gave me your number." Eric was looking at the doctor, wondering why he was asking so many damn questions. He'd broken no law in seeking treatment outside the state of Illinois.

"Still, why come to Indiana?"

"I'm originally from South Bend, I know the area. It's not that far away."

"But far enough."

"Yeah, far enough." Eric shook his head, then smiled slightly. "Why did you go to all of this trouble? Why didn't you just do the exam, and let me find a psychologist on my own?"

"Like I said, I was in the Vietnam war. No one thanked me for going. No one asked if I had issues from having been there. To this day I sometimes have nightmares about it." He shrugged. "Believe me, I'm not just being nosey. I don't ask nearly this many questions of other patients and not even of soldiers when it's not during some war. I want to do all that I can to help the troops. Believe me, you're not the first soldier to come home and have this problem. You're not even the first to cross the state line to see me. Lieutenant, you'd be surprised at how many soldiers I treat from the Chicago area."

Eric couldn't help laughing. "Is that what you think of automatically, that we're all depressed?"

"Not necessarily depressed but post traumatic stress. You wouldn't be human if killing didn't affect you."

Eric's head shot up and his eyes narrowed as he glared. "I never told you that I personally killed anyone."

"You didn't have to. Listen, if the problem persists make another appointment and we'll try something else. While you're here I'll send the nurse back in to draw some blood. Is that okay?"

Eric looked at the man, at the compassion and knowing in his eyes. He accepted the hand that was offered and shook it.

"Have faith." The doctor smiled as he closed the door behind him.

Chills followed the man's remarks, and Eric was left staring at the closed door. Those were the very words that had haunted him the last few months he was in Iraq and had haunted him since his return. Why had his life been spared?

Chapter Six

The bottle of pills felt like lead in her hand. It was obvious Eric was hiding them from her. Gabrielle glanced at the Indiana phone number. Antidepressants. She bit her lips, wondering what on earth had happened to her husband in the year he'd spent away from her.

She thought of the way they were now, the way they had been for almost nine years, before his last tour of duty. This was nothing like it. The war had changed them and their relationship. The first two tours had been seven months each. Gabi didn't know if it was the fear that had kept them connected, knowing he was more than likely going to be sent back, or the fact that they needed to value every second of Eric's leaves. Now that the year long tour, the thing they'd dreaded was over, and Eric was home for good, things were out of sync. As much as they still loved each other, Gabrielle didn't know if it would be enough.

She checked the negative pregnancy strip and for the first time she heaved a sigh of relief. Maybe it was best that she couldn't seem to get pregnant. The rational part of her brain knew they didn't need a baby right now.

Sure, their lovemaking had improved. Their social life was even getting better, but Gabi could tell Eric was playing a part for her, pretending to be having a good time, joking and making small talk with their friends. But the times when she'd catch him with empty eyes and a lost look nearly tore her heart out. Trying to talk to him was proving nearly impossible. He kept saying he wanted to forget. But all he was doing was shutting the door on her and pushing her farther away.

Gabi looked down at the pills. And now this, she thought, another secret. He should have told her about this. Just the fact that Eric had bothered to leave the state of Illinois and cross over into Indiana told her that he was trying to keep it a secret from her. She was a nurse, for heaven's sake. Couldn't he, shouldn't he, be able to talk this over with her?

"Why are you prying around in my things?"

"Prying?" Gabi turned to face her husband, holding the pill bottle in her hand. "I wasn't prying."

"Then what happened, the pills just appeared in your hand?"

"I was putting away your underwear. I've always done that since we've been married. What's the problem now with me doing it?"

He stood watching her, the look on his face unreadable "Eric, what's wrong? Talk to me."

"Why does everyone keep insisting I need to talk? I don't. Why aren't you ever satisfied? You were pissed we weren't having sex often enough, so I went and got some pills. For the past two months I've been using them and, we're having sex more often. Now what's your problem?"

"I wasn't aware that you needed help in order to touch me. I didn't know making love to me was such a chore." Gabi saw him flinch. At least he had the decency to be bothered by his choice of words.

"Eric, did you forget I'm a nurse? These pills don't help with your prowess; maybe if they were Viagra." She tried to smile to take some of the sting away from her words, but the knowledge that something was very wrong prevented her from it.

"The doctor didn't think I needed Viagra."

"I was only kidding."

For a long moment neither of them spoke. Then Eric spotted the stick she'd used to check to see if she was pregnant and he frowned. "It's negative?"

"Yeah."

"Good."

"Don't you…?" She stopped. He was right, it was good they didn't have to worry about that. "I can't keep doing this."

"Doing what?" Eric asked, tilting his head to the side.

"This, us, not talking, snapping at each other, not trusting, lying, making love as though it's…" She looked at him. "I can't keep doing this."

"What are you saying?" Eric crossed the room and sat in the chair, waiting for her to speak.

"I'm scared, baby, you're so different. Half the time you treat me as though you hate me, as though I've done something to offend you. You've changed so much, you're almost mean and it's scaring me."

"I was in a war."

"And now you're not."

"It's not over."

"I know that, but you behave as though you blame me for the war. I didn't start the war. I didn't give you orders to go. Sure, you were the one over there fighting, but I was the one over here praying, begging God to spare you. I was the one dreaming of you being in danger.

"You never told me."

"You never let me tell you. You have no idea what I was going through here. I've tried to be sympathetic to your feelings but it's getting to the place where I don't know what to say. I never know what kind of mood you're in. It's like I'm trying to walk on eggshells without causing a crack. I can't do it anymore."

"Do you think I'd hurt you?"

"Maybe not physically but you're killing me just the same."

"How, Gabi? Just because I went to see a doctor on my own, because I thought I needed a little something to help me cope?"

"It's not your need to see a doctor or to take an antidepressant; it's your need to hide it from me. We never hid anything from each other before."

"A lot has happened, Gabi. Be glad I'm keeping it all inside."

"Maybe you shouldn't."

"What should I do, unburden myself and burden you with it? Would you like for me to give you the nightmares I'm having?"

"Yes."

"No, you don't mean that. You only think you do."

"My shoulders are wide enough, try me."

"Why can't you stop picking at it? I've told you a thousand times it has nothing to do with you or our life together. I love you, that hasn't changed."

"But you have." She stuck the pills back in the drawer and started for the door. Eric's hand on her arm pulled her back. "Eric, don't you know I'm aware you're pulling out?" His lids shuttered and closed.

"I'm trying."

"I know you are," she answered.

"Just give me some time."

Gabi licked her lips, and closed her eyes, willing away the tears. She wouldn't use those on her husband. "I'll start dinner, okay?" she said, taking her hand and removing his fingers one by one from her arm. "I haven't been taking the pills." She saw the look of fear in his eyes. "If you want to make love to me, you will not pull out anymore."

"You can't force me."

"And you can't force me not to try and hold on to the best of us." She took a deep breath. "Eric, please talk to me before we get in trouble. I don't like what we're doing to each other, lying, playing games. This isn't us. I don't want us to destroy all that we've built. Do you?"

"No," Eric answered, "I don't want to lose us. Just hang in there with me, baby, have my back. I need you."

"I'm trying to have your back, but I need you too. Try to remember that, okay?" Gabi walked away feeling dejected. She was trying, she really was, and telling Eric the truth about the pills had taken that boulder from her shoulder. She shivered as though a cold wind had kissed her cheeks. One tear fell from her eye and made its way down her cheek. For the first time ever she wondered if her marriage would last.

"Have faith."

I can't, she mentally answered the voice, wondering if it were really her guardian angel that kept telling that to her. It wasn't like she was a bible stumper. She'd not been to church in years. She'd prayed more during the times Eric was in Iraq than she had her entire life. And it looked as if God had not heard her or she'd prayed the wrong prayer. True, he'd come home alive but he'd not come home whole. They were both trying but the strain was taking a toll.

Eric took from the drawer the bottle that Gabi had replaced. He held it for a moment, then flung it against the wall so hard it cracked and pills spilled out onto the wooden floor.

He was a marine, damn it, a man. He shouldn't have a need for this nonsense. He could imagine the disgust his wife was feeling now finding out his weakness. And if the sight of the pills alarmed her, how in the hell could he ever tell her the need for them? He knelt on his knees and crawled across the floor to retrieve the pills, hating himself as he did so, shame filling him when he caught his reflection in the mirror. He should be kicked out of the corps for this. He wouldn't blame Gabi if she stopped loving him. He hated crutches; it was a weakness.

Eric popped one of the pills in his mouth and swallowed it without water. He closed his eyes, a sinking feeling in the pit of his stomach warning him what was coming. The sinking flowed into his chest before he swallowed another. With a heavy heart he went into the bathroom, tore off and wadded a handful of toilet paper, wrapped the pills in them and went to his closet and stuffed them in the pockets of his dress blues. The shattered plastic container he threw in the wastebasket, making sure to keep it in plain sight so Gabi would see it. Eric closed his eyes against the knowledge that he was adding another lie on top of the ever growing pile.

His gaze fell on a lone pill he'd missed. He bent to retrieve it, thinking of the reports that had come across his desk a few hours earlier. Ten more marines killed.

A knot formed in his belly, Eric wiped the pill against the side of his pants and popped it in his mouth. He didn't need dinner and he didn't need to look at the pity or the tears in his wife's eyes. He needed to sleep, to escape. He lay across the bed and gave in to the heaviness of his spirit.

For ten minutes Gabrielle had been calling off and on for Eric. His not answering her was rude and she was irritated. She didn't hear the shower running so he couldn't use that as an excuse. Gabi didn't want to eat dinner without him. She wanted to be with him even if he wasn't the best of company. She was hoping eventually he would break down and allow her in.

The fact that he was sprawled across the bed asleep didn't really surprise her, but the fact that he was still in uniform did. He was such a stickler for everything in its place, a by-the-books guy. His lying there as though he didn't care was definitely not the norm. She sat on the bed beside him, glancing at the wastebasket and the now destroyed pill container. She'd not meant for her husband to throw away the pills, not if he needed them. She only wanted to be kept in the loop.

"Eric, wake up, baby, you need to eat." When he didn't move she lay next to him and started crying softly. She didn't know how to fix the problem because she didn't know what the problem was.

Suddenly her husband was holding her, murmuring to her, telling her how much he loved her. She looked at him; he was still asleep.

"Gabi, I'm coming home to you, baby, I promise."

"Eric," she said, shaking him, determined to wake him. He was scaring her. "Wake up."

"Don't worry, baby, I love you. I'm coming home and we're going to start our family."

She looked at him as the tears ran down his cheeks. God, what happened to him there? She kissed him, held him, and his eyes opened.

"Baby, what's wrong," he asked. "Why are you looking so sad?"

"I'm scared. You're talking in your sleep and I'm scared for us. You won't talk to me. Tell me what happened. I don't know how to help you if you don't tell me."

Sobs tore out of her husband so loudly that it frightened her. She'd never seen him cry.

"Eric, talk to me." She held him in her arms. "Tell me what's wrong, what happened." He was holding her so tightly that she could barely breathe.

"Gabi, why me? Why did I live?" He shook his head. "There was so much blood, I couldn't help them. It was my job to look out for them, to keep them safe and they died. Why didn't I? I was thinking of you, how much I loved you. I was daydreaming about making love to you. I should have been doing my job. But I was saved anyway. I don't know the answer and it's killing me. I have to find the answer."

"The answer to what?"

He was crying, the tears falling into her hair but his face was blank. Then Gabi realized her husband was still asleep or at least he wasn't awake in the normal sense. She glanced down at the broken bottle as fear clutched her. She rooted around for pills, swallowing her panic.

When she found none, fear gripped her tighter as she dumped the contents of the wastebasket on the floor. Nothing, not one. Oh, God, no, Gabi prayed, slapping Eric's face, calling his name, attempting to make him sit up.

"What's wrong?" His voice was groggy, his eyes blurred. "What's going on?"

"The pills how many did you take?"

"Two." He blinked as though having a hard time remembering. "No, I took three."

"You're lying, the bottle is empty."

"I only took three, Gabi. I put the others away."

"Where?" she asked, not believing him but wanting to.

"Look in my dress blues, the jacket pocket. They're there wrapped in tissue-"

Before he could get the rest of the words out she was racing for the closet, pulling the wadded tissue out, spilling the pills on the bed. She glanced at the broken bottle, then at her husband who'd fallen back asleep. He wasn't going to die, he hadn't overdosed. She picked the pills up carefully, rewrapped them and put them back into the pocket and rehung the jacket.

Gabi sat against the head of the bed. Eric was now compounding his lies to her with even bigger ones. She wondered if he'd deliberately broken the bottle so she'd think he'd dumped the pills. She shook her head and rubbed his sleeping face.

"I'm going to try and save us, baby, I swear I am." Right now all she wanted to do was sit there beside her husband and make sure he was safe.

"*Have faith,*" the voice whispered.

"I'm trying," Gabrielle answered.

Gabrielle's head dropped and she snapped awake. She glanced over at the clock, surprised she'd even nodded off. Ten minutes made her know she needed more. Her eyes were gritty and her body ached from sitting in that position the entire night. But she'd been too afraid for Eric to dare even lie beside him. She'd been too afraid of falling asleep. She shrugged, not beating herself up over the lost ten minutes. Nothing had happened.

She sighed. It was now or never. She almost wished she could have the talk with her husband in his drugged state. At least he wasn't yelling; he was more reasonable, more loving, more like himself.

Gabi smiled at such foolishness. This talk would be done now in the light of day with her husband completely conscious. She would just have to deal with whatever mood she found him in. She wasn't giving up on Eric or them. She was determined to make it work.

But first she was going to get answers to some much needed questions, things that had bothered her. Gabi had to know exactly what she was dealing with. She'd already decided she wasn't going to work today. She wished Eric could call in sick, take the day off but he couldn't. She knew what he would tell her if she asked: He was a soldier, an officer, he'd never take the day off. It was time, she thought, and prayed for strength. They'd have an hour. She woke her husband.

He looked at her, then the clock. "The alarm didn't go off," Eric said, looking toward the clock then at her. "I had another hour."

"I know. We need to talk. Take your shower and come down, I'll have coffee waiting."

"Why are you dressed in the clothes you had on last night?" he asked.

"I haven't been to bed."

He squinted, "You okay?"

"No, I'm not okay," she answered and got up, going downstairs to clean up the uneaten dinner. Within seconds she heard Eric trailing behind her.

"What's going on? Are you angry because I didn't eat dinner? I fell asleep."

Gabi glanced around, her gaze following Eric's to the kitchen. It was morning and the dinner was still on the stove. She'd not wanted to move from her husband's side to put it away. Gabi turned. "You had a little chemical help in falling to sleep. Don't you remember anything that happened last night?"

"You mean the pills you found?"

"I mean after you took the pills, after I came down to make dinner." She looked closely at him, not knowing if he were once again lying, and that bothered her more than anything. He was taking away the trust she'd always had in him. That she wouldn't allow, not even from him.

"Look, I'm sorry about last night, dinner. I'll help you clean up."

"Don't." Gabi stopped him, putting out her arm to block him from going around her. "Just shower." Her voice came out in a horrible screech. She sounded like…damn, she sounded like a drill sergeant.

"Eric, I need a few minutes alone. You know all about that. But I'm not going into a bar to pick up a man. I'm going to clean my kitchen, so please, just go and shower so I can think." She turned and walked away.

Eric glanced after his wife, bits and pieces coming back to him. He'd thought he'd been dreaming. He did remember crying in her arms. Damn. He shuddered hard. What kind of a man was he to be falling apart? What kind of a marine?

He breathed in and blew it out, then marched back up the stairs. He blinked, remembering something else: Gabi slapping him in near hysterics, her running to the closet and dumping his pills on the bed.

Oh God, she thinks I tried to kill myself. He groaned and stripped, dropping his rumpled uniform into the hamper. It didn't take a genius to know that more than likely Gabi was angry about his hiding the pills and probably worried that he'd thought about taking them. Well, he'd put her mind at ease about that. He had no plans on taking his life.

Chapter Seven

Eric took his time in the shower. He knew what was coming and he couldn't say he blamed his wife. The little he remembered from the night before told him that. Still, he didn't want to have it out with Gabi. With a shot of pain he wondered if he should continue pushing her away when she started the conversation.

That always worked, he thought with regret. The constant hurt in her eyes flashed before him. She was right; he was being mean, but it was working. There was a method to his madness. Whenever he pushed her away, she dropped the conversation about his dreams or what he'd done in Iraq. She didn't even pressure him to give her a baby. It was working but in making it work, he was losing her.

A tremor trailed down his spine as he thought of the cost of protecting Gabi from all the horrors. But he'd do what was necessary. She was his wife and he would make sure she didn't know the things he'd done. Unable to postpone it any longer, Eric made his way down the stairs, trying to avoid Gabi's eyes. "I don't have time for breakfast," he said, sitting and picking up the cup of coffee Gabi had poured. Despite his words, she placed toast and scrambled eggs in front of him.

"I'm sorry if I upset you last night," he said softly.

"Oh, and exactly what are you sorry about?"

Gabi put down her cup and stared at Eric. She wondered if he even remembered the things that had occurred, his anguished sobs. She held his gaze, the look in his eyes telling her he didn't remember. Fear clutched her at the thought of what she was going to do. She'd worried that Eric had cheated on her while in Iraq. Maybe that was the reason he'd been treating her so awful. If that was it, if he hadn't fallen out of love with her, perhaps she could forgive him. Perhaps they could get around that and get on with their lives. First she had to see just how much he did remember. God forgive her, but she was going to test her husband. She had to know what was going on. "Eric, what are you sorry for."

"Everything." He shrugged his shoulder carelessly, thinking that the best answer, since he still wasn't clear on all that happened.

"I want more specific details. Are you sorry that you tried to choke me?" she lied. Tears filled her eyes and ran down her cheeks. "Are you sorry that you said you didn't love me?" She nearly choked on her sobs. Yes, she was testing Eric but the pain was real. For a moment she almost didn't ask him the last lie, but she had to know. Tears streaming down her face, she stared at him. "Are you sorry that you wanted me to forgive you for cheating on me in Iraq?"

Gabi's voice had dropped. She said her last accusation softly, as though she couldn't get the words out, but still he'd heard her. It was as though time had stopped. Eric dropped the cup, "Tried to choke you, baby?" he said, reaching for her and pulling her into his arms. "I'm so sorry, I don't even remember."

"What about the other things?"

"I couldn't have said those. I never cheated on you. How could I have said I didn't love you. I do love you, you can't doubt me on that." He was examining her neck. "I would never knowingly hurt you," he said, his voice hoarse. "Baby, I'm sorry."

"You didn't choke me." Gabi backed away.

"What!"

"You didn't touch me. Not to harm me anyway."

"Then why did you say that?" He moved backwards away from her and glared. "Did I tell you that I had an affair?"

"No."

"What the hell are you doing? Stop playing games with me."

"You said you were sorry for everything and I wanted to see if you even remembered what to be sorry for? You don't."

"You were testing me?"

"Yes."

"Why, Gabi?"

"Because something is very wrong with you. You're not yourself. You're lying to me, keeping things from me and I needed to know what else you're keeping from me."

"You think I cheated on you? Is that what this was about? Did anything even happen last night?"

Gabi looked at him, then sipped her coffee. "You were having a nightmare. You said you were covered in blood, that they'd died and you were responsible. And you said you were looking for answers."

He moved toward the door. "I have to go. I can't be bothered with this nonsense." He couldn't believe he'd confided all of that to Gabi. What must she be thinking of him? He didn't dare look at her. He had to get out of there, but she was blocking his exit. To get out he'd have to bodily lift her up and move her. He groaned. He wasn't going to go that far.

"Gabi, I don't have time for this right now."

"If you want our marriage to succeed you'd better make time to be bothered with this 'nonsense.'"

"Damn, Gabi, why don't you let it go, drop it."

"I can't, because last night you were sobbing. Last night I thought you'd taken an overdose of pills to end your life. I thought I was about to lose you." She glared at him. "As hard as it would be to lose you to death, it's even harder to lose you while you're still alive. Think about that."

Gabi closed her eyes. "You're hurting and I'm not going to just pretend that you're not. Since you don't want to get help, I want you to know I'm going to do everything in my power to make things right. I'm not going behind your back anymore. I'm going to talk to your parents, let them know what's going on. I'm going to find a counselor and if that doesn't work, I'm going to the chaplin at Great Lakes. I'm not letting us end without a fight. I love you too much for that. You're my world. If you're not willing to fight for your sanity, I'll do it. I'm fighting for us."

Eric couldn't believe Gabi and yet he could. She wanted to save him, the same as he wanted to save her. Only she was forgetting it was his job to do the saving. He was the man in the family and he was not surrendering his position to her. He'd had enough things go wrong since returning home. Allowing Gabi to wear the pants in the family was not going to happen. He glared at her and she glared right back. Okay, he wasn't intimidating her at the moment.

"Gabi, you're making too much out of those damn pills. It's no big deal." He tried to make his voice soothing and smiled. When she didn't smile back, he groaned again. He saw her hands clenched at her side. His baby was in her ass-kicking mood.

"You're intentionally deceiving me." Gabrielle waved her index finger in his face. "First, you don't tell me about the pills. Then when I accidentally, and I mean accidentally, find them, you go and hide them and break the bottle so I'd think you tossed them."

"I didn't, that wasn't intentional," Eric protested, but he couldn't look at her. Maybe he hadn't broken the bottle to deceive her, but he'd known from its placement in the trash that she'd think he'd thrown them out. He hadn't imagined she'd think he'd taken all of them.

Eric rubbed his hands over his face, no longer knowing what to do. "Gabi," he started. He stopped at the look of menace in her eyes. She was on a roll and he knew from experience that he could do nothing but listen to her until she was done.

"I'm going crazy around here. You have me on a merry-go-round and I can't take much more. This has to stop today, now, Eric. We can go to counseling to try and fix things before it's too late. I'm not going to wait around for you to become psychotic, to maybe attack me in my sleep. I do understand that you've been in a war, that you've seen terrible things. I understand that, but you're going to have to meet me halfway, help me help you."

Eric stared at his wife in disbelief. This was the craziest thing she'd said since he'd returned home. "You think you know what I've been through? You think because you've watched news reports you know what happened?" He shook his head. "You have no idea."

"Then why don't you try telling me?"

"Gabi, I'll deal with my problems my way. Leave me alone about it. You're not to go putting my business out in the streets."

"It's my business, too, and I'm doing whatever I think is necessary, so I'm letting you know up front."

Damn, how Eric wished he could just have it over and done with. If only he could tell her the real horrors he'd committed or that he'd practically seen the fear in the eyes of the men that he'd killed. He'd been that close to them. Would she want to know that he'd seen the fear in the faces of his friends, or that they'd seen it in his? And the babies. How could he tell her about the babies?

Eric shivered as he glanced at his wife, knowing that she wouldn't want to know that on occasion the so-called enemy had appeared to begging for their help. Eric wasn't all together sure if many that were killed had not intended to surrender. It wasn't his job to go over each and every kill or they would all be dead. That much he knew, but still those times stayed with him.He wondered how much any American would really want to know. Gabi was patting her foot impatiently, waiting for an answer.

"Why aren't you answering me?" she asked.

"I'm wondering how much you really want to know."

"I want to know everything that happened to you from the day you left home until the day you came home. I want to know the moment you stopped loving me and when exactly you decided it was okay to treat me like crap."

Eric twisted his mouth to the side. "I never stopped loving you and I never decided to treat you like crap."

"That just happened?"

"It happened because you won't get off my back, like now." His voice remained soft and he lifted his eyes to hold her gaze. "I have seen and done things that are going to take me more than a few months to let go of. Since I've been home you've been bugging me to have a baby. I know I promised you that when I came home we would start our family.

"It was wrong of me to not just tell you that I didn't know if I wanted a baby. I tried to tell you in other ways, but you wouldn't stop. And as for thinking you were stupid..." He shrugged. "Of course I knew me being fully aroused and hard inside you and then my slipping out leaving you empty would not go unnoticed by you. If you couldn't tell the difference then I'm in bigger trouble than I thought. No, baby, I didn't think you didn't know. I didn't think you were stupid. Is that what you want to hear?"

"It's better than not knowing anything."

"Are we done?"

"One more question."

He couldn't help the sigh that slipped out of him. "Please," he pleaded, knowing it would do no good. She would ask her question anyway.

"Sometimes I get the feeling that you're blaming me for something, but I don't know what. Do you think I cheated on you while you were gone?"

"Of course not." Eric frowned, wondering what had made her think such a thing. He tried to draw her into his arms. She shoved him away.

Gabi was determined not to allow Eric to sweet-talk her out of getting answers. She'd meant it. She was tired of this. "Then tell me, why are you trying so hard to shove me away, to make me know my place? I know you're an officer, but you're always throwing that around as though it's supposed to mean something to me. The only thing that means anything to me is that you're my husband. If I've done something wrong, then just tell me. How can I apologize for my actions if you don't tell me what I've done?

A thick sadness flowed through Eric like honey that had been left out too long and was now pouring slowly. He couldn't move if he wanted to. Gabi was taking him back to a place he didn't want to be. He closed his eyes and it was as if it were just happening.

They'd all seen the truck coming and had known before impact it was the real deal. Eric could see it all clearly. The part that bothered him the most was the split second his mind had been on Gabi and not on the truck or his men. He'd been daydreaming about making love to her when the truck had started toward them. And then there was the thing he could never forget, the hand that had shoved him away and not the others. Was it any wonder he was having a hell of a time living with that? He didn't deserve to live any more than they had deserved to die.

Eric shivered when Gabi touched him and his arms went around her and pulled her close. He heard the sob catch in her throat. She'd never understand how important it was to him to be a man she could depend on. If his men couldn't depend on him, how could his wife?

As much as Eric loved Gabi, if he could go back and change things he would. He didn't like thinking that his reflexes had been impaired because of his love for her. Like now. She was rubbing his head and he was breathing in her essence. She was going to make him lose it completely and give in to her wish that he unburden himself, and when he did, the telling would hurt her.

"Baby, talk to me," Gabi crooned.

He couldn't, not now. He held her so tightly that the muscles in his arms trembled. How was he supposed to tell her that when his men needed him most he'd been lost in his thoughts of her?

Maybe if he'd spent those few seconds crying out a warning to his men... Even after he'd finally begun firing and ordered his men to do the same, thoughts of Gabi had still been on his mind. When he'd been shoved away, when he'd lain beneath the bodies of soldiers and thought he was dying, he'd still thought of her. He'd wondered how she would survive his dying. And he'd thought how much he'd miss her.

"Eric," Gabi called softly, unable to control the tears in her voice. "Eric, am I right? Are you blaming me for something? If so, won't you please tell me what it is?"

He froze, then opened his eyes and looked at his wife, wondering if she was right about him blaming her for the death of his men. If that were true, it hadn't been intentional. Damn, it wasn't her fault that she'd captured his heart and soul so completely that even in the face of death his thoughts had been of her. He was whipped. That was his fault, not hers.

"Eric."

He rubbed his hands over his eyes, then over his bald head. "Please leave it alone, Gabi, leave it alone."

When Gabrielle pulled back and yanked a handful of his shirt in her hand, twisting it and thunking him on the head, he wanted to laugh. He couldn't believe she was getting physical with him.

"I'm not going to lose you, Eric," she promised.

Laughing, Eric shook his head and pulled her in for a kiss. "You're something else, you know that? I love you and I'm going to try harder, I promise. Now I have to go, baby." He kissed her again, lifting her and this time setting her down away from his escape.

He walked out the door, thinking until the moment he was actually driving down the street that Gabi was going to come out and stop him. He'd meant it when he said she was something else. She was, and he was grateful for that. This was the reason he'd prayed so hard to come home, to be with his wife.

Life was so damn hard, he thought. He'd changed so much. He wished like hell that there'd never been a war, that he'd never gone, that it was over and everyone could come home. Eric even wished for the time when the Iraqi people could start rebuilding their country and their lives and live free from terrorists, but that wasn't likely, that much he knew, not when every day more senseless acts of violence were committed.

The one thing that made Eric proud was that in some small way maybe he'd managed to help. Now if only he could keep his thoughts in that vein, then maybe the memories of the not so good things wouldn't overwhelm him, and he wouldn't treat the woman he loved like crap.

Eric groaned, hating the things he'd done since his return home almost as much as he hated the things he'd done in Iraq.

Gabi had every right to be angry with him. He had been treating her like crap. He couldn't believe she'd hit on part of the problem, something he'd hoped never to admit to her. It wasn't Gabi's fault he'd missed her like hell, that much of the time when he had a free moment he was so damn horny for her that he could close his eyes and imagine loving her. And it wasn't her fault that he feared he would never see her again. It definitely wasn't Gabi's fault that the president had declared war on Iraq and that he'd had to do his duty not once but three times, that the horrors he saw had increased with each tour.

He blew out his breath knowing it wasn't Gabi's fault that he'd reneged on his promise because he couldn't get the image of those booby trapped blankets out of his mind. No, none of it was Gabi's fault. It was Eric's for loving her so much that he'd almost gone crazy being so far from her for so long.

Eric closed his eyes against the pain. He'd wanted to come home to her so badly that it had mattered more than anything.

Now he was feeling guilt that he was home and that guilt was eating him up inside, tearing apart his marriage and making the woman he loved doubt him. He was lying to her, hiding things and even thinking of being with other women. None of it was right, but no one had written a manual on how to come home from a war and feel whole.

Eric had to do something and do it quickly. Gabi was pressuring him again to get help, threatening to find a therapist herself if he didn't. Go to a counselor? He almost laughed at the thought. He was a marine; he would deal with his problems himself without a shrink.

Gabrielle stood at the door watching Eric drive away. The taste of Eric's kiss lingered on Gabi's lips. He'd thought with his kiss he'd sweet-talked her into keeping quiet. Well, he hadn't. She knew he would be angry when he found out she'd made good on her promise. She didn't care. She sucked in a breath admitting the lie to herself. She did care, but she needed to help her husband. Sure, at the moment he was fine but there were far too many mood swings for her to handle alone.

As her fingers dialed the number, Gabi prayed, hoping that her guardian angel would be able to look out for both her and Eric. "I love him," she said into the stillness. "I can't lose him."

"Hi, Mom," she said when Ongela Jackson picked up the phone. "I need your help."

Eric sat in his office doing mostly paperwork. He had thought a lot about the conversation he'd had with Gabi. He was desperate to find a solution. Maybe he'd call her later and take her out. They were in serious need of some fun. He was smiling when Sergeant Benson walked in and rapped his knuckles on the open door.

"Lieutenant, we have the men ready to load up on the bus. Did you want to say anything to them before they take off?"

That question had been put to Eric several times in the last couple of months, every time more men left the base to be shipped off somewhere before landing at their final destination, before they too joined the war.

Why did anyone think he had anything to say? Because he'd been there three times? Because he'd commanded troops over there? Why didn't they ask Mike to make the speeches? He was good at that sort of thing, giving the 'for God and country' speech.

Eric cringed. He wasn't. That was more than likely the reason the task was falling to him more and more lately, to make him buck up and get with the program. He felt the subtle manipulation as he thought over what he was supposed to say to the men. He felt disgusted with himself and the war. Sure, he believed in fighting for his country, for defending the rights of others, but it bothered him that the cost had become much too high.

"Lieutenant?"

"Sure, I'm coming, Sergeant. Just give me a second." Eric fiddled with a couple of papers, willing his mind to shift gears. He followed the sergeant out of the office and stood before the men.

They were so young, too damn young, he thought, their faces trying hard to look every inch the marine, to not show fear. He didn't have it in him to give it the old 'fighting for your country, what a privilege' routine.

Eric put his hands behind his back and looked at the soldiers.

"Be careful over there. Take nothing for granted and above all, stay alert. This isn't a game. Men will be killed on both sides and it makes no difference who has the just cause. Both sides think they're right. Taking a life is no fun. It will transform you forever. Having someone take your life is even less fun. This is not a movie. You don't get to redo it. Just remember what I've said and watch your back. If you err, let it be on the side of staying alive. I'll pray that you all maintain some of your humanity. Good luck, men. I hope that I'll get to tell you 'job well done' on your return home."

The sergeant was eying him. Eric didn't blame him. He doubted if any officer had ever given the little speech he'd just given. But he wanted the men to be careful. He wanted as many of them as possible to come back alive. Eric was getting tired of burying soldiers and he was sure the people in Iraq were getting just as tired of burying their dead.

Chapter Eight

The positive sign appeared only seconds after Gabi applied the urine. A pang of jealousy hit her and for the count of ten Gabi allowed her own desires to surface before shoving them into the background where they belonged. She sucked in a couple of breaths to fortify herself for what had to be done.

Looking up from the strip, she reminded herself that she was a professional, she was a nurse. She would do her job. Two minutes, she told herself, just two minutes and it would be over. She had only to walk down the hall to the exam room and deliver the news.

Gabi opened the door and smiled. "Congratulations, Mrs. Cape, you're pregnant."

"Will my insurance pay for an abortion?"

"Excuse me?" Gabi couldn't believe what she was hearing. She tried to remain composed.

"An abortion, will my insurance pay for an abortion?"

Try as she might Gabi couldn't prevent the tremors that rocked her for a moment. This wasn't her decision to make. Still, she couldn't answer the patient. She'd give anything to be pregnant. Despite Eric saying they didn't need a baby, she wanted one. She wanted a part of Eric that was good, for she feared what their future would hold.

"Well, will it?" the patient asked, staring at Gabi.

Gabi pushed away her pain and envy and held her breath for a long moment before directing her gaze to the patient. "Don't you want the baby?"

"If I wanted it I wouldn't be asking about an abortion. Look. I'm sorry, but I have six kids already. The last thing I need is another baby."

Gabi pulled her bottom lip into her mouth and bit down, trying to remind herself that it wasn't her job to moralize; her job was to take care of her patients to the best of her abilities.

"Just go to the front desk and ask the receptionist for a referral." Even those words were hard for Gabi to get out.

"Does the doctor have to approve it?"

"Yes, but the first step is to ask for the paper--work. You don't have to worry, they're always approved, and your insurance pays for it. It's your right, your decision."

"Why can't you get it, the referral, I mean?"

Gabi looked at the woman for a second and began tearing the paper from the examine table. "I don't do the paperwork."

"You've given me other referrals."

Gabi sighed. She didn't want to say the words because she knew how it would sound, but the patient was pushing her for an answer. Gabi sprayed the table with disinfectant, trying to keep her gaze from landing on the patient. "I don't do paperwork for abortions."

"You don't believe in them?"

"I believe every person has the right to choose what's best for them."

"So why won't you do the paperwork?"

"I believe I have the right to choose whether to be a part of an abortion."

"Are you judging me? You don't know my situation."

"No, I'm not judging you. It's just I already have enough sins of my own to atone for." She saw the woman's skin blanch and knew she'd used the wrong words. "I'm not judging you, so in the same respect you shouldn't judge me." Gabi raised her shoulder. "Some people can't work with corpses; I prefer not to fill out the paperwork for abortions."

Gabi blew out the air in her cheeks and attempted to smile. "I'll take your chart to the front desk and ask Joannie to put through your request. Good luck."

"I have six kids."

"I know," Gabi answered and attempted once again to smile as she glanced over her shoulder. "Everyone has to do what's right for them."

Another Man's Baby

Yes, Mrs. Cape had six kids and Gabi had none. It wasn't fair. Gabi wanted a baby so badly and couldn't seem to get pregnant and Mrs. Cape didn't want a baby, yet she found herself pregnant. It wasn't fair. *Why, God?*

"*Have faith.*" She heard the words again and became angry. Have faith in what? she wanted to shout. Anytime I pray for something things get twisted. I don't get what I prayed for, so why bother? She carried the chart to the front desk, not meeting the eyes of the patient as she stood on the other side.

"Joannie, Mrs. Cape needs a referral to the family planning center," Gabi said and walked away. She heard Joan explaining that the referral would be approved in five days, asking if the patient would like the referral mailed to her home or whether she would prefer to come back and pick it up.

A chill made Gabi look up. She did believe in choice. It was just that she chose to have a baby and couldn't.

For the rest of the day she did her work automatically, looking at the clock often, hoping the time to go home would hurry.

Gabi stretched and looked up from the paperwork on her desk. On hearing a sound she looked to her right, surprised to see Jamilla lounging against the door of an exam room. Before she could turn away something about the way Jamilla was leaning into the patient caught Gabi's eye.

She glanced around the hall and shuffled papers, thinking it would break the trance her friend appeared to be in. When it didn't, Gabi's gaze was once again drawn to her co-worker.

It was obvious what was happening. Jamilla was flirting with one of their regular patients. For a second longer Gabi watched her. It was so easy for Jamilla to flirt. While she was thinking that, Jamilla tilted her head back and the patient's lips came down.

Gabi wanted to turn, to move, to do anything but remain where she was. She scooted her chair back, trying unsuccessfully not to scrape it on the floor.

Once on her feet, instead of moving away, Gabi found herself standing there watching them. Mr. Rivers was married, and his wife was also one of their patients. What the heck was Jamilla doing?

Mr. Rivers looked up and caught her watching them. He brushed his hand down the front of Jamilla's body and Jamilla moved into his hand, laughing deep in her throat. What was wrong with them? They were standing in the hallway of a medical office, and doctors and other patients were around.

"Gabi, I didn't know you were standing there," Jamilla said lazily, finally taking notice of her. "Mr. Rivers just needed a nurse visit. No charge." She grinned at him, then at Gabi.

Gabi's mouth flew open when the man grabbed Jamilla's behind and rubbed it as though Gabi were not standing there. She just looked at Jamilla when the patient walked through the exit door. Without a word, Gabi walked away. Another person in her life who wasn't what she seemed to be.

Jamilla ran in front of her. "Gabi, why did you look at me like that?"

She gave her such an odd look that Gabi stopped. "I didn't want to embarrass you," Gabi answered.

"Why should I be embarrassed?"

"His wife is our patient, in case you forgot."

"And?"

"And I thought you might not have wanted me to see what was going on."

"Why?"

Jamilla was getting angry. She was rolling her neck around on her shoulders, standing back on her legs and snorting her words out through her nose.

"So what, you think you're better than me because you have a husband?"

"I never said that." Gabi rubbed her forehead at this entire conversation. It was giving her a headache. She didn't want to talk to Jamilla about this. The day had been hard enough already.

"Jamilla, your private life is not my business."

"But you have an opinion."

"Skip it." Gabi walked away only to have Jamilla run in front of her again, almost causing Gabi to collide with her. "What are you doing?" Gabi was annoyed and didn't even try to prevent the annoyance from coming through in her voice.

"Why are you tripping?" Jamilla stood with her hands on her hips and a smirk on her face.

"Jamilla, I'm not tripping. I'm not even saying a word. I'm trying to go home. Look, you're my friend. I'm not judging you."

"But you are."

"I'm not judging you, but if you're asking me if I would do the same thing, then the answer is a big fat no. I would never mess with another woman's man. As women we should stick together. It's hard enough as it is to make a relationship work without someone else getting in the middle of it."

Gabi watched as Jamilla's eyes narrowed. She'd ticked her off, that much was obvious, but Jamilla had asked for it. She'd tried not to get into this and definitely not here at work. "Come on," Gabi said, trying to soften things. "Can't we talk about this later, maybe go out for lunch or something?"

"Why don't you make it dinner? Bring Eric," Jamilla said and Gabi couldn't help seeing the look that crossed her friend's face. When Jamilla stuck her tongue out of her mouth and moved it in a suggestive manner, it ticked Gabi off.

"I don't play that, Jamilla. Friend or not."

"What if your husband wanted to play?"

"Jamilla, if Eric wanted to play, believe me, he wouldn't play in your house." Gabi was so angry that she wanted to snatch the weave off Jamilla's head and beat her with the hair. She was steaming.

"Ladies, your voices are carrying. I could hear you two rooms down."

A groan built in Gabi as her eyes shuttered in embarrassment. "I'm sorry, Tracie. Look, Jamilla, I'm sorry, I'm tired."

"Me too," Jamilla answered. "Girl, I was playing with you about your husband. He's fine and all, but I won't mess with him, you don't have to worry."

She did the innuendo again with her tongue and the sucking motion with her jaws and walked away. Gabi's hand automatically rose as she took a step behind her, determined this time to wring Jamilla's neck.

Her hand was brought down to her side with such force that Gabi frowned and turned around. She glared at Tracie before realizing the woman had saved her from making a professional mistake. She swallowed and looked away. "Thanks."

"Go home, Gabi, you've been under a lot of stress lately. I started to take over when you had Mrs. Cape. I knew she was pregnant and wanted an abortion. She'd called earlier about it. I'm sorry, I should have mentioned it." Tracie put her hand on Gabi's arm. "One day when it's right," she emphasized, "you and Eric will have a baby."

"I told him," Gabi sighed, letting out the breath she'd been holding. "He knows I haven't been taking the pills."

"Good, the two of you have a good relationship. I'm really praying for you to make it. I hope you're both praying as well." Tracie hugged her hard, releasing her quickly.

"Thanks," Gabi said again and walked toward the locker room for her purse. This thing with Eric was spilling over into other parts of her life. She should have never confronted Jamilla. She'd always known Jamilla was a little loose with men. She'd looked over it mainly because the entire year Eric was gone Jamilla had been by her side helping her fight the loneliness.

Why did it bother her today? she wondered. Jamilla had never known the meaning of hands off another woman's man. But until today she'd never so blatantly gone after a patient's husband, and definitely not there in the office. *That was just wrong*, Gabi fumed as she got in her car and drove away.

Eric tried joking with Gabi to no avail. She was much too quiet. She didn't seem angry with him but something was wrong. Well, something was different anyway. Something was always wrong with them it seemed.

"What's up, baby?" he ventured.

"Nothing," she answered, stabbing a piece of her salad as though it were the enemy.

"Something I did?"

"Nope."

"Work?"

Gabi stopped with the lettuce halfway to her mouth and he waited.

"I thought you wanted us to keep anything that was bothering us to ourselves."

He flinched and tightened his jaw. "Okay, if you don't want to tell me, then don't. I was just asking. I thought we sorted things out this morning." He waited but she didn't answer, just continued eating.

This was his fault. He'd shut her out and now she was doing it to him. "Women." He rolled his eyes and sighed loudly, hoping to get a rise out of her. Nothing. He didn't want this for them. "Gabi, tell me what's wrong, baby."

"I don't think you want to know."

"Is it that bad?"

She sighed, "Eric, why are you bugging me about this? Like I said, you won't talk to me, but you can't stand that I won't talk to you."

Okay, so she was being evil, giving tit for tat as she was fond of saying. He ate a few bites of salad in silence, but it was bugging him that his wife was clamming up. "Gabi, tell me what's wrong."

She sighed again and he ignored it. She was looking as if this time she might tell him.

"Jamilla and I got into a fight today." She tilted her head back. "I almost hit her. Tracie stopped me."

Surprise kept him silent for a second while he stared at his wife. The stress of their marriage was getting to her, Eric knew it. Otherwise Gabi would never have lost her cool like that. He took in a breath. "Tell me what happened."

"She was flirting with one of our patients. She kissed him and he had his hands all over her."

"Why does that surprise you, Gabi? Jamilla likes men. She's never hidden that fact."

Gabi was glaring at him. Not wanting to be the next person Gabi wanted to hit, Eric smiled at her. "What else?"

"The man's wife is also our patient."

"Oh."

"She was so bold about it, so nasty."

"It wasn't really your business. Why did you fight with her over it?"

The tension in Gabi increased. Eric could tell from the way she clenched her jaw and the stiffness of her shoulders that she was getting angry with him. "It's not as though you didn't know how she is," he offered.

"Has she hit on you?"

"Of course she's hit on me, you know that. That's what she does. But I've never been interested. Now tell me why you chose today to fight with her over her nature. She can't help it."

"What makes you think that I started it?"

"You have to admit you were probably not in the best of moods when you went work. I just thought…"

"Well, you're wrong. Jamilla approached me. I kept telling her I didn't want to get into it with her, that it was her business, but she insisted." Gabi stopped and glared for effect.

"And that made you want to hit her?"

"She insinuated that she'd like to get with you. She made lewd gestures, not once, but twice."

He could feel the smile coming and wanted to stop it. His baby wasn't in the mood for jokes. "You got jealous?" He laughed. "Thanks, baby, I'm glad."

"I didn't do it for you."

For a moment there was complete silence before Eric said softly, "I know. I also know something more had to have happened. What was it, baby?"

"I had a patient today," she almost whispered and Eric breathed a sigh of relief. He'd been afraid she was going to question him about his inability to talk to her. "Go on," he coaxed. "What happened to your patient?"

"She was pregnant."

Now he knew where this was going. He felt a pain in his abdomen as a knot of anxiety radiated across his midsection, strangling his abdominal muscles.

"And?" he asked.

"I went to congratulate her. When I told her the test was positive, she asked for a referral for an abortion."

"Oh."

For a moment Eric's cheeks burned as Gabi glared at him. He waited.

"She doesn't want the baby."

"Gabi, it's her decision."

"I know it is."

He watched while she closed her eyes against the pain. Gabi wanted a baby in the worst way. Damn. He went back to eating his salad. "Anything else happen?"

"No, that was about it."

He waited for her to say more. When she didn't, his guilt overwhelmed him. He fished for a mandarin orange. "I think you'd make a very good mother." His wife lifted her face and she stared at him, waiting.

"I was thinking maybe it's time for us to start working on that baby."

"I thought you said it was good I hadn't gotten pregnant."

"You agreed with me," he answered her.

"Yeah, I know, but look what we did. We were lying to each other. I was planting my pill box so you could keep count of the missing pills and you were pulling out. As much as I want a baby, I don't know if we're at a place where we should try."

She gazed at him and Eric saw the tears well up.

"I decided today that if you don't want a baby, I'll have to learn to live with that. I'm sorry I lied to you, and tried to trick you into getting me pregnant."

"And I'm sorry I lied to you and tried not to get you pregnant."

They both laughed and relief rushed to Eric's soul. As much as he wanted to protect Gabi from possible pain, he wanted more to make her happy. Giving her a baby would make her happy. He'd have to learn to pray in order to keep that baby safe. "I do want that family we talked about."

"Are you sure?" Gabi asked, holding her breath. "You were so determined before."

"I think we're allowed to change our minds, aren't we?"

"Baby, are you sure?"

He could see the hope spring to life within her. As badly as she wanted a baby, she'd evidently made up her mind not to pressure him about it.

"I'm not sure," Gabi whispered softly, holding her head to the side, looking at him with a funny expression on her face.

"You're not sure?" He saw her disappointed face in his mind every month when she did a pregnancy test and found out that she wasn't. He knew how much she wanted a baby, how much she'd wanted a baby before he left.

"I've been an ass, Gabi. You no longer have to worry about me. I think this morning you brought me back to my senses." He was teasing her, wanting to see the light that he'd taken out of her return, to see the sparkle in her eyes.

"Eric, I don't want to force you into anything." His smile tugged at her heart and she smiled in return. "Okay, I know I've been singing a different tune lately. But I'm serious. I'll respect your wishes. I know how strongly you felt about our not having a family. I should have given your reasons more consideration. You've been through a lot and I shouldn't have pressured you. I love you and I don't want to do anything to jeopardize our marriage."

"You're not. We've talked about this for years. My reasons were things that I will have to learn to let go of. It never had anything to do with my love for you."

"Are you sure?"

"I'm sure."

"Do you really want a baby, for real?" Gabi held her breath.

"I do want a baby, I want lots of babies with you." Eric saw the smile breaking out and the dimples in Gabi's cheeks. She'd been trying hard to hold back her joy from the moment he'd told her he was ready to start their family but she wasn't having much luck.

"Eric—"

He laughed and finally got up and went to her. He pulled her up. "You've been putting up with a lot from me the past few months. You've been so patient. I love you and there is nothing I want more than to have a baby with you. I also agree with you about something else, I know I should get some counseling. I think I'm about ready."

"You're not doing this just for me, are you?"

"Not just for you," he grinned. "I love you and I'm definitely going to enjoy making a baby with you."

"Eric…"

Before she could say another word he was holding her in his arms, capturing her lips, covering them, tasting the sugar cookie scent of her. He pressed her body close to his. "Baby." He wanted to say so much more, but now was not the time.

Chapter Nine

Three months of trying and his wife wasn't pregnant yet. Now that he'd had some time to adjust to the idea Eric wanted a child with Gabi.

"Dr. Samson, look, before you start psychoanalyzing me again this is a serious question. It's physical, not mental. I can't get my wife pregnant."

"Are you trying?"

Eric refused to answer that question or to be amused.

"You've only been home a short time, Lieutenant. The last time I saw you, you didn't want a baby. What changed your mind?"

Eric narrowed his gaze and stared at the doctor for several seconds. "I thought I said I wasn't here to be psychoanalyzed."

"I was just curious."

"I'm trying to get my life and my marriage back on track. I'm trying as hard as I know how to remember that there are good things in life. I'm also trying to shove all bad memories out of my mind."

"Are you expecting that having a baby will give you all of that?"

"Again, Doc, are you a urologist or a psychologist? I always wanted a baby."

"Not the last time I saw you."

"Not that you need to know this in order to perform the tests but things have changed in my life. Like I said, I'm attempting to regain control of my life. Now, I need to know what's wrong. Test me, see why I can't give my wife the one thing that she's asked me for."

"Okay, Lieutenant. I'm sorry if I pried. I'm sure there's nothing wrong but we'll do a semen analysis." He gave Eric the information for the lab and looked at him. "Is everything else going well with you?"

"I thought you just apologized for prying."

Laughing, Dr. Samson clapped Eric on the back. "Okay, you've got me. I guess I do like playing amateur psychologist. Are things okay with you?"

"There're not perfect but they're getting better."

"Do you need another refill?"

Eric didn't answer. He wanted to say no but he didn't want to give the pills up just yet. "Will they harm the baby?"

"No."

"Will they prevent me from making one?"

"No."

"Then I guess it wouldn't hurt to have a refill just in case. Listen, any chance the lab can take me today? It's hard for me to get here. Sometimes I just need to do as much as I can while I'm here."

"I send the specimens to a lab in Chicago. It would have probably been easier for you to have gone to a doctor there."

"I didn't want to. Besides, you've already been in my business. I don't need any more people prying into my life."

Dr. Samson smiled at Eric. "Okay," he said, "understood. Do you mind if I ask one more question? I was wondering if you've given any thought to talking with a counselor?"

"I've thought about it," Eric answered, not going farther. He had thought about it. For three months he'd thought about it, and luckily since he was doing everything in his power to make a baby, Gabi had miraculously gotten off his back about talking. She was happy for now and that was pretty much all he wanted, well, what he wanted for things that he had any control over anyway.

With a quick call everything was taken care of. Eric was given an order to take to the lab in Chicago. He'd gone and had given his sample and was headed home. He was genuinely smiling, knowing that he truly wanted a baby. He'd not waited around; he'd done something about it. "Boo-yaa," he said softly.

Eric had known Gabi was going to be waiting for him and he was right. The moment he turned off the key she was running down the drive toward him. He opened his arms and lifted her off her feet. "How did your doctor appointment go?" Eric asked Gabi, giving himself time before talking about his own appointment.

"They're going to run some tests and I'm going to do a basal chart for my temperature. We'll have to make love more often," she grinned. "If there's a spike, you need to get in there and get the job done."

Gabi was grinning, happy, the way she should have been all this time. He crushed her lips with his and moaned, the sweet taste of her filled him with wonder. Damn, he'd almost messed up their marriage. It was getting better now that they were both on the same page.

"We're really trying now," Gabi burst out before her in-laws had a chance to do more than give her a quick hug.

"So I take it you and Eric are working things out? I'm so happy to hear that and I'll be even happier to hear the news that you're pregnant," Ongela said, grinning.

"It won't be long, I'm sure. We both went to the doctor for physicals, just to make sure everything's in working order. But we're not worried, we're young, we're healthy and we're in love." She turned around and found Eric grinning down at her. He kissed her and she tingled. When she tried to turn away, he deepened the kiss, making her knees turn to mush. This was more like it. This was what she'd expected when he returned home, the two of them loving each other, unable to keep their hands off each other.

"Are you two planning on trying for that baby now or are you going to give us the dinner we drove hours to eat?"

"We'll feed you," Gabi teased, "then you can just drive the three hours back. You don't have to worry about spending the weekend with us."

The four of them laughed, knowing the trip was so long that they always stayed for a couple of days. Now that they'd both taken early retirement it made it more convenient. Having grandparents who could come for a week at a moment's notice was going to be a huge bonus, one Gabi was looking forward to.

For three days life was the way it was supposed to be. It couldn't get any better. Then the phone rang and the mood changed.

Listening to Eric's end of the conversation, Gabi heard him ask, "Why can't you give me the results on the phone. Let me speak to the doctor."

She sidled next to him, trying not to allow disappointment to seep into her eyes. She was a nurse; she knew the routine. A sinking feeling hit the pit of her stomach. She slid her hand down to her belly, hating the flatness that mocked her. Her gaze connected with her husband's. She saw a flicker of panic behind his eyes and tried for a smile. She had to put on a brave face. Her in-laws were in the middle of leaving and her husband was about to freak. He was a marine, but above all he was a man. He didn't want to hear this kind of news.

He glanced down at her and she saw the fear in his eyes. "It's okay," she lied, "this is how it's always done. Don't worry. It's no big deal." Her heart thumped twice, then settled down, the motion signaling the death of her dreams. Gabi pasted on a smile. She had to be brave for Eric. She turned to his parents who'd heard the conversation. "Don't you two worry. We promised you grandbabies and we're keeping that promise."

Gabrielle wanted so badly to go with Eric, to be there to hear the news, to buffer her husband's pain. She wanted to protect him. "Baby, it's my day off. I want to drive to Indiana with you. We can stop in Calumet

City and see your parents, make a day of it. We could even take the train in."

"Gabi, I don't need you to hold my hand." Eric stared at her with a stern expression on his face.

"That's not what I'm doing."

"You said there was nothing to worry about. If that's true, why are you so anxious to go with me? I'm a big boy, I can go to the doctor alone."

Gabi moved toward Eric to hold him, but he moved away. "Don't shut me out again," she said softly. "We need each other. No matter what happens we have us. Just remember that. I want you more than anything. I want us to stay strong. Promise me that. Promise me that no matter what happens in the doctor's office we will be okay."

Eric's eyes narrowed and he glared at Gabi, knowing this wasn't what she had in mind. She wanted solidarity but she was castrating him with her words.

"Gabi, I'm not trying to be mean and I know you're trying to be supportive. But that's not what I need from you right now. Let's not play games with each other. We both know what the results are going to be. I need to do this alone. You're treating me as though I'm an invalid. I'm a man, Gabi, a marine, an officer. You need to remember that and respect it. Whatever happens in my life I can deal with it. The problem is, can you?"

He didn't stop glaring at her. Ignoring the hurt in her eyes, he saw the tremor around her lips. "If you want to mourn with someone, Gabi, do it alone. That's not my style. I was doing this for you," he lied. "I could care less if we have kids. Don't worry about me, I'll be just fine."

He shook away the pain that was stabbing at him. Hadn't Gabi just asked him not to go there? He had enjoyed the last months as much as she had. It had taken him a long time to get to the point where he was comfortable with the thought of bringing a child into the world. But damn it, some power was playing games with his life and he didn't like it. First saving his life, then taking it away. What was he, just a chess piece on a board? Was he being used for some powerful entity's amusement?

He glanced back and saw Gabi watching him from the window. He wasn't going to tolerate his wife looking at him with pity. He was a man, damn it. He would live through this. But would he and Gabi make it through what he knew would be a hard time? They'd barely begun to repair their marriage. Would Gabi still love him if he couldn't fulfill his promise? he wondered and felt a chill slip over him. The hand pressed again on his spine and this time he expected the whisper he heard: "*Have faith.*"

His throat closed and he could feel a burning in his lungs. "Whoever is out there listening, please," he prayed. "I don't know if there is a God. Is that the reason You're jacking my life around? If You exist, tell me, show me. Whoever is in charge I need You to listen. I know I don't have any right to ask anything of You. You saved my life and that should be enough, but…please, whoever You are, just allow me to give this one thing to my wife. She wants a baby so badly. You know it and I know it. I want to give this to her. Please, just this once, listen to me."

"*Have faith,*" The voice said again and Eric was determined to try.

"I'm sorry, Lieutenant. But there are lots of babies needing adoptions," the doctor said, not looking directly at him.

"I know that, Dr. Samson, but that's not what my wife wants. She wants my baby." Eric was doing his best to remain calm but he could do nothing about the clenched teeth.

"But there's—"

"Thanks," Eric said, not waiting for the doctor to say more. There was nothing more to say. He wasn't going to have a civilized chat about his not being a man. The one thing his wife wanted was the thing he couldn't give her. Damn. Their trying to have a baby had taken them back to where they'd been in their relationship before he'd ever set foot in Iraq, before he'd seen so many horrors that he wanted to forget. It had been the way it was before he'd caused Gabi so much pain. Now what would they do?

Eric left the office and Dr. Samson knowing he would not bother coming back again. From now on if he found himself in need of a physician he would find one in Illinois. At least Gabi was aware that he'd driven to the doctor for the results. He wasn't hiding things from her anymore. A lot of good having faith had done. He'd tried to have faith the entire three hour drive into Indiana. What good had it done?

Eric turned off the key in the ignition but remained sitting there trying to make his body move, go inside, get it over with, tell Gabi she'd never be a mother. Eric sucked in his hurt and made his way into the house, almost hitting Gabi who'd been behind the door waiting for him.

"Hey, baby what happened?"

He saw her fear. She was afraid and determined to hold it in for him. When she reached her arm out and gently massaged his arm he knew for certain she was already aware of the outcome. He swallowed, not wanting to prolong her disappointment but get it over and done with. "I got the results." He stared at her, wishing it were different. "I'm sterile."

Eric waited, saw the disappointment settle around Gabi, saw her resolve. She was struggling with trying to say the right thing to make him feel better and trying so hard to push her feelings aside. A fake smile appeared on her face but she couldn't do anything about the glittering tears that swam in her eyes. Eric had to give her credit, though, she was being brave.

"It's okay, baby," Gabi whispered through the tears as she rocked her body back and forth.

"It's not okay."

"Eric, there's nothing we can do about it. Maybe we just need to have more faith," Gabi said, remembering the words that had been whispered to her for the past months. She wrapped her arms around her husband, felt him shudder and held him tight. "It's going to be alright, I promise you."

"Don't make promises you can't keep, Gabi."

"This one I can. Come on, we're in this together." Gabi wanted so badly to take her husband's pain inside herself and carry his burden. She saw the hurt in his eyes and her heart broke for him. For a moment she forgot how to breathe. Eric didn't need any more pain. Gabi didn't think he could handle it."

"But you've wanted a baby for so long."

"So what? Maybe it's not meant for us to have a baby. That doesn't mean we can't be happy. I've wanted you a lot longer than I wanted a baby and I have you. Just so the two of us are together I'm happy."

Eric could feel Gabi trembling in his arms. He held her tighter as his throat started to close with pain. He groaned as he held her, wanting to believe she didn't care, but knowing how this news had devastated her. What he wouldn't give to be able to change things, or to do as she asked and have faith. But having faith was not going to change things. He was sterile.

"Gabi, baby, you know you're just saying that. I know how this news makes you feel. I know how it makes me feel. You work around babies all the time, what are you going to do?"

"I'm going to keep working around them, I'm a professional."

"And what if another patient wants an abortion? Knowing what you know, that I can't give you any babies, how are you going to feel?"

"The same way I felt before." She pulled away to look at him. "This doesn't change us. We're still here." She shook her head. "Don't…"

"Don't what?"

"Maybe we should talk to someone to help us get through this."

"You mean I should talk to someone." He moved away. "I don't need to talk to anyone, Gabi, I just talked to you that's enough."

"Honey, don't do this again, don't shut me out. Baby, you were ready months ago to talk to someone. So what? We can't have a baby, big deal."

He narrowed his eyes and glared at her. "It is a big deal and we both know it. Don't patronize me."

Gabrielle took a deep breath to steady herself. Inside she was screaming, her nerves frayed. But now was not the time to give in to histrionics. "Yes, it's a big deal but it's not something that has to destroy our marriage. We love each other, we'll get through this."

"But you want a baby," Eric walked to her, laid his hands on her abdomen and looked at her. "You're never going to have that with me. Maybe we should give it up. Maybe you should find someone else. I'd understand."

"Are you crazy? There's nothing for you to understand. How can you even suggest I find someone else? In a couple of months we will be married ten years. Do you think that means nothing? What if the problem was with me? Would you leave me? Do you think I'd even let you? I'll tell you now, I would never allow you to leave me and I'm not allowing you to attempt to just give me away. That's not your choice. You don't pick whom I love."

"But, Gabi-"

"Don't you but Gabi me. Now I know for sure you need help if you think I would ever leave you for something like this. I wasn't lying when I said there are things I want much more than a baby. I want you. I want us to be happy, to be like we were before you went to that damn war. I want that more than anything in the world."

Gabi came up on tiptoe, kissed her husband and wrapped her arms around him. "I want you, baby."

Eric rubbed his hand across her abdomen and gazed down at her. Gabi's look was genuine, she loved him.

"We're in Chicago, there are specialists here. The doctor you saw is only one opinion."

"He's a specialist."

"So what? He can't have the things available to him that we have here. Even my office could rerun the test."

"I don't think so." Eric cringed at the thought of the people in Gabi's office knowing his business. "I don't want everyone in your office giving me funny glances."

"Okay, okay, calm down," Gabi whispered soothingly, patting his arms. "This is a gigantic city. We'll find someone we can trust. We're in this together and we'll figure something out. But before we give up and accept the word of one doctor we're going to get a second opinion. We, Eric, not you. We're a team and we'll get through this as a team."

Gabi held on to Eric, embracing him until he returned her love. "Come on, baby," she whispered softly, leading him to the bed, undressing him and making tender, sweet, exquisite love to him. "You and I are a team. We'll always be a team."

She worked her magic on him and Eric believed. Maybe the drive from Indiana wasn't long enough to have found faith, but right now, here in the arms of his wife, he knew with her help he would try to have faith. Maybe his making love to Gabi was all that he needed in order to have faith, he thought as he drifted to sleep with Gabi lying on his chest, her arms around him.

Eric reached out for Gabi but her side of the bed was empty. He opened one eye and looked around the darkened room. The red glow of the clock showed it was only two A.M. He heard water running and got up. Why the heck was Gabi showering so early? He smiled into the darkness. It didn't matter why she was doing it, he thought, making his way toward the bathroom to join her.

His hand on the knob, Eric stopped. There was more than the sound of water running. There was sobbing coming from the bathroom, gut-wrenching sobs that tore his heart out. His hand fell from the knob and Eric walked back toward the bed.

So this was how they were going to get through this. His wife was going to lie in his arms and make love with him, and then later cry in the bathroom.

Pain vibrated through every cell in Eric's body. He climbed into the bed wishing he could comfort his wife. It was killing him knowing she was in the bathroom crying her heart out. "Why did you save me?" Eric whispered under his breath. The effort of the words was like sticking knives through him. "Why?" he repeated.

When the bathroom door opened, Eric pretended to be asleep. Gabi lay close to him, her hand touching him, making it impossible to stop the shiver that claimed him. Instead, he turned toward her, held her in his arms and breathed in her scent.

"I love you, Eric," Gabi whispered softly.

"I know, baby, I love you too, he answered.

Gabi's hand searched his body and found him, and he held the moan inside. He didn't know if he had the energy to make love to his wife, even if they both needed it right now. What was the point? Nothing would ever come of their lovemaking. He could never give her the baby they both wanted.

"Eric, it's okay."

"You were crying."

"Just for now, baby. I'm not going to lie to you. The thought of a baby that has your beautiful brown eyes and could be taught so much by you has always been a dream. I know how much your parents want to be grandparents, so yes, I did cry. I didn't want you to hear me because it's over. It's out of my system. Besides, you know me, Eric. I cry once, then the problem's solved. No big deal."

"It's a big deal to me."

Gabi buried her sweet-smelling face in his neck and Eric sniffed in amazement. Since Gabi was fifteen she'd had this special essence that was hers alone. It was partially her scent that had wrapped around him and captured his heart. He couldn't believe it. Even freshly showered she still smelled like sugar cookies. His hand moved under her hips and he shifted to get into position. But before he could enter her, he deflated like a balloon. Embarrassment scored his soul.

"Baby, you're just tired."

He refused to answer her. He was a man on a mission. When his own manipulations didn't work, he nearly choked on his words. "Gabi, I think I need a little help here."

Eric's eyes fell on the bedside clock as he rolled off Gabi to allow her access to caress him. When he looked again, an hour had passed. He'd become hard as long as his wife was touching him, kissing him, covering him with her soft lips, but the moment he attempted to enter her all the air went out of his sails and his erection was non-existent. Gabi wasn't saying much but he could tell she wanted to stop trying. She was tired and now so was he. Damn.

This time when Eric rolled off of Gabi, he flipped over to his side.

"It happens, baby. Every man has an occasional problem."

He wasn't yet thirty, he wasn't supposed to have an occasional problem. His wife saying that it was okay didn't help Eric one little bit. He moved away from Gabi toward his side of the bed and closed his eyes. "Good night, Gabi," he said and pretended to sleep.

Gabi lay in the dark unable to sleep knowing her husband was on his side of the bed, also not sleeping. She'd attempted to wrap her body around Eric but he'd moved several times until she'd gotten the message and moved to her side of the bed. Thread by fragile thread her marriage was slowly unraveling and there wasn't a darn thing Gabi could do about it.

She waited, listening for the voice to tell her to have faith, but this time the silence was all that greeted her. Even the voice no longer believed. Gabi wanted to cry so badly she could feel it in her throat, her eyes, but she couldn't cry, even softly, without her husband hearing. And he didn't need another thing to feel sad over. Of all the ways she'd imagined their life to be, this had never been even a remote possibility

Chapter Ten

Eric was holding on by a thread, determined not to allow his failure as a man to alter his marriage. But so many failures were piling up on him, making him doubt, first his failure as an officer to keep his mind on the danger at hand, and now his failure as a husband to Gabi.

He wondered about the God Gabi prayed to. If He did exist, for what purpose were the lives of mortals? Were they all just created for His amusement?

Eric didn't believe in Darwin's theory either. It made no sense. He'd always reasoned that if man had evolved from apes, why were there still apes? Why hadn't all apes evolved? Why weren't they extinct?

But he did believe some supernatural being with power that Eric didn't have had somehow put things into play. Maybe the power could be ascribed as God. Eric didn't know, but if He would stop screwing around with his life he'd think it over. Hell, he might even begin to believe.

He looked out over the base and up at the sky. "I'll give it a shot," he said. "Some being saved me, that much I know, and some being is screwing around with my life. Please stop," he said simply. Why not? That was as much a prayer as any he'd heard. He didn't see a need to beg or grovel and bowing down on his knees wasn't in his plans. This would have to do.

He let out a breath. "Give me something," he said softly, "show me You're God and maybe I'll believe. I need to feel like a man again. Give me the ability to give my wife a baby and I'll believe. If You want me on my knees you'll get it. Make the impossible, possible. Change what can't be changed and we have a deal. I don't go back on my word." Eric smiled at the sky. "I'm a marine officer and my word is my bond."

Eric chewed on his lips and sighed, blowing out the air that he was continually taking in. He shook his head, just a little. No mythical being was going to be able to solve his problems. It was all nonsense.

"Lieutenant, we need some help at the recruiting stations."

Eric looked toward his commanding officer and saluted. "Sir, I've never done recruiting." He felt a knot in his gut knowing what was coming. He didn't want to do it.

"You're a marine, you can do it."

"What am I supposed to do?"

"You're going to Waukegan and they will decide where you're needed most. We're trying something new. There's going to be a crossover with the other branches. We want you to work in teams, perhaps with another officer from the recruiting stations. There are still a few wrinkles in the plans. But from now on Waukegan will be your home base. You may not necessarily remain there, but it will be your new home.

Eric took a look around Great Lakes and blinked. "How long, sir," he asked.

"Until you get the job done."

"What specifically is the job?"

"You're going to all of the schools in Illinois and even in the field, to the homes of ROTC students. The enlistment is dangerously low. We need you to instill some pride, get the quota up. Bring us some bodies."

Eric shivered. That was what he feared most about the assignment, bringing bodies. Hell, it was bad enough that he had to look into the faces of college kids. Now he had to talk high school students into signing up to die. He shivered. *Is this what You saved me for?* Another thought followed. Maybe it wasn't Gabi's God at all that saved him. Considering his new assignment he rather doubted that it was.

For three weeks Eric was traipsing all over Illinois talking at schools, and not just to the ones with marine programs, but air force as well. If they had ROTC he was talking. He'd finally landed in Joliet and was working primarily with Master Sergeant Leon Ross. Lucky for Eric they got along from the moment Eric arrived.

Eric glanced at the sergeant, grateful that the atmosphere had been different from that of the temporary posts he'd been sent to. There was none of the hidden animosity, as though Eric were stepping on someone's toes. They were military but they had worked beyond that and were on the verge of forming a friendship. Now they were taking their show on the road to the homes.

"Lieutenant, are you ready to go?"

"Sure, let's do this." Eric looked at the man and observed the premature lines on his face. Eric had thought him much older than the fifty-five he said he was. He looked to be at least sixty-five. Then again, doing what he was doing could age a person big time.

"Ma'am, I'm Lieutenant Jackson and this is Master Sergeant Ross. Your son is in the ROTC program at Lincoln High School. We want to talk with him about making the service a career."

"A career," the woman screeched at him. "What kind of career? There's a war going on."

"Of course there's a war going on, ma'am. And we do our duty to defend our country."

"My son's only eighteen."

"He's old enough to join without your consent."

"He's not joining."

"Could you please tell me why he's in the ROTC program at school if he has no intention of serving his county?"

"It wasn't like there were a lot of other programs open."

"But joining ROTC is a choice, not a requirement."

"He wanted a uniform to impress the girls, okay?"

Eric looked at the woman sternly, hoping to stop her tirade. They had not been invited inside, and he doubted that they would be. He took a peek inside the home, looked at the neighborhood, then back at the scowling woman. "Is your son planning on going to college?"

He noticed the slackness around the woman's mouth that told him they couldn't afford college. Of course not. When it came to gathering data the corps was the best. They'd done their work carefully. The recruiters had been instructed to concentrate on the low to middle income homes, with particular emphasis on Latinos, blacks, and poor whites. They were their target, someone to whom they could offer a chance at an education, a cash bonus, an opportunity to travel.

Eric ignored the feeling of ants crawling over his spine. He had a job to do. He was a marine and he was going to do it.

"We have a sign-up bonus," Eric said softly, "up to ten thousands dollars if your son meets the qualifications, plus full tuition to a college of his choice. If he makes the service a career he can retire with a very nice pension in his forties. We'll even help him get a home. He'll get to travel to foreign countries, things he'd probably never be able to do on his own. We'll be there for him every step of the way."

"Will you be there for him if he comes home with both legs blown off?"

"If that should happen we have very good hospitals throughout the country. Veterans are never alone. A disabled veteran has a lifetime pension."

"Just like the one hundred dollar a month pension my husband received from serving in Vietnam and being sprayed with Agent Orange? No thanks."

"Ma'am, Eric said, talking around the knot of disgust in his throat. "Casualties happen in war. We all hate them but we're trying to do a job, to protect our country, to protect you and your family. Serving our country is an honor and a privilege."

"How much are you getting, Lieutenant?"

"Excuse me?"

"How much of a bonus are you getting for every young person that you deliver? Fifty dollars? A hundred? How much is my son's life worth to you? Tell me, are you going to go to Washington and try to recruit the senators' sons?" She stopped and looked around.

"Or are you concentrating on the people who don't live in five hundred thousand dollar homes?"

"That's not what we're doing…I would go to Washington if I were given orders to." Eric blinked, determined to do what he'd come for, to sign up another marine. "I wouldn't be a marine if I didn't believe in what we're fighting for."

"Lieutenant, please leave my home. I don't believe you, I think you're lying. You look at my son as a quota. You get a bonus when you sign up a kid. You will not be the one worrying about him every night, praying he'll come home alive. You'll not be the one to bear the pain if he doesn't."

"I feel the loss of every soldier," Eric answered, allowing his gaze to linger on the woman. "That is not a lie."

"Not like a mother or a father. They have to be your babies for you to feel it. And a flag-draped coffin will not make me feel any better. You should be ashamed of yourself."

Eric stared straight ahead; he was ashamed of himself. "It's my job, ma'am. I'm a marine."

"And I'm a mother," the woman said and slammed the door in his face, making Eric jump.

Damn. Eric clenched his teeth and breathed out hard. "How many more on the list, Sergeant Ross?"

A glance around the smoky bar had Eric wishing he had not come. He should be home with his wife. If he could have anything in the world that he wanted, it would be to erase the last eighteen months from their lives. He blew out a breath, shaking his head as he did so.

"Whose shit list are you on?"

This time Eric did grin. Then he laughed, looking directly at Sergeant Ross. It was obvious Eric's new assignment had something to do with him screwing up, probably the little speeches he'd been giving to the troops leaving for the war. This was the higher ups' way of reminding him who and what he was.

"It's that obvious, huh? I think since I've been home maybe the general thinking is that my mind needs a little readjusting. Having me recruit kids doesn't sound like the way to fix anything."

"No, it doesn't, but it does let you know who's boss."

Eric held up his glass and clicked it with the other marine. They drank, not mentioning the frosty reception they'd received in all of the homes. None of the parents wanted their kids to join up. Neither Lieutenant Eric Jackson nor Master Sergeant Leon Ross blamed them. But it wasn't their job to tell civilians their thoughts. They were both soldiers and they had orders to increase enlistment. To be honest, a part of Eric wanted to get someone to join, so he could end this assignment. The longer he was in the field without results, the longer he would be made to stay in the field. It was a vicious circle with only one end. Besides, both men knew the moment trouble broke out everyone would expect the soldiers to take care of it. How were they going to do that if no one wanted to make a commitment?

"I'm not signing back up." Sergeant Ross spoke softly with some regret tinging his voice. "I already have my years in. My wife's worried that things may get so desperate they'll ship me over. I promised her when this contract is up I'll come out. I've got another two years."

"I have a year left." Eric glanced around the bar before returning his focus back to the sergeant. "I always intended to make the service my career, to retire, just like I've been telling the kids, have a nice pension and a good job and live comfortably."

"What changed your mind?"

"Probably the same thing that changed yours." Eric stopped dancing around the issue and looked the sergeant in the eye.

"What changed mine is my nineteen-year-old son enlisted, wants to follow in my footsteps. He's made me so damn proud. But I'm scared as hell that…I don't want my son to die. Not just in a war. I don't want him to die, ever. I want to see him marry, have kids of his own." He took another sip of his drink. "You got any kids?"

"No," Eric admitted, "not yet." There was no need in saying not ever.

"Well, wait until you become a father. Those civilians were right; you don't understand until it comes right in your face."

"Did you tell your son not to join?"

"How the hell was I going to do that? He respects me. He'd think I was the biggest hypocrite in the world to go out and tell other kids to join and then tell him not to. But to tell you the truth, I keep hoping my wife will go off, tell him no damn way. He broke up with his girlfriend. I don't know if he thinks that will win her back or what. I just know that he wants to go and there ain't a damn thing I can do about it. I'm serious, I'm not signing back up."

"Neither am I," Eric admitted. "Damn," he added, taking a long swallow. "It must really be hard on you being a recruiting officer."

Eric waited in vain for an answer while Leon Ross looked past him, his eyes dead and haunted. "I should call my wife," Eric said at last, not making a move to reach for his cell. "She's probably worried about me." Still he didn't call, knowing that his phone was off and Gabi couldn't contact him. He closed his eyes and swallowed.

"*Have faith.*"

In what? Eric wondered. The voice was coming more frequently. He'd put off counseling but if the voice continued he'd go just to find out the meaning of the voice. The base had a counselor but it was the last place Eric would go for mental help. When he left the corps it would be with honors, not as a mental case.

"Want to dance?"

Eric's eyes traveled up the lean brown feminine body standing before him. "Sure, why not?" he said, putting his glass on the table and moving to take the woman in his arms.

An hour of dancing passed more quickly than Eric could have ever imagined. He was on his second drink with his dance companion, his fourth for the evening, two over his usual limit. He was feeling no pain and no guilt that he was making his wife worry.

"I love a man in uniform."

Eric smiled. He'd heard that line a thousand times. His usual response was, 'So does my wife.' Not tonight, though. Tonight, he didn't want to mention Gabi or acknowledge the fact that she was sitting home worrying about him. He was tired of her worrying about him. He was her husband, not her son. His eyelids closed and he swore he could see her sitting on the sofa in front of the television, not concentrating on the picture, but thinking of him. He didn't want to see the pity in her eyes tonight. He wanted to forget that he couldn't be a man for her, that he couldn't give her a baby.

"Thanks," Eric said at last. "I'm glad that I wore my uniform."

"What's your rank?"

"General," Eric lied.

"Really?"

"Really." Eric smiled at the woman. "Have you ever been with a general?"

"No, but I'm always ready to try new things."

"I bet you are," he said, smiling into her black eyes, looking at her chocolate brown skin and neatly weaved hair.

He held out his hand to her. "Come on, let's dance some more." When she laid her head on his shoulder he thought of Gabi and the fact that she would smell the woman's scent on his body, on his clothes. So what? he thought. So what? He'd had a hell of a day.

"Lieutenant, are you ready to go?"

Eric looked toward the sergeant. "I'm having a good time," he replied lazily.

The sergeant glanced down at his watch. "My wife is probably worried about me, sir. She can't sleep until I get home."

The message was loud and clear. Eric and the sergeant had talked about their wives. His dancing for over an hour apparently had the sergeant worried and rightfully so. Eric was more than tempted, he was ready. And if he had his own car he might have followed through on it. He smiled in the sergeant's general direction, wondering what would happen if he stayed away all night.

"Lieutenant?"

"I thought you were a general," the woman spoke, laughing.

Eric hunched his shoulder and grinned at her.

"It doesn't matter. I've never done a lieutenant either."

"Mercy," Eric said and smiled, walking away. "Maybe next time."

Chapter Eleven

For three hours, Gabi had sat in front of the television not watching the programs, repeating over and over to herself that she would not call Eric. He was a big boy. He knew she was worried about him. She was trying her best to give him space to work it out on his own. Between finding out he was sterile and not being able to maintain an erection the last few times they'd made love, things were not good. Talking only seemed to make it worse, so she didn't talk, not about anything important anyway.

The click of the lock blasted through the quiet house like a bullet. Instead of the tension draining out of her body, more settled around Gabi's shoulders. She wanted to run to Eric, examine him, and make sure he hadn't been hurt. Not tonight, she thought. She'd wait until he came to her.

"Gabi, why aren't you in bed?" Eric asked, coming to the doorway of the living room.

The slurred speech made her head jerk up. "Did you drive home like that?" she asked before she could stop the words.

"No, Sergeant Ross drove me. I'll need you to drive me in tomorrow. My car's at the office."

Eric stood there staring at her, a look on his face that struck at the core of her heart. She was losing him and he was doing it deliberately. Saving a marriage took more than one person; it took two. Gabi no longer knew which way to go. If she talked he got angry; if she didn't, she got angry.

"You hungry?" she asked instead. "Did you eat?"

"No, I didn't eat. You got something on the stove?"

"I have a plate for you in the fridge. I can warm it up for you."

"Thanks."

So polite, she thought, the two of them could be room- mates. She passed him on her way to the kitchen and caught the scent of perfume, stopped and looked at him, frowning at the lipstick on his shirt. She shook her head and headed toward the kitchen. Not tonight, she thought. Tonight she wasn't in the mood. Tonight she would warm his dinner and pretend that he wasn't reeking of alcohol and another woman's perfume.

"Eric, I made an appointment for a physical for you. You have Saturday off, so Friday you need to fast. No drinking after work because they're going to draw blood."

"How do you know what the doctor is going to order?"

"It's a physical. It's not hard to figure out. Why are you being so suspicious?"

"I just don't know what reason you have for going behind my back and making an appointment for a physical."

Gabi couldn't keep the sigh from escaping. "Look, it's no big deal. My insurance requires it for both of us."

"Then this is for insurance purposes?"

She glared at him. "I want to make sure you're healthy. They're doing me a favor, blood tests, X-rays, EKG, the works."

"What, no test for STDs?"

Gabi stood up and looked down at him. "Should they test you for STDs?" She grabbed her keys from the hook and walked out the door without saying goodbye. Her body was shaking with the effort to maintain control.

Gabi fumed the entire way to work. Nothing was going as it should. She'd talked with Ongela and had been advised to wait it out, to give Eric more time. She would give Eric all the time he needed but she wished he'd give her just a little help, just behave as though he liked her. She was beginning to question it. She wondered what she'd done to make him stop liking her.

Opening the door of the clinic, Gabi paused. This used to be her home away from home. She'd always loved working here but now even the office felt stifling. Her relationship with her co-workers was deteriorating almost as rapidly as her marriage. Trying to remain sane at home and at work was becoming a for real juggling act. Gabi stopped as she saw Traci heading for her. She took a deep breath, wondering what was coming now.

"Gabi, where were you last night?"

What an odd question. Gabi looked at Tracie and witnessed a flicker of something pass across the woman's face. She didn't know what was up but her skin crawled. "Why?" she asked instead of answering the question.

"I saw Eric last night in a club in Joliet. At first I thought it was you dancing with him." Tracie hunched her shoulder. "But after an hour or so I could tell it wasn't you."

Gabi's spine stiffened as she ordered her body to obey her commands. She was not going to break down and she was not going to let Tracie think she didn't know Eric had been out dancing with another woman.

"Eric went out for a few drinks with the sergeant he's working with. He told me he had a good time dancing and had a few too many drinks. He didn't mention seeing you there, though."

"I guess he was a little too preoccupied."

"Probably," Gabi answered, not taking the bait. "I'm sure he didn't intend to be rude. Next time you run into him you should speak, he'd love it. I am surprised that it took you an hour to notice the woman he was dancing with wasn't me."

Gabi reached for the next chart, smiled, and called the patient into the room. She was grateful she didn't have to give shots at the moment. She was feeling much too volatile to stick anyone with a needle.

Tracie was supposed to be her friend. And what she'd done Gabi didn't consider friendly. It was a dig, pure and simple. But there was not a damn thing she could do about it, and she refused to wear her feelings on her sleeves. She thought of Tracie telling her she could tell she and Eric were fighting because Gabi had not been oozing with stories about him.

Gabi took the patient's blood pressure and replaced the cuff, her mind still on Tracie's comment. She would have to make sure their lunchtime conversations contained dewy-eyed comments as she lied about something wonderful Eric had done. She had no choice but to lie as he'd done nothing wonderful in months, not since finding he was sterile.

Gabi stuffed the laundry into the washing machine, determined not to bring Eric's shirt to her nose, determined not to try and place the scent. She closed her eyes and felt the knife jabbing away at her. She couldn't believe Eric was cheating on her. Cheating was one of the two things she wouldn't tolerate. They'd talked about this before they were married.

Eric knew that she wouldn't stand for a man putting his hands on her and that she wouldn't stand for her husband cheating. She'd told him that. She'd grown up with cheating and spousal abuse in most of the foster homes she'd been placed in. She wasn't going to take either.

As much as she loved Eric, she'd been telling him the truth when she told him that she would leave him. Tit for tat, baby, she thought to herself.

Gabi couldn't help it. She brought the shirt to her nose, the perfume stinging. She wasn't crying, she told herself. "I'm just having an allergic reaction," she said softly as the tears fell from her eyes and streamed down her cheeks.

"Girl, your husband's a good dancer."

"Isn't he, though?" Gabi grinned at Jamilla, wondering where she'd seen Eric dancing. She was grateful she had her hand wrapped around her Coke. She sucked the icy drink through the straw and into her mouth, fighting the urge to fling the liquid on her co-worker.

"Yeah, he danced with me once last night but then this hoochie got him and wouldn't let him go."

"Can't say as I'd blame her," Gabi answered and took a bite of her sandwich.

"I was going to ask him to give me a ride home but he left before I got a chance."

"Too bad. Were you there with Tracie?" Gabi asked, ignoring the shards of glass piercing her soul, or her blood that had to be running down her arms and her legs.

Gabi looked at the floor expecting to see a puddle of her blood, but there was nothing.

Where's your 'have faith' now? she silently asked the voice in her head. *Seems when I can use you telling me that, you aren't here. Why? Is it because my husband is screwing around on me and there is nothing you can say? Well, let me tell you this: Having faith ain't gonna cut it. If he's screwing around, his ass is out.*

For the rest of her shift Gabi avoided Tracie's looks of pity and Jamilla's smirk. She wanted to kill Eric for humiliating her like this. Sure, he was hurting, but so was she. But she wasn't running out to clubs getting smashed, or dancing. She was sitting home worrying about her husband and wondering how to fix their marriage.

The sound of babies crying in the waiting room renewed the pain Gabi was carrying. She'd begged off working with the pediatrician but that didn't prevent her from seeing or hearing all of the babies coming in for their checkups.

Her stomach lurched when Tracie walked toward her. There was a determined look in Tracie's eyes, the same look they all had when they had to tell a patient bad news. "What's the matter?" Gabi asked before Tracie could open her mouth.

"Come into the back with me. I need to tell you something."

"Sure." The voice that came from Gabi's mouth did not sound like her at all. It sounded like someone who had stuffed their mouth full of rocks. Tracie turned, giving her a inquisitive look, no doubt wondering why Gabi wasn't following behind her. Her feet wouldn't move, that's why.

Gabi gave a weak smile and ordered her brain to send the proper command to her feet. She followed Tracie into the kitchen, surprised when Tracie kept walking out the back door of the clinic and into the parking lot. The numbness became all encompassing. This was serious.

"Let's walk across the lot to Dominick's."

"But…"

"It's okay, we won't be gone that long."

"Tracie, you're being so mysterious. Just spit it out, tell me what's wrong." Gabi stopped walking, wanting to get this over with.

"Jamilla is angry with you."

"You mean that little confrontation we had about Mr. Rivers? I apologized."

"She was angry with you long before that. She's jealous of you and she's out to hurt you. I just wanted to warn you to watch your back."

"What can she do to me?" Gabi stood in the middle of the parking lot knowing exactly what it was Jamilla could do to her.

"She's going after Eric. It's no secret that the two of you are having problems. I've seen him without you several times now in the same club in Joliet, and so has Jamilla."

As they walked into the store, Gabi decided to forget the pretense of coming there to shop and leaned against a wall. "Are they… She took in a breath. "Do you think she's sleeping with him?"

"You would know that better than me." Tracie blushed and looked down. "I'm just telling you so you can put a stop to it."

"Eric wouldn't cheat on me."

Silence.

"He wouldn't." Gabi swallowed. "I don't even know why I asked you if they were sleeping together. I don't think even Jamilla would go that far, we're friends."

"With friends like that you don't need enemies."

"Tracie, the entire time Eric was gone, Jamilla was a good friend to me. She kept me from being so lonely. I owe her."

"You owe her nothing. She wanted someone to party with, and you were alone and lonely. She wasn't hanging with you for you, but for herself. Now that Eric's returned she's jealous."

"Of what?"

"Of what you had."

Gabi blinked. Tracie had said *had*. A soft groan slipped out of her. She didn't have enough friends to lose any. And if she admitted to the truth, she wasn't feeling confident enough about her marriage to do nothing. The thought of making amends with Jamilla came to her. Maybe if she did something to let the woman know there were no hard feelings, maybe Jamilla would play in someone else's back yard.

"I was thinking of having a cookout, inviting everyone from the office," Gabi lied, having just thought of it on the spot. She shrugged her shoulders. "I shouldn't have called Jamilla on Mr. Rivers. Maybe it's up to me to make amends." She glanced expectantly at Tracie.

"You can try. But if you're hoping Jamilla will have a conscience and keep her hands away from your husband, I'd say that's a long shot."

What Gabi was hoping was that Eric would keep his hands off Jamilla. She wanted to remind him that Jamilla was her friend.

"Having the party is not all about Jamilla. I need some normalcy in my life. I need a party, I need to have some fun."

This time when Gabrielle smiled, she meant it. She had not thought about how much she needed fun until the words came out. A party might not be the thing to fix her marriage but she was sure hoping it helped her state of mind.

The moment they were back in the office she went to her co-workers and invited them for a weekend cookout. When she told Jamilla there was a moment's hesitation.

"You sure you want me to come?" Jamilla asked. "You've been treating me funny for weeks."

"I'm sorry if you thought that. And yes, I want you to come." Gabi grinned. "We're friends, I don't care what anyone thinks." Something flickered in Jamilla's eyes and she stared at Gabi.

"You don't care what anyone thinks about what?"

"Nothing, I just meant we're friends." Jamilla gave her another strange look.

"Remember, Gabi, a dog that will bring a bone will carry one. It's not always the hoochie you have to watch out for around your man. It's the old bats that pretend they're so sanctimonious, the ones who want to make you think butter wouldn't melt in their mouths."

Gabi saw Jamilla glaring in Tracie's direction and knew she was aware of their trip to the store.

"Chill, Jamilla, no one's said anything. I just want to have a party, and I want to thank you for getting me through the year Eric was gone. You were a good friend," she said moving closer, hugging Jamilla and noticing Jamilla didn't hug her back. "Can you come?" she asked as she backed away.

"Don't worry, I'll be there. With bells on," Jamilla added.

A sinking feeling settled around Gabi's heart as she walked away telling herself that Eric would not disrespect her by going after Jamilla. *But Jamilla will go after him.* The words surged through her mind. The thought to cancel the party came to her but Gabi released it. She really was in need of a party.

It had been a long week waiting for the party. Instead of tension decreasing at work it had increased. Now Tracie was also avoiding her. Gabi couldn't help wondering from time to time about Jamilla's words. She couldn't help wondering if maybe it was Tracie who was lusting after Eric. Sure, Tracie was twenty years older, but what did that matter? Jamilla could be right.

Another Man's Baby

Now Gabi stood in the middle of her home and surveyed it, making sure all was as it should be. She had enough food and drinks to feed three offices. She smiled. The house was pretty and she was in a festive mood. Eric hadn't given her as much resistance as she'd expected. In fact, he'd invited several of the guys from the base and even Sergeant Ross and his wife.

When the first guest arrived Gabi's spirits lifted and continued in that vein with each new arrival. The music and laughter were just what she needed. She mentally patted herself on the back, glad she'd thought of it.

When she heard Jamilla and Tracie's voices, she was ready for them. Opening the door she could feel her smile slide down her face as her eyes opened wide. She did a double take, tried not to gawk and couldn't quite cut it.

"What?" Jamilla asked.

"Nothing, nice outfit," Gabi answered, moving aside to allow them to enter.

"Thanks." Jamilla turned and in spite of the music the room went silent for a moment as everyone took in Jamilla's outfit: hot pink daisy dukes and a hot pink halter top that had to be three sizes too small. The boob job Jamilla had gotten two years before was working overtime. More of her breasts were pushed out of the small square of material than was covered. She was so damn close to being naked that Gabi wondered if her home could be raided by the police for indecent exposure.

"Hey, you two," Eric said, coming to stand alongside her. "Want a drink?" he asked. Then he stood back, gave Jamilla a once-over, stopped, looked again and smiled. "That's some outfit, Jamilla," he said softly and Jamilla beamed. Tracie threw Gabi a look that screamed I-told-you- so.

So maybe the party wasn't such a good idea. Gabi lifted a bottle of beer from the tray Eric was carrying. He looked at her for a moment but didn't comment. He knew she never drank beer. She thought it smelled like urine. Now Gabi twisted the top and brought the bottle to her lips. She turned from her husband and brought the bottle down. It still smelled like urine.

For the next three hours Gabi did her best to ignore Jamilla trying to press up on her husband every chance she got. To anyone else the party was a rip-roaring success. Everyone was laughing, joking, eating, drinking and having a good time, even Eric. Gabi couldn't remember hearing him laugh that much since before the war. She wanted him to laugh, only she wanted him to laugh with her.

Walking toward Eric to see if she could coax a dance out of him she paused when she saw Jamilla bump into him. He'd just picked up a fresh batch of pina coladas that Mike had made. The bump was deliberate. If Jamilla's jutting hip hadn't told her that much, the smirk on her face when she saw Gabi watching her did.

"Eric," Jamilla screamed, "you got liquor all over me. You put it on me, now get it off." Mike relieved Eric of the tray and handed him a towel.

As Eric's hand move to swipe the sweet drink from Jamilla's barely concealed flesh, Gabi stepped between them and snatched the towel away. She glared at Eric and Jamilla before tossing the towel to Jamilla. "You're a big girl," Gabi hissed, "I think you can take care of that by your-self." She turned back to glare at her husband. "I need you in the kitchen."

Eric grinned as he followed the sway of Gabi's hips into the kitchen. He'd been thinking all evening how good it was for the two of them to be throwing a party. This one was a success in more ways than one. Eric had been unable to take his eyes off his wife the entire night. Every time she came into view he got an instant erection. He wanted her so bad his teeth ached. Too bad it took a party to do that. But he wasn't going to complain; anything that got him over the hump was welcomed.

"What are you doing?" Gabi snapped the moment they were in the kitchen.

He looked at her, his mouth watering at the sight of her breasts jiggling a little as she poked a finger in his face. He took her finger and kissed it. "What's up, baby?" he said, patting her behind. "Aren't you having fun?"

Her eyes narrowed. "Are you kidding me? Stop flirting with Jamilla."

"Jamilla, please, it's you I want, baby," he said, pulling her close, nuzzling her neck. "But it makes me feel good to know you're jealous." He slapped her behind and laughed going out the kitchen.

She couldn't believe it; he thought she was kidding. It was time for this party to come to an end. Gabi went back to the front of the house, turned off the music, and began emptying plates. When the guests started drifting in to see what had happened to the music, she began handing them their belonging, hugging them and telling them how glad she was they'd come.

"What's up, baby?" Eric came to stand beside her.

"Party's over," she replied between clenched teeth.

"Good," he smiled and began helping with the cleanup. *So, Gabi is as anxious as I am to make love*, he thought. He stared at her behind for a full five seconds before turning away. He was rock hard. It was good that she was kicking everyone out.

"Is that for me?" Jamilla looked down at Eric's crotch, pressing herself close to him, hugging him and kissing each cheek.

Eric followed her line of vision and grinned. "Nope, that's for Gabi," he whispered, then laughed out loud. "Good seeing you tonight."

The last guest gone, Eric locked the door, then walked slowly behind Gabi, his arms sliding up her hips, her body sending heat flooding through his veins. He was hot. It had been way too long.

Mercy, he thought, grinding his pelvis against the round mound of Gabi's behind. When she turned in his arms he stopped short. The look in her eyes wasn't one of love or lust; it was fury. When she took a step back, he knew what was coming but was too late to prevent it.

Whack!

Eric's hand came up and he rubbed at his cheek. Gabi had slapped him so hard that he was positive his teeth were loose. Besides that, his ears were ringing. "What was that for?" he asked, not pretending ignorance. He really didn't know.

"Are you really that stupid or you just plain don't give a damn about hurting me anymore?" Gabrielle shouted somewhat incoherently.

"What are you talking about?"

"You. You were all up on Jamilla and you got an erection. I saw her looking at it and you grinning like a fool at her."

"Baby, you've got it all wrong. I swear it wasn't like that. I've been thinking about you all evening, wanting to make love to you. I could barely wait until everyone left. That's for real."

"If you think you're touching me tonight I know you're crazy."

"Don't you want me?" Eric stared at her, shock going through him. What had happened here?

She walked away, giving him a look of disgust, as if he were the lowest form of life on the planet. When he heard the lock click on their bedroom door, he tried to see things from Gabi's side and shook his head. Women! There was no making them happy. Gabi was hurt when he wouldn't touch her and now she was angry when he wanted to. Damn, he was not in the mood for begging.

"Gabi," he yelled, running up the stairs. "Come on, open up, baby. Please listen to me. Don't shut me out," he begged, "It wasn't what you thought."

"Go to hell," was the only answer he got back. And hell was where he already was.

Chapter Twelve

When Eric woke his wife was gone. Though he called out, he knew from the empty feel of the house that Gabi wasn't in it. It wasn't as though either of them had to go in to work. It was Sunday, the day they used to spend lying in bed and making love.

He groaned, wondering when his marriage had degenerated into what it now was. He would never have believed this would happen to them. Eric showered and dressed, skipping the coffee Gabi had made, turning the pot off instead. When she was this pissed, he didn't think it wise to drink anything until he talked to her.

When Gabi returned she'd sought refuge in their bedroom. She wasn't ready to face her husband but now it was becoming downright silly. She'd made lunch and now was forced by hunger to sit in her husband's presence. They sat across each other at the table barely speaking. Gabi could tell that Eric was trying not to look at her and it was breaking her heart. She didn't know if it was because he was sorry or guilty. She couldn't tell.

"Where were you?" Eric finally asked.

"Church."

"Church?"

"Church," Gabi answered. "Don't look so surprised. I went a few times while you were gone."

Eric's eyes closed and he groaned, rubbing his head as if that would make the situation better. "What's happening to us?" he asked finally. "Are we still in love?"

"I am," Gabi said so softly that he had to strain to hear her. And Eric noticed that she said it as though she were afraid she was the only one in love. What had he done to her? He hated his actions. Though part of him wanted her to leave and find someone who could help her fulfill her dreams of a family, a larger part of him would never be able to bear it if she did.

She was watching him with the oddest expression on her face. Then he noticed the lone tear roll down her cheek. "Don't do that, baby," he whispered, going to her, falling on his knees and pressing his head against her chest. He felt the trembling of her body and looked at her. Instead of the one tear, there was now a flood.

"I love you, Gabi, forgive me, baby."

"Are you sleeping with Jamilla?"

"No."

"Are you cheating on me?"

"No."

"What are you doing?"

"I don't know." He wiped the tears from her eyes, kissing her face, her nose, her eyes and finally her lips.

"Talk to me please. I feel so alone," Gabi whispered.

"I know and I wish I could tell you everything. I feel so dirty, Gabi, so inhuman, I wonder how on this green earth I deserve to have you. I should have died in Iraq. I should have never come home. I've done nothing but hurt you since I returned."

"Don't ever say that. I would have died too if you had not come back."

"But you're dying now. You're slowly dying a little every day. I can see it and I know I'm doing it to you. I want to stop. You have no idea the lectures I've given myself. Each time I leave this house with you in tears, I swear I'm going to stop it. Then I have to go to work, and I have to talk some kid into signing up." His body jerked and a shudder made him close his eyes tight.

Eric ran his thumb over Gabi's arm and felt her tremble beneath his touch. "You're the only clean thing in my life. Sometimes I want you so

bad to fill me, to take away all the dirty spots, to fill me with your good-
ness. I want to tell you every horror I've seen and have you kiss me and
tell me it's okay. I want you to make it all better for me. Then I come to
my senses and think, 'No, I can't defile her like that.'"

"But that's not how I look at it. You're my husband and you're shutting me out. I want to help you."

"Why are you still with me?"

"You're my husband."

Eric thought he saw a flash of pity and stood to walk away from her.
He shook his head. "I'm still a man, Gabi."

She pulled on his sleeve. "I know you are, I never thought differently.
If you're thinking not being able to give me a baby makes you any less a
man in my eyes, think again."

Her words stabbed him and he flinched. "It seems you went to that
conclusion awfully quick."

"Don't turn this around, we both know that's what you meant. I've
tried telling you I don't care. All I want is for us to survive this."

"If you don't care, why do I always hear you crying when you think
I'm asleep?"

"I'm not crying because I can't have a baby; I'm crying because I'm
losing you."

The two of them stood staring at each other only inches apart. Eric
wanted to reach for her to assure her that she wasn't losing him, that he
was the same as he'd always been but that was a lie. He'd never be the
same after all the things he'd done. Right or wrong, what he'd done was
etched on his soul and he didn't know how to erase it. "Why did you go
to church?" he asked, holding her gaze, swallowing his hurt when she
came toward him.

"I went to pray for us," Gabi answered softly, touching him, caressing
him, the tears still streaming down her face.

"Do you think it'll help?"

"I hope so. All I can do is have faith." She glanced upward at him.
"I'm not sure if I know what that means. I'm thinking it's the same as

patience, but I'm not sure. And… I'm running out of patience. Is the therapy helping?" she asked, switching the subject.

"No," Eric answered truthfully, because it wasn't, because he wasn't going and when he'd gone he hadn't talked. He couldn't tell anyone the things that weighed on his soul, not ever.

"Maybe if you try talking to me, tell me what's bothering you. You never know, just talking to me might help." Gabi looked down, her shoulders trembling. "You treat me like the enemy. I love you, Eric, I swore to love you for always, to have your back as you had mine. But you no longer have my back. You're hurting me and I can't take much more."

"Another threat?"

"No, baby." Gabi stared at him and shook her head slowly. "You can't or won't talk to me but I know one of us needs to talk. You're pushing me away and one day I'm going to believe you no longer love me. One day when you push, I'm going to push back. All I ask is that you be honest with me, give me a reason to believe you love me, give me a reason to even want to have faith. Talk to me."

Eric rubbed at Gabi's ever increasing tears with his thumb. "You never used to cry."

"I never had a reason to cry before."

With her words Eric crumbled, pulling Gabi hard against him. He held on to the one good thing in his life that he was pushing away. "I love you, Gabi, you have to believe that. I'm trying to find my way back to you. Just hang in for a little while."

Her shoulders shook. "And baby," he added, "I do have your back, I've always had your back. Even this, my hurting you, has been because I had your back."

He saw the doubt creep into her eyes and slipped a finger under her chin, raising it to meet his lips. He'd kiss away her doubts. He'd make love to her until she would know with every fiber of her being that he could not stop loving her, that even if he died, he would be thinking of her, sending her his love.

As Gabi's arms wrapped around him, it wasn't lust that fueled his desire but love. He lifted his wife into his arms and carried her to their bed. Then he kissed her slowly, going over every inch of her again and again, using his tongue, his mouth and his kips to tell her what he couldn't say with words. He wanted his lovemaking to soothe her wounded spirit, to lift the burden she carried.

And he would do it even as he added another pebble to the mountain of guilt he carried in his soul. He'd be damned if Gabi thought he didn't love her. Sure, almost on a daily basis he thought that she would be better off without him but still he didn't want her to stop loving him.

For the next few weeks Gabrielle had renewed hope. Things were not as they had been between her and Eric, but the decay had at least ceased. She treasured each moment they were together. But still there was something eating away at Eric, something that he wouldn't share with her. Gabrielle had almost tired of changing the channel when Eric became lost in news of the war. She didn't want to be his warden, only his wife.

When he'd wake up in the middle of the night drenched with sweat, his eyes wild, she'd hold him, pleading with him to let her in. There were times he'd seemed on the verge, then he'd look at her, shake his head and tell her that he'd work it out in therapy.

Therapy had been Gabi's idea but it didn't seem to be helping. As much as she didn't want the irrational tinge of jealousy it ate at her anyway. Knowing that Eric could sit in an office and tell things to someone else that he couldn't tell her burned at her pride.

Gradually Eric began staying out again. Only now he'd kiss her on the forehead when he returned home. And he'd hold her, his way of assuring her of his love, she supposed, but it was no longer enough.

Blind and stupid were not roles Gabi had ever expected to play and she couldn't do it now. Not when more and more often Jamilla would comment at work about having seen Eric, having danced with him. Gabi had promised Eric she'd give him more time to find his way back to her.

But she'd also made a promise to herself that she wouldn't be dogged. She'd broken that promised to herself. It wasn't that Gabrielle doubted Eric's love, but dogged was still dogged no matter how you looked at it.

Gabrielle chopped garlic, onions, tomatoes and green peppers to top the frozen pizza. Eric was watching her. His eyes held a question but there was no answer Gabi could give. She no longer knew what he wanted.

"You're looking tired," He said.

She popped the pizza into the oven, opened the fridge and took out a bag of salad. She was waiting before she answered him, not wanting to snap. As soon as the salad was rinsed she dried her hands and turned to face him. "Why do you say that, because I'm only making frozen pizza and salad for dinner?" She opened the cabinet and took down two cans of broccoli cheese soup, opened them and dumped them in a sauce pan. "Is that better?"

"No, it has nothing to do with the food."

"Then what? I don't understand what you're asking me." Gabi bit her lips, trying to remain calm, not wanting to lash out at him and say, "Hell yes, I'm tired.' She waited.

"Your soul seems tired."

She blinked. Her soul was tired. "How can you know my soul is tired? You're not here often enough to know that." God, if only she could have bitten back the words. Gabi waited, she didn't feel like fighting any more.

"Do you still love me, Gabi?"

Immediately tears flooded her eyes but she refused to allow them to fall. "I've done nothing to make you think I don't love you."

"You've given up."

She began to tremble. If he was deliberately pushing her buttons he was doing a damn good job. She slid into the chair at the kitchen table across from him. "Given up on what exactly?" she asked, narrowing her gaze and staring at him.

"On me."

"What is it that you want me to do?"

"Fight for us."

Pain flooded Gabi's body, radiating to every cell and membrane. She'd done this once too often. Her eyelids shuttered close and she clenched her teeth together, determined to regain control.

"Why don't you call me on my bull anymore, demand that I stay home?"

"You're not a little kid and I'm not your mother." She rubbed her face, then opened her eyes. "Do you really think I want you home with me if I have to beg you?"

"I didn't say beg, I said demand."

"I'm also not a marine officer. Eric, you know right from wrong. You know if I decided to take to the streets you would have a fit."

"So why haven't you?"

"Is that what you want me to do?"

He shrugged. "I'm just curious, that's all. You say I'm not me anymore but you're not you anymore. You would have never allowed me to get away with any of this before."

"Your behavior is now my fault? You come home three to four nights a week late from chasing tail and it's my fault?"

"Do you really believe I'm doing that?"

Gabi could only glare.

"That's what I mean. You think I'm stepping out and you've resigned yourself to it. I don't want a martyr, Gabi."

"Why don't you try telling me what it is you do want? You've been home long enough to get over whatever happened. You've asked me to be patient, to have your back. I've done that, and now you're complaining."

"Having my back is not giving up on us." His head tilted. "I have a question for you."

"What?"

"Tell me, what is the prescribed time for getting over things you thought you would never do? What is the time frame for getting over taking someone's life?"

"It was war."

"What is the time frame for feeling guilty about recruiting kids to send them into this madness?"

"It's your job."

"That wasn't the question. I want to know how long you think it's proper to feel the way I do."

"I have no idea. Why don't you talk it over with your therapist?"

"Right now are you hurt or angry, Gabi?"

"I'm pissed."

"Then why don't you go with that? The long-suffering wife is not a role you wear well and it's not one I want to see."

Gabi stood to check the pizza. "So, you want me to go stone ghetto on your ass? Let me repeat, I'm not your mother and I'm not your commanding officer. If that's what it takes to have your back, then I guess I no longer have your back." She slid the pizza on the platter, cut wedges, placed the plates on the table and proceeded to eat.

So that was what he wanted, Gabi fumed. Her husband had no idea. She resisted the urge to smash the pizza into her husband's face. He was making her tired. Pick a mood, any mood, she thought, and stay with it.

"Are you still praying for us, Gabi?"

"No," she answered and continued eating.

"What happened to having faith?"

"Fairy tales, Eric. I've stopped believing in them. I count it lucky that the one prayer I prayed was answered. You came home…alive. Perhaps I should have prayed for more."

Eric didn't have an answer for Gabi's statement. He wondered if that was the reason that his life had been spared. Was it because of Gabi's prayers, because of the prayers of his mother? He shuddered. That couldn't be the reason. The entire United States was in constant prayer over the safety of the troops, or so he'd been told on many occasions.

"I do love you, Gabi." Eric gazed at his wife, somehow knowing this time she would not return the endearment. They ate in silence.

"Want to watch television with me?" Gabi asked at last, unable to bear the deafening silence. Her breath hitched and she swallowed. "I mean, if you're staying home."

"What's on?" Eric's eyes held hers. He'd seen her swallow, saw the quiver as her breath became trapped in her chest. He wanted to tell her again how sorry he was that he was no longer the man she'd married and loved.

But how many times could you tell a person that you were sorry, especially when he didn't know if he would stop hurting her. She was watching him. It made his heart hurt and he ached for them. For a moment he wanted to ask her to continue praying for them. He wanted to pray for them himself but he didn't know how.

"Gabi, what do you want to watch?" he asked again.

"I taped a few episodes of *Spouses Cheating*," she said, spooning the broccoli cheese soup into her mouth. Gabi watched as Eric's eyes lifted and he stared at her.

"Sure, why not? I'll make popcorn."

Gabi could feel Eric's eyes on her as they watched the taped shows of spouses catching their partners in the act of cheating. "Hey," she said, turning toward him, "would you like to go dancing this weekend at that club in Joliet you've been going to?"

"I didn't tell you I'd been to Joliet."

"No," Gabi said, reaching for a handful of popcorn, then turning deliberately toward the television. Eric turned also.

"Are you having me followed, Gabi?"

She frowned, looked at Howard Deeds, the host of the show, and smiled. She stared for a long moment at the couple hitting each other, screaming and generally making fools of themselves in front of the millions of people watching the show.

"I would never do what those people are doing," Gabi said, not quite answering her husband's question. "I can't imagine wanting the entire world to know I'd been played for a fool." She reached for more popcorn. "So, do you want to go dancing?"

"How did you know I'd been to Joliet?"

"Tracie and Jamilla were there. Jamilla said you danced with her."

"And?"

"And nothing." Gabi looked at him as though he were nuts, pretending that she wasn't dying inside. "I just wanted to know if you wanted to go dancing with me. We haven't been out in a while. I'd like to go."

"Why the club in Joliet?"

"No special reason. I just figured if you liked it, it must be good. If you don't want to go there we can go some place else."

She was playing it cool, but not cool enough. Eric saw the tiny quiver around her lips. He stared at her throat, saw her swallow several times and knew what she was asking him: Have you cheated?

Well, it depended on how one looked at it. He remembered Jimmy Carter saying once that he'd cheated in his heart. Eric understood now exactly what the ex-president meant. He'd also cheated in his heart. He ran his tongue over his lips, thinking Gabi would be better off without him. He was not doing anything but hurting her but somehow he couldn't seem to release her.

"I don't want to go dancing," he answered at last. He saw the way Gabi bit her lip and hated himself for hurting her deliberately. "Maybe we can catch a movie, maybe a comedy." She smiled and it was all that he could do not to go to her and gather her in his arms. He'd only thrown her a crumb. Eric was ashamed of himself, but the spiraling was happening so quickly that he didn't have the momentum to stop it. He was afraid now to touch her, afraid that he'd not be able to complete the act.

Another Man's Baby

"Do we have anything for an upset stomach?" he asked as the acid churned in his belly from the guilt that was eating him up. Nothing had lessened since he returned home. Instead it was increasing—his guilt over the war and his guilt over the hurt he was heaping on his wife. Eric didn't know how much more he could take.

"Yeah, there's a bottle of antacid in the fridge. Did the dinner upset your stomach?"

"No," he said, leaving the room to get the antacid, wanting to tell her it was the guilt that was eating a hole in his intestines. Maybe it was a good thing Gabi had forced the physical exam on him. Eric didn't think he was in such good shape.

Gabi watched Eric's back as he walked away. She was shaking so hard that she wrapped her arms around her body. Her cooking wasn't what had upset her husband's stomach, she decided. It was more than likely the show they were watching. If he was uncomfortable watching it, that was just too bad. If you didn't cheat, it shouldn't bother you. She reached for the pillow from the sofa and screamed into it, muffling her sound with the fabric. A movie would do them good. At least they'd get out of the house.

Chapter Thirteen

Eric hung up the phone and heaved out a breath. He'd made a decision. It was time to get some help. He'd been home almost a year. His semper fi attitude was not solving the problem; it was only making things worse, not better. Marines prided themselves on their straightforward approach to mission and steadfast dedication to accomplish it. Things did not have to be spelled out for them; they knew what it meant and what to do about any situation. As much as Eric believed in *semper fidelis* with heart, soul and mind, he could finally admit he needed outside help. He'd to do what he'd promised Gabi. He would actually try and talk to the counselor he'd been pretending to go to.

But first he would talk to his father. He sighed and closed his eyes. He was sick of his new assignment. Recruiting didn't suit him. He would miss Sergeant Ross, but he didn't want to continue there. However, no new orders had come down for him and when he'd questioned it he'd been told that his orders stood as they were until further notice. It was beginning to look as though he'd been forgotten.

He was seriously thinking about giving up his commission early. Another ten months and that would be it. He would be free, but free to do what? He didn't think when he took off his uniform that it would make a difference in how he felt. It wouldn't stop the memories or the nightmares. Eric closed his eyes and willed away the memories, something that was working less and less. He sure hoped his father had an answer.

"Thanks, Pop," Eric said, climbing into the passenger side of his father's Escalade and leaning back into the butter soft cushion.

"You're my son, why are you thanking me?"

Eric attempted to smile. "Tell me how you and Mom survived. I need to know."

"You're talking about Vietnam?"

"Yeah." Eric wished he didn't have to ask but he needed to talk to someone and his father was the only one he wanted to ask.

"I've never talked about it, Son."

"I know."

"Your mother and I separated for three years. She moved to San Francisco."

"Three years! Why didn't either of you ever mention that?"

"It wasn't any of your business. You're our son, but that was between husband and wife."

"Why did she come home? I can't believe after three years she would."

"Neither could I. But I had to try. I went there and begged her on my hands and knees. I stayed there with her for six months, winning her back, making her fall in love with me all over again."

"And she did."

"That part was easy; she'd never truly stopped loving me. But it took a long time for her to trust me or my love. She refused to even consider having a baby for several years. And after you were born she refused to have any more."

"Why?"

"She told me straight out that she was trying to protect herself. She said if anything ever happened she wanted to give you as good a life alone as she could with the two of us. She said she would not allow herself to struggle alone raising kids that she could not provide for."

Eric watched while his father's eyes darkened with pain.

"I'd hurt her." Terry shrugged. "The pain was so deep that every day since I've worked hard to regain the things we'd had. And even now I know that while she gives me ninety-nine percent of her heart, she keeps that one percent tucked safely away, wrapped in cotton. He smiled. "I know it shouldn't matter, not that tiny percentage, but I want it all. I'll never stop trying for that other one percent. I had it once so I know how it feels and I want it again."

"Did you ever talk to Mom about the war?"

"By the time we got back together, it wasn't the war. It was all the things I'd done to hurt her. She couldn't have cared less what I'd done in Vietnam, it was what I'd done to her."

"Did you cheat on her?" Eric asked.

"Yes."

"Did she find out?"

"Why the hell do you think she left me?" Terry groaned loudly, then gave Eric's hands a couple of pats. "Are you cheating on Gabi, Son?"

"In a way," Eric answered honestly. "I'm not giving her what she needs and I know that. Have I slept with another woman, no, but I've been thinking about it and I have been doing more than I should. Right now in our case, I don't know if that would be the worst thing. I think Gabi might be better able to forgive that than my shutting her out."

"Then let her in, tell her what she wants to know."

"I can't, Pop. I don't want to see the look in her eyes."

"What did you do over there, Son?"

Eric closed his eyes. "I don't want to see the look in your eyes either."

"Eric, your wife is right. You can't hold all of this in forever. Do something before it's too late."

"I am. I made another appointment with a therapist and I intend to keep it."

"Are you going to talk?"

"At least I'm going to go."

"Don't wait until it's too late, Son. The last few times we've seen Gabi it's like the life is slowly seeping out of her. I remember that look on your mother's face. I don't want to see it on your wife's. We love her too, Eric, she's our daughter. I don't want to see her hurt. And I don't want to see you hurt if you lose her."

"I have no idea why she hasn't left me."

"Sure you do, she loves you and you know it. That's your safety net, that's what's allowing you to shit all over her."

Eric flinched. "I'm not..." He stopped. He was. "Did it bother you this much?"

Another Man's Baby

"Killing is never easy, at least not for those who have a conscience. We were both in kill or be killed situations but at least you have the support of the nation. We, the Vietnam vets, didn't have that. The entire country was against us. As black soldiers we were supposed to be fighting for the freedom of others but we'd left our home where we had few rights and returned to find we still had few or no rights. I came home during the riots, right after Dr. King was assassinated. It wasn't an honor during that time to be a marine, or an American, and being black was like…" He sighed and shrugged. "It was a triple threat. I'm surprised your mother and I ever made it back." He glanced at Eric and slowly shook his head at his own memories.

"Dad?"

"I'm not saying you had it easier," his father continued. "You didn't and I know you don't want to talk about it, but remember, I'm here if you do. I was a foot soldier, a grunt, just following orders. You were in command and had to give orders. 'Heavy is the heart that wears the crown.'"

Eric laughed. "I didn't wear a crown."

"I couldn't think of anything else that would fit. You know what I mean."

"I know. Thanks for not telling Mom that you were meeting me." His father smiled but didn't answer. Eric thought over his parents' relationship. Things he'd never known colored his observations. It was as though a light bulb had gone on.

"Is that why you take Mom to San Francisco every year?"

"Yes," his father smiled. "I take her there because that's where she fell in love with me again. But it's also for me. It's a reminder to me that I'm the guardian of her heart. I'll never hurt her again."

"But the two of you fight like crazy," Eric laughed.

"All married couples fight. Besides, I never promised not to fight with her. I just promised not to hurt her and I haven't."

"Dad, I really am trying with Gabi. I'm determined not to let our marriage disintegrate."

"Good. We want you to be happy, Son. We want Gabi happy."

142

Eric had always known the extent of his parents' feelings for his wife. It had always amazed him that they'd accepted her so quickly. Now he suspected there was a reason for that immediate acceptance. "You two really do look at Gabi like a daughter, don't you?"

"Why do you think we fell in love with her so quickly? I'd always wanted more children." Terry paused, sucking in his own hurt. "Your mom always wanted a daughter." He smiled. "In fact, she prayed for twins, a girl and a boy. She loves Gabi as much as she loves you. If you make her lose Gabi she's not going to forgive you."

"I don't want to lose Gabi, Pop, but you're putting a lot of pressure on me."

"I'm telling you how it is. You're a military officer, buck up."

Eric couldn't help laughing. In a way his father was treating him as though he were a little kid. He'd given him a verbal spanking. And Eric was grateful. It was just what he needed.

Less than a week later temptation vied with duty. Eric groaned. Just when he'd decided to stop going out to the club, he was being asked to go again. He shook his head at the sergeant. "I don't want to go to the club anymore. My wife doesn't like it at all and I don't blame her.

"I wouldn't ask if it weren't important. I'm so worried about my son I just need to unwind."

Eric couldn't help thinking of the many times the sergeant had been there for him, being the designated driver while Eric drank a little too much and danced with any hoochie who pushed up on him, going farther than he should but not far enough that he'd be lying to Gabi when she asked if he were cheating. Other than giving a woman or two a ride home on occasion, Eric had never left with any of them. Sure, some of them had thought when they asked for the rides in their suggestive voices that he'd give them a different kind of ride. But Gabi's picture hung from his rearview mirror, always there to remind him, to stop him.

"Let me call Gabi and tell her I'm going," Eric finally acquiesced. "But I can't stay out late. I really need to repair my marriage."

Gabi couldn't believe what she was doing. She'd found the matches for, Foxes Jazz Club in the bathroom at work and had known immediately either Tracie or Jamilla had left them there for her to see. One might be trying to help her, but the other would be trying to stick it to her. Since Gabi's perceptions were off, she no longer trusted her own instincts, or the motives of either woman. Still, she wrote the Joliet address down, leaving the matches where she found them, not even mentioning them.

When Eric called to tell her he wasn't coming home, she'd had enough. Her shoulders sagged with heaviness, and depression wove its way though her spirit. She'd sworn never to do this.

Gabrielle thought of Eric asking her to fight for him. She shouldn't have to fight for him. He didn't have to fight for her. This was the end of what she was willing to put up with. She'd had her man's back. She'd done all and more that she knew to do. She thought of how much she would miss Eric's parents. They were Mom and Dad to her, but how long would that last?

Gabi felt a shiver as she pulled into the parking lot of the club, noting there was nothing special, nothing that should have kept Eric coming back for over three weeks, especially after she'd kind of called him on. Maybe he just didn't give a damn. She spotted his car and braced herself for what she would find inside.

Gabi was trembling, looking over her shoulder for a moment, wondering if Howard and the TV crew of *Cheating Spouses* would blast through. She swallowed and bit her lips. She'd sworn she'd never follow any man, not even this man who was slowly crushing her soul with his indifference.

She ordered a Coke from the bar and sat in a dark corner booth to watch, wishing like hell that she hadn't come. She should go home. When you went looking for trouble, you always found it.

She heard a loud laugh and didn't have to strain to see the person. She knew from hearing it most days of the week that it was Jamilla.

At first Gabi pressed into the cushions to not be seen and then thought better of it. She had every right to be there. She watched Jamilla dancing, her hands trailing all over the man in uniform. Gabi's heart froze. The man in uniform was trailing his hands all over Jamilla as well. They were dancing so nasty that they might as well have stripped and had sex right there on the damn dance floor.

Gabi downed her Coke, wishing it was something stronger but glad that she'd be at least clearheaded enough to drive home when this night was over.

She headed toward the dance floor, not knowing exactly what she was going to do when she stopped walking. She'd not rehearsed it, had hoped she wouldn't find her husband here.

The smell of sugar cookies pulled Eric's head away from Jamilla's chest. He blinked and looked up, not as surprised as he would have thought to find his wife walking toward him. He glanced over her shoulder for the camera crew, wondering if that was the reason she'd begun watching *Cheating Spouses*.

Jamilla caught his lack of interest in her and stared first at him, then in the direction he was looking. At first Eric had thought to keep dancing with Jamilla, keep touching her and allowing her to touch him. Then he saw the smirk on Jamilla's face.

His gaze fell on Gabi. He couldn't hurt his baby like that. Hell, he'd disrespected her enough already. He wasn't going to have another woman think he'd dis his wife for her, not in front of her face. Hell no, that wasn't going to happen.

Eric dropped his hands from Jamilla's body and walked toward Gabi. "Hey, baby, he said, drawing her into his arms, whispering into her ear as he did. "If you make a scene Jamilla will think she won." He felt the tension uncoil slightly in his wife's body.

"Where's the camera?" he asked. He wrapped his arm around Gabi and groaned as she wrapped her arms around his back. And then he tensed as her nails dug into his flesh. He wanted to move away. She was ripping into him so hard he could feel the blood seeping out. She deserved her anger. She felt brittle, as though she might break.

"Gabi, ease up, baby, you're hurting me," Eric whispered in her ear.

"And you're killing me," Gabi answered.

Eric closed his eyes. Damn, what the hell was he doing? Once again, he thought maybe it would be best for Gabi if he were not in her life, if she were able to find someone with whom she could have the babies she wanted.

"Listen, Gabi, I-"

"Shut the hell up," Gabi said in a hoarse whisper. "Don't you dare defend your actions."

He'd started it and he would have to play it out. Gabi walked over to where Jamilla was sitting and he wondered if she would continue to play it cool.

"Jamilla, listen. I don't mind your dancing with my husband, but as for your touching him the way that you were, I don't play that. Understand?" she said.

"Talk to your man." Jamilla struck a pose and turned her palm out to Gabi.

"Oh no, you didn't!" Before Gabi could say another word Eric was kissing her, kissing her right there on the dance floor with all the passion he hadn't shone her in weeks. Hell no, Gabi thought. Does he really think it's going to go down like that? His grip was tight around her and his lips fused with hers.

People were clapping, Jamilla looked embarrassed and disappointed. The skank.

Eric twirled Gabi around, kissed her again, and sat her on her feet a distance from Jamilla. "You've won, baby. Let's go home."

"Won? Won? What the hell have I won?" She glared at her husband.

"Your dignity, baby. Let's get out of here."

If she didn't have her dignity who did he blame for that? Surely not her? Gabi had had it. She was not fighting over Eric, but she sure as hell was going to kick his ass when they got home. She was so angry that she thought again about the drink she hadn't had, glad now that she hadn't. In this condition she was mad enough to run Eric over in the parking lot. If she'd had a drink she didn't think she'd practice any self control.

"You okay, Gabi?" Eric asked. "I mean to drive home?"

She glared at him. "Are you worried about me?" She pushed his hand from the door, put her key in the ignition, and gunned the engine. Despite her resolve, she couldn't stop the tears from flowing. What a low life, trashy thing to do. Did he have to screw around with someone she knew, someone she worked with, a so-called friend? Tit for tat, baby, she thought as her mind devised a plan. I told you what I would do if you ever cheated on me.

"Have faith."

"Shut up," Gabi screamed, "just shut up. This is my life, stay out of it. I'm not having faith, I'm kicking his ass out." She gunned the car, opening the window to dry her tears. She refused to have it out with her husband with tears in her eyes.

Gabi pulled into the drive fast and ran straight to the bedroom and began ripping Eric's clothes from the hangers and throwing them down the stairs. She was in the midst of throwing his underwear when he came in behind her.

"I didn't do anything."

She hurled a vase of flowers at Eric, but missed him and hit the wall. She kept throwing things. She'd never known this side of herself existed. She'd also never known she could hurt this much, that Eric could hurt her this much. She'd been doing everything in her power since he'd returned home, going along with his problems, trying to be understanding.

"Calm down, Gabi."

Gabi stopped throwing things and glared straight ahead. "I want you out, Eric. I want you out now. It's over. I don't want you here anymore."

Eric scratched his forehead, knowing good and well that this was what he'd brought on, hoping that she'd leave him. Maybe then he could stop feeling so damn guilty. Now that it was happening he didn't see how he could leave her, especially when she was so upset.

"Gabi, I wasn't going to go to bed with her."

"Go to hell, Eric."

"Listen, where do you think I'm supposed to go tonight? This is my house too."

"I don't care where you go, just go."

"Look, I'll sleep in one of the other rooms. This house is big enough for both of us." Before he could move Gabi was pounding on him, hitting him with her fists, kicking him, screaming the entire time. He'd brought her to this.

"Stop baby," he pleaded, but his talking seemed to be doing one thing and one thing only, making her angrier. "I'll leave now," he said and turned and walked down the stairs, sliding down the last few, ducking as Gabi aimed another vase at his head. He was shouting, "Stop!" at her but she was so busy throwing that he had to run out of her firing range. He didn't stop running until he was sitting in his car listening to the racket she was still making inside the house. He wondered if she'd change her mind and cut up all of his clothes. He should have left her alone, not said a word until she'd cooled down.

Damn, he'd been asking for this. What had he expected was going to happen? Eric groaned and sat there to wait it out. It was three hours before the lights went out and still Eric waited another hour before reentering the house. He opened the door quietly and stood there. Gabi's energy was so strong that her pain wrapped around him and nearly choked him. He took a step toward their bedroom and stopped, wondering which room to sleep in. He stood a better shot of Gabi's not killing him if he stayed in the basement. But he didn't want to be that far from Gabi.

Eric picked up his scattered clothes as he went. As near as he could tell, there were not any shredded items and he didn't smell the stench of bleach. He picked all the clothes up, then listened at his bedroom door. Damn it. And damn him. His wife was sobbing.

"Gabi," he said, pushing the door open. "Don't cry."

"Eric, just leave me alone. You didn't worry about me when you were feeling Jamilla up, so don't bother worrying about me now. I don't need your sympathy, I can do without it."

"Baby."

"Close the door," she yelled and tossed a pillow at him. He blew out a breath and closed his eyes as he closed the door. Okay, it was time he seriously sought help. He might be drowning in doubt but there was no need for him to take Gabi down with him. Marine or not, he couldn't fix this problem alone. He couldn't blow it up and make it go away. He went to the bedroom next to theirs, dropped his pile of clothing in a chair and undressed without turning on a light, not bothering with putting away his clothes. He was dead tired.

"I want a divorce."

Eric poured a cup of coffee. "Why?" he asked, deciding to go on the offensive. "Because I drank a little too much and flirted, or because you think I'm no longer a man?" The words hurt when they came out. He'd said them to manipulate her, but realized when the words hit the air that that was how he was feeling, like half a man and not even a half man worthy of having his life spared.

"Don't run game on me, it's not going to work," Gabi said, looking evenly at him. "I want a divorce because for whatever reason, you don't want to be married to me anymore. You've been home almost a year now and things are getting worse between us. You've been shoving me aside, trying to make me ask for a divorce and now you've got it. I don't want to do this anymore. I want a divorce."

"What about counseling?"

"What about it?"

"Shouldn't we try that first?"

"Too little too late."

"You don't love me anymore?"

"Not enough to allow you to treat me like this." Gabi looked directly at him. "Why is this bothering you now? You've wanted this for months, you've just been too much of a coward to say the words." She took in a deep breath. "So have I."

"I didn't mean to hurt you, Gabi."

"Yes, you did." Gabi laughed hysterically. "I'm not naïve. You did this deliberately. There was no reason for you to do it like this. All you ever had to say was, 'Gabi, it's over.' You say I don't think you're a man. Guess what? I don't. But it's not for the reason you think. A man would have just 'fessed up and told me what he wanted. I've been asking you for months, allowing you to walk all over me, to yell and act as though I have no right to question you. I'm tired, Eric. I can't do this anymore." As Gabi walked toward the door, she glanced at the clock. "I have to go."

"This is important." Eric walked slowly toward her, desperation in his voice. His father had warned him, the voice had warned him. Now he'd waited too long. He'd lost Gabi. "I've called in, Gabi, can't you do the same? We need to talk." He walked closer before putting out his arms. If he could only hold her, he could make it right. "Gabi," he whispered and reached for her. She stopped him.

"Eric, if you touch me, I swear I will slap the taste outta your mouth. Now step off."

He backed up, knowing he'd gone way too far. "Can't we be civil to each other? Shouldn't we set some ground rules?"

"We had rules, you broke them."

"I'm going to get counseling."

"Good for you," Gabi said, glaring at him. "I hope it helps you."

"Gabi, please call in, this is important. We need to talk. I talked to my father. Ask him if you don't believe me. I told him how rotten I've been to you and that I was going to stop. Come on, baby, you've been wanting to talk."

"I don't believe you." Gabi laughed. "*Now* you want to talk? What was it you told me, baby? You don't have time for this nonsense? Guess what? Neither do I."

Chapter Fourteen

Taking a deep breath Gabi let it out and walked into her office. She needed her job but she didn't need the crap she was going to have to deal with. *Please God, don't let that skank get up in my in face, or I will not be responsible for what I might do to her.*

She shouldn't have prayed. The first person to cross Gabi's path was Jamilla.

"Can we talk?" Jamilla said, coming up to her.

"Sure." Gabi took a step back just in case she needed the swing room.

"I'm not trying to take your man," Jamilla said.

"Excuse me? You can't take my man. If you could he wouldn't be my man, now would he?" Gabi walked away to take care of her patients, ignoring that Mrs. Darden had her twins, ignoring the smile they gave that made her heart melt like butter. No, Gabi was determined to turn her emotions off. She refused to let the fact that she and Eric couldn't have a baby and now would never even have the opportunity to adopt one together, get to her. And she for sure wasn't about to let Jamilla think that she was worried about her stealing her husband. The nerve of the heifer.

Heat from the mug of vanilla, cinnamon latte warmed her hands. Gabi wouldn't deny that she was enjoying the coffee Eric had made especially for her. Nor would she deny that she was enjoying the wary truce between herself and her husband. He'd actually waved a white flag in front of her face for days until she'd calmed down enough to talk to him without wanting to fling something at him.

"Gabi, breakfast is ready. Did you want me to bring you a tray…or would you like to eat at the table…with me?"

For a moment she twisted her mouth to the side in contemplation.It was strange, for three weeks they'd lived together in separate rooms. They were getting along better than they had before she'd kicked him out of the bedroom. Eric was almost his old self, funny, considerate, coming home at a decent hour.

"I'll eat with you. Just give me a second to say goodbye to Mom."

"Thanks, baby?"

Gabi's head snapped up quickly and she narrowed her gaze on Eric, not speaking but telling him with her eyes that they were not yet at the calling her 'baby' stage."

"Thanks, Gabi," Eric said, getting the message.

"Gabi, he's trying so hard," Ongela said, her voice wistful. "Come on, honey. You know you don't want to divorce him. I know he's been hurting you, but, Gabi, he'll die without you."

Gabi sighed and took in another breath, letting that one out also in a sigh. She listened to her husband setting the table. She swallowed as she returned her attention to Ongela. "No, I don't want a divorce. I love Eric, but I'm tired. You forget, Mom, we've had these calms spots before. It's like he's an addict trying for a while to remain straight, wanting to be good but eventually going back to old habits and falling off the wagon."

"Not this time, Gabi. I don't think it's going to happen that way. He's scared. He's been here several times begging me to talk to you, asking his father for advice. He loves you, honey. He doesn't want to lose you."

Gabi couldn't help it, she wanted to believe in her husband just as much as her mother-in-law. But that was part of the problem. If she was going to compare Eric to an addict she'd have to compare her own past behavior to that of an enabler. She'd sat back waiting for him to change back into her husband, not holding him accountable for his behavior, making excuses, and hoping, always hoping things would get better. Gabi was sick of it all and disgusted with herself for having allowed her husband to walk all over her repeatedly in the past year. She brushed away the tears that started to well in the corners of her eyes.

"Mom, I don't know if I can trust Eric anymore. I've had it with his on again off again behavior. Yeah, right now he's being the old reliable Eric. But we both know the reason why. Divorce. That word stopped him. Think about it, Mom. He's a marine. He considers divorce a failure. He can't have that." A heaviness filled her chest at the possibility that her words might just be true.

"He loves you, honey."

"I'm not so sure anymore. If he loved me he wouldn't have treated me like this. I've tried to be understanding."

"It's the war, Gabi. It make men behave strangely. The Vietnam war changed Terry."

Gabi wanted to scream, 'Enough.' Ongela was calling her daily in an effort to keep her from actually filing for divorce. She'd have to give it to Ongela. She was relentless in her efforts to keep her and Eric together.

Sucking on her teeth for a moment she tried to think of a different approach, something that would make her mother-in-law hear her. "Mom, I've tried being understanding. You know I have. Tell me how long you want me to put up with Eric? If I forgive him, what happens if next time he decides to bring some woman home and screw her in our bed? Are you still going to tell me to hold on, to stay with him?"

"I'd never do that, Gabi. I would never tell you to take Eric's cheating on you."

"But, Mom, that's what he's been doing. Maybe he hasn't had sex with anyone yet, but he's cheating on me just the same. He wouldn't talk to me, he spent all of his time with other women. What do you call that?" Gabi sniffled and dried her tears when she heard Ongela crying on the other end of the phone.

"Please, Gabi, just hold off on the divorce. You said you two have a truce. Let's see how this plays out. Maybe you can forgive him. Don't you want to be able to forgive him?"

Of course she wanted to forgive her husband but she was afraid for a good reason. She'd meant it when she'd said she was done with her past behavior.

"Do this for me for, Gabi, please. I don't want to lose you. I love you."

Fear raced through her at Ongela's words. More than her marriage was at stake. She stood to lose her entire family. "I love you too, Mom," Gabi whispered. "And I don't want to lose you either." New tears were running down her cheeks. "I want to forgive Eric. I really do. But, Mom, he has to show me this time it's for real. This time he has to mean it. I'm not going to keep giving him more opportunities to hurt me."

"So you're going to forgive him?"

Gabi couldn't help smiling at her mother-in-law's manipulation. Ongela had broken her. She loved her and was always there for her. How could she refuse her? Still, Gabi didn't want to give in quickly. "I'll hold off on going to a lawyer and I'll see how it goes. As long as we have a truce I'll wait it out."

"Gabi, everything's on the table."

Gabi was grateful for Eric calling her. She loved Ongela and always would, but this was her marriage. Ongela had made some good points. They had an almost ten year marriage at stake. She had to be sure before she took a final step to dissolve her marriage. She'd do as she'd promised. She would wait and see what happened next.

"Mom, I have to go," Gabi said, breaking into Ongela's pleading. "Eric has breakfast on the table." She hung up the phone before Ongela could say more. Eric peeped his head around the corner, his eyes questioning. They stared at each other for a nanosecond before Gabi followed Eric to the kitchen.

She was grateful they weren't fighting, but she hadn't said she didn't want a divorce; neither had she sought out a lawyer to make it happen. She'd decided to give it another week or so and see how it went. After all, Eric had started seeing a counselor. There was hope, she thought as she finished breakfast and went out to the garage and backed out. The car bounced, then jerked. Gabi stopped the car abruptly. Something didn't feel right. She backed up a little more, going slowly, hearing another thud.

She got out and looked at all the tires, then groaned. A flat tire. She almost kicked the car but didn't. Instead, she backed up a little more and pulled Eric's car out. "Eric," she yelled. When he poked his head out the door, she asked, "Are you going anywhere? Can I use your car?"

She saw the surprise in his eyes. She'd never asked to take his car before, but why shouldn't she? Her money helped to pay for it. It was her car also.

"Of course," Eric answered. "Want me to go with you or would you just like me to change the tire?"

Gaby stared for a moment at her husband. Even when they were being nice to each other there was this degree of uncertainty that she didn't like. But still it was better than what they'd had. She wasn't forgetting Jamilla or any of the rest, but she was willing to continue the truce. Her in-laws initial call begging her not do anything hasty had postponed the trip to the lawyer for that reason.

She noticed Eric was still waiting for her answer. "Change the tire for me, please. Thanks," she added. "Maybe when I get back we can pop in a movie."

Her heart stopped at the full-fledged grin he gave her. "Good," he said, "I'll call for pizza."

Just like old times, she thought. It was Saturday and Eric wasn't going anywhere without her. They were going to stay in tonight to watch a movie, together. Gabi smiled all the way to the store and all the way back. She didn't even stop smiling when the oranges she'd bought spilled out of the bag when she hit a quick stop. For a change her mood was bright. It had as much to do with her mother-in-law asking her to hold on as it did with Eric's attempts to make things better. The coffee he'd made for her brought a smile to her lips. She'd have to admit, he was trying.

Before she was even out of the car Eric was opening the door to help with the bags. "Hey," he said, taking the bag from her and walking toward the kitchen.

Gabi smiled, deciding to leave the rest of the bags for her husband, and began rummaging for the oranges. She jerked her hand back when she felt something strange. It was slick and limp. She bent and looked under the seat. All the air went out of her lungs. She spotted what she'd felt and also a splotch of red silk. An inner knowing filled her with dread, making her numb. She reached for a tissue and pulled the used condom out. Then she took more tissue and fished for the silk. Her world went black when she held the panties in the tissue. She felt she would die on the spot.

"I'll get the rest of the bags," Eric said. "What are you doing all bent over? What's that you've got in your hand?"

Gabi looked up, her eyes brimming with tears. These she couldn't stop. The cut was too deep, the pain too raw. She couldn't believe what she held in her hand, that Eric would do this in their car. This was past nasty. She flashed the panties and the used condom at her husband.

"This time I'm serious. I want a divorce. I want you out of my life. The truce is over." She took one step, then another and another. With each step another part of her died. There was nothing more for her to do but continue the seemingly endless steps until she reached the door of her home and went inside.

"Gabi," he was calling but she ignored him.

"Gabi, please."

"*Have faith.*"

Not now, Gabi thought, *I'm not in the mood.*

"I don't know how they got in the car, Gabi, you've go to believe me." Eric was right behind her shouting, then whispering, talking softly, then back to shouting.

She couldn't fight, she couldn't even talk. Gabi walked up the stairs slowly; she was going to be sick. She prayed to make it to the bathroom, not wanting Eric to see that weakness in her or have him offer to help. She'd rather die than have him help her now.

When she was done, the only thought in her mind was to make it to the bed before she passed out. When Eric lay alongside her in the bed, she couldn't even summon up the energy to tell him to go away, that it was over, that they were done. Tears slid beneath her lids and at that moment she wished he had died in Iraq.

She drifted off as she heard the voice she'd been hearing for the past year, the voice telling her to have faith. She was sorry, but she'd run out of faith. She'd run out of everything.

Eric trembled. This was bad. It was as though he were holding a corpse. There was nothing left in Gabi; not even her sugar cookie scent remained. He wrapped his body around hers and prayed, not sure if he believed his prayer would be answered. But this he hadn't done. He'd not had sex with anyone in his car. Hell, he'd not had sex with anyone but his wife. Sure, he'd come damn close to doing it, but something had always stopped him. This, he thought as he held onto his wife. This was what had stopped him, what it would do to Gabi if he did. Now he hadn't and she was still hurt beyond reason. He didn't think she would ever forgive him.

Eric ran possibilities through his mind. Maybe Sergeant Ross had taken his car. But Eric knew that hadn't happened. He thought of the people who'd been in his car in the last few weeks. Several women he'd given rides to but none as far as he knew had taken off their panties. There had been no reason to, and the condom, it had been used. He held Gabi tighter, wanting someone to believe in. "God, oh God, please," he moaned as he felt Gabi's sprit sliding farther and farther away from him. "If You are real, help me, please."

When she woke, Eric tried to talk to her again but Gabi looked through him as though he didn't exist. He watched as she packed a bag.

"Are you leaving me?" he asked, fear making his words harsh. She refused to look up. "Baby, please," he said, dropping to his knees and putting his arms around her. "I swear I didn't do it. I don't know how those things got there. Don't leave me." She was shivering, and he held her, pulling her close, his head resting on her empty womb. "Don't leave me, not now. You said we were a team, that we could get through anything together."

"I said *we*, not *me*. There is no more we, not after you and some tramp...you screwed in our car. How could you, Eric? That was past nasty."

She heaved and he could feel the little life that was in her seep out.

"If you love me even a little bit, just let me go. I don't want to look at you. I can't be around you. Just let me go. You've done enough to me, Eric. I can't take any more." The tears were a steady stream down her cheeks.

He raised up, tried to read her eyes, but they were dead, as dead as the eyes of the soldiers on the battlefield. He was scared. He didn't want her driving in her condition. What if...

"Let me go."

Eric moved back. "Where are you going?"

"I don't know," she answered.

"Will you let me know when you get where you're going? I'm worried about you. That's all I want, to know you're safe."

"You should have been having some of this worry in the past months. Too little, too late. This never had to happen. I feel..." She moaned and an agonized sound came from her throat as she allowed her gaze to linger on him. "I feel so betrayed. My very soul has died. I can't tell you what I'm going to do because I don't know. I only know that I can't be in the same house with you." She picked up her bag and left the house without once looking back.

Before the door could open to her frantic ringing, Gabi was pushing on it. The tears had returned and she couldn't control them.

She almost fell when the door open. She looked up at Eric's mother. "He had an affair. I found panties and a used condom in his car, our car. How could he do this to me?" she cried and fell into Ongela's arms.

"Oh, God," she moaned. "I feel like I'm going to die." She heard Eric's father coming from the den and sobbed even harder.

"Where's Eric," he asked. "Is something wrong?"

"Us. We're wrong. We're really getting a divorce."

Gabi was aware of the looks Terry and Ongela were giving each other. She shrugged her shoulders. "I don't have anywhere else to go. I know that you're Eric's parents, but I feel you've been mine as well and I...I...I need you." She broke off, sobbing, falling to the foot of the stairs and remaining there despite their attempts to move her.

"Let me call Eric. We need to get to the bottom of this." Terry headed for the phone.

"No," Gabi screamed through her sobs. "Don't call him."

"But he'll be worried, honey. He probably has no idea where you are, does he?"

Her father-in-law's soothing voice was not going to placate her. "I can understand if you don't want me here," Gabi sobbed. "After all, I'm only your daughter by marriage but if you call him or if he calls and you tell him I'm here, I'm leaving."

"Gabi, you're our daughter. We love you. Marriage or not, you're always going to be our daughter. Now calm down and tell us what happened," Ongela soothed.

"I already told you."

"I know you two have been having a rough time of it since Eric returned home, but you seemed to be doing so much better the last time we came up to see you." Ongela held Gabi's face in her hands. "Honey, I just talked to you this morning. You seemed fine. Does this have anything to do with that phone call you made to us a month or so ago?"

Gabi returned to crying. "It has everything to do with it." For a moment she wondered if she should tell his parents, though Eric hadn't wanted them to know. "Since we learned that we might have a little more problem than we thought having a baby...I mean...since Eric can't... We've come close to this point. I know a lot of this is from the assignment he's on now and from the war but he won't talk to me about any of it. It's been rough but I was determined to hang in there." She looked at Ongela accusingly. "I tried telling you what was happening." She closed her eyes and scrunched up her face, then beat her closed fist on her chest. "God, oh, God," she moaned, unable to continue. "I can't talk right now. I just want to lie down."

"Is there something I can get you, Gabi? Or maybe you can just talk to me?" Ongela had tears in her eyes.

"Not right now," Gabi said and hugged the woman to her, wishing that she had a mother of her own, that she didn't have to borrow Eric's. But she didn't have a mother and Ongela was the only real mother she'd ever had. "I'm sorry I came here. I didn't have anyplace else to go."

She started up the stairs. "Please don't tell Eric," Gabi pleaded and went into the bedroom where she'd shared so many passion-filled nights with her husband. As she dissolved into a puddle of pain and tears, she knew that she needed this. She would have to go through the torture of betrayal before she could ever work her way to being whole again.

Eric paced back and forth rubbing his hands together. He'd waited all day for Gabi to at least call. She would, he thought, because she was so considerate. All the things he'd valued, he'd thrown down the toilet in the last few months. If only he could go back.

As darkness fell his fear increased. It wasn't like Gabi to allow him to worry. '*You hurt her.*' He tried to reason with the voice. "I know I hurt her," he groaned aloud. "I was trying to protect her. I thought she would be happier with someone else, someone who could give her babies."

It finally hit him where Gabi was, with his parents. She had only two close friends, Tracie and Jamilla. At least they had been her friends. Jamilla was out of the running on that and maybe Tracie too. There was only one place Gabi would have gone in the state she was in.

As he dialed the number the knot of tension in his body eased. "Hello, Mom," he said the second he heard his mother's voice.

The phone was slammed so loud in his ear that Eric jerked it away. He no longer had to wonder. His wife was there in his parents' care and as usual they had taken her side. Eric didn't care; he only cared that she was alive and well.

He continued calling his parents. Sometimes the phone would just ring; other times his mother would pick it up, not answer, and slam it back down, making Eric wish he'd never bought them the caller ID for Christmas.

By the time he remembered his father's cell number, more hours than he cared for had passed. Gabi was the one who kept up with things like phone numbers.

"Dad," Eric said when his father answered. "Don't hang up on me, please."

"Don't talk to him," Eric heard his mother say in the background. "We promised."

"He's my son. Now stay out of this. You can go be with Gabi, but I'm talking to Eric."

"Tell him what a disgrace he is," Eric heard his mother shout in the background.

"I will," his father agreed.

Eric waited. At least his father was willing to talk to him.

"Is it true?" his father attacked, the disgust in his voice coming through loud and clear. "Did that child find a woman's panties in your car and a used condom? Couldn't you find anywhere else to do your dirt? Did you have to disrespect your wife by doing it in her property?"

"Dad, don't I even get a trial?"

"What kind of trial do you want? That poor girl is brokenhearted! I've never seen her like this. You're wrong for what you've been doing to her."

"I know that, Dad." Eric slid to the floor and stretched out his legs in front of him. "Don't you think I know how wrong I've been?"

"I warned you."

"I know that too. But I didn't do this. I swear I haven't slept with anyone other than Gabi."

"She said you've been going out, staying out to all hours, going dancing, drinking. Did she lie?"

"No."

"She said you've come home stinking of other women. Did she lie?"

"No."

"She also said her friend has been coming on to you, that she caught you with her in a club feeling her up. Did she lie?"

"No."

"Then, Eric, you're going to have to explain to me how you're innocent in this. I don't see that you deserve a trial. You've been cheating on your wife and you got caught. Now the best thing for you to do is just 'fess up to it. That's going to be the only thing. Gabi isn't stupid and neither are we. Tell the truth, then ask for forgiveness."

"I have asked for her forgiveness, but, Dad, you've got to believe me. I didn't have an affair. Everything else Gabi said is true. Everything else she thinks I did, I did it, and it was stupid. But I didn't have an affair."

"Why did you do all of this? It seems calculated."

For a second the breath went out of him and Eric could hear his father swearing.

"Eric, did you hurt this girl deliberately? When you talked to me you told me none of this. You said you were going to stop. True, we never discussed exactly what it was you were doing but it seems like you didn't stop."

Eric's throat was tight. He could hear the shame in his father's voice and it pained him. His father had always been so proud of him. He didn't want to lose that but he couldn't lie to his father to prevent it. He'd have to tell the truth and rebuild from there.

"It was deliberate in the beginning," Eric said softly. "I was trying to protect her, Dad. I thought she would be happy with someone else, someone who could give her babies. She's wanted them so badly and I couldn't give them to her. I was trying to push her away, get her to leave me, to stop being so damn nice, to stop loving me so much."

"It looks as if you've got your wish."

"I know but I can't stand the thought of her not loving me. I can't live without her." Eric's voice broke. "When she caught me with Jamilla it knocked some sense into me. I had already decided not to go back to the club. That night I went with a friend who needed me. One last fling, that's all it was going to be. But we were working things out after that. She was almost ready to forgive me, to believe me. I'd decided to stop pushing her away. I'd realized I would never be able to push her from my heart. We were on the right track." Eric shook his head even though his father couldn't see him. "I'm not guilty."

"You're guilty, Son, just maybe not of this particular crime."

Relief washed over Eric. "Are you saying you believe me?"

"I've always known when you were lying and I know you're not lying now."

"What about Mom?"

"Your mother right now doesn't want to hear anything you've got to say. You know how she feels about Gabi. You've been mistreating that girl and your mamma is not going to take that lightly. In fact neither of us will. She's staying here with us for a while. She doesn't want you here."

"Dad?"

"No! She doesn't want you here. She needs someone to look out for her."

"What about me?"

"When Gabi tried to get you to stop this nonsense, you told her you're a man. It's true. You're a marine, an officer, a grown man, Eric. You'll have to look out for yourself."

When his father hung up, desperation slowly stole over Eric. His parents were disgusted with him. Gabi must be in pretty bad shape for his father to come down on him so hard. Still, he'd gotten the information he needed. Gabi was safe.

A week passed before Gabi felt up to returning home. She packed her bags and stood by the door with Eric's parents. It was time to say goodbye.

"I'm going to make him regret this." Gabi looked into her mother-in-law's eyes. "I'm going to make him sorry he hurt me."

"Baby, he is sorry," Ongela replied, trying her best to keep Gabi calm.

Gabi shook her head. "Not as sorry as he's going to be."

"Gabi, you're talking revenge. Don't do it. It's only going to tear you two even farther apart; it's not going to help you get back together."

"Nothing can do that."

"You can get back together if the two of you start working together." listening to each other. Have a little faith, just a little, Gabi. That's all it takes."

"That would be all I'd have to give, but right now it's not faith that's needed. You don't have any idea what your son has done to me. I know you want us together and I'm not even asking you to keep secrets from him, but I've never broken a promise to Eric. I promised him if he hurt me, I would hurt him."

"If you're talking about sleeping around to get back at him it's the wrong move. You're going to feel like dirt afterwards. Men aren't like women; they can't forgive that as easily."

Gabbie's mouth dropped open. "You think I should just forgive him?"

"Don't you want to be able to forgive him one day?"

"I feel nothing for him," Gabi said softly, and she meant it.

"That's not true, Gabi, or it wouldn't matter to you to even the score. If you truly didn't care you'd just forget this."

"Maybe I care enough to make him hurt the way he hurt me." She kissed her mother-law-law's cheek. "Thank you so much for giving me refuge and for giving me a family. I can never repay you, but I'll love you always," Gabi said and kissed her again before marching out the door.

"What do you think she's going to do?" Ongela Jackson asked her husband.

"We both know very well what she's going to do. Did you encourage her behind my back? Was the little thing the two of you did here in front of me just for my benefit?"

Ongela was insulted. "Of course I didn't encourage her. I advised against it. Yes, she'd brought it up before but I always told her not to do it. I don't want to see those two apart."

Terry Jackson swore under his breath. "I think we should call Eric and warn him."

"No." Ongela put her hand out to stop her husband from calling their son.

"I thought you said you told her not to go for revenge," Terry said.

"I did, but Eric deserves to sweat a little bit after all he's put her through in the past year he's been home."

Terry raised his brows. "You do know there are always two sides to every story, don't you? You won't even give Eric a chance to explain things to you. He said he didn't have an affair, that he doesn't know how the things got in the car. I believe him."

"Even if that's true, there are other things Gabi told me, personal things, things I'm not going to repeat to you."

"Remember, Ongie, you've only heard Gabi's version."

"She told me all the things she's done as well. Besides, Terry, I don't believe Gabi will be able to go through with it. I know how much she loves Eric. But I think Eric need to think that she might do the same things he's done."

"What things did Eric do that would warrant him suffering? He's been through enough, Ongie."

"He's done things to that child since almost the moment he came home. For over a year, Terry, that child has put up with his nonsense and every time she talked to me about it I advised her to give Eric a little more time."

Terry flinched. "While you've been talking to Gabi, I've been talking to our son. I know Eric wasn't touching Gabi shortly after he first came home, if that's what you're talking about. But he told me about that. He wasn't sure he wanted a baby. He was trying to protect her. It's the war, it's got him freaked."

"That still doesn't justify the way he treated her."

"Damn. I didn't want to tell you this. Honey, he didn't want her to know about the babies that were used as decoys. Ongie, they booby trapped live babies with explosives. The thought of that messed our son up. That's why he didn't want any babies. But he tried to put that behind him because he loves her so much and because she wanted babies so badly. But I'm guessing he told her all of that when he changed his mind and agreed to have a baby." Terry saw the look on Ongela's face and groaned. "Gabi didn't know about that, did she?"

"No…neither did I. Of course I've read about it as I'm sure Gabi has but to go through it, to see it. My God! My poor son, my poor baby."

"Now that you know, can I call Eric?"

"Terry, I'm not kidding. As bad as I feel about what Eric had to go through, there was still no need for him to have put that girl through all that he has.

"But, honey—"

"No buts. We're going to stay out of this."

"Ongie, honey, it's hard. Neither of you has ever been in a war. I can understand where he's coming from."

"Did he talk to you about it, about what happened?"

"No, and I didn't ask him to. He just mentioned a couple of things and I filled in the details. Don't forget I also fought a very inhumane war. Eric will talk when he's good and ready.

"He'd better get good and ready soon or I'm afraid it's going to be too late. He's going to have to do something drastic to keep his wife."

"But Gabi loves him. Even you said she still loves him."

"Of course she loves him, that's why it hurts so much. He's destroyed her spirit and her soul. If Eric wants that girl, he'd better learn to open his mouth and tell her what he's dealing with inside. Saying he's sorry is not going to cut it this time."

Terry walked to his wife and held her in his arms. "I hope they make it."

"Me too." Ongela looked up at her husband. "We've all just got to have faith that they will."

Chapter Fifteen

From the moment she found the panties and condom in Eric's car, Gabrielle had felt like the walking dead. But she was determined to get over it. Part of her wanted to quit her job and get one in the hospital but she refused to allow Jamilla to run her away. She went to work every day and did her job, the same as she always had. She laughed and joked with the patients and even pretended in front of Jamilla that her life was just fine.

Gabi no longer cared that Eric wasn't going out. He no longer mattered to her. She'd filed for divorce and he'd been served. Still, he refused to leave the house.

In light of the situation, Gabi was trying to convince herself that Eric had never come home, that the past year she'd been living with a ghost. That was easier to do than she'd originally thought. It felt as if she had, because there was no way her husband would have ever put her through the things that Eric had put her through in the past months.

Her nerves felt raw, exposed. Gabi had dropped the stubborn ten pounds that had always refused to leave. If she'd known what it would take to get rid of the pounds she would have gladly kept them and added another ten.

She'd had one objective in the past weeks, one reason for going on. And its name was revenge. Gabi was going to make her husband feel the same pain he'd inflicted on her. She ignored the voices telling her not to do it, that it was wrong, that two wrongs didn't make a right. She didn't care.

Gabi was empty and knew she would be even emptier after what she was planning to do but it didn't dissuade her from her plan. It hadn't been all that hard to execute. Two phone calls and the plan was in motion. She was taking a page from Jamilla's book, for she was somehow sure that the panties belonged to Jamilla. She'd considered sending the panties to a lab, along with the condom, but had burned them both before she could give in to such a vile desire. She refused to allow Eric or Jamilla to take her down that road. What she was planning was bad enough.

Tit for tat, she'd promised her husband and Gabi planned to keep her promise. She'd called the one person who would be able to plant the sword in the middle of her husband's heart. It should hurt that she was doing this, but it didn't. She was dead inside. Twice Gabi had visited a downtown club, *The Orgasmic Stallion*, and picked up books of matches that she had left casually next to lit candles in different areas of her home.

She'd had the bait laid out for her with the matches from *Foxes Jazz Club* she'd found in the bathroom at work. Now she was doing the same. For a moment Gabi cringed. What if she'd never written down the address, of the club? What if she'd never followed Eric there? What if she'd not found him with Jamilla? But she had taken the bait and she had gone to the club, and as someone had intended, she'd found her husband in Jamilla's arms. Now it was her turn to return the favor, to make Eric wonder.

For two weeks she'd visited *The Orgasmic Stallion* alone. For two weeks she'd visited Reggie there. If Eric didn't take the bait soon she might have to devise another plan. She knew Reggie was getting ideas in his head, ideas that she'd purposefully planted. Another week of this was about all Gabi could take before dumping her plan, before doing anything more drastic.

"Lieutenant, everything okay with you?"

Eric glanced over toward the sergeant's desk. "Yeah, thanks for asking. How're we doing? Are the numbers up?"

"A little here and there. I guess our going to the schools is finally paying off. There's noise about our driving down to Belleville in a week or so." He shrugged. "All the branches are going to go out together en masse."

Eric saw the grimace that passed over the man's face. They both mostly believed in their mission, but they were having a hard time doing it. It was a tough job and if a marine couldn't do it, then it couldn't be done. "How's your son, Ross? Is he still stateside?"

Eric noticed that the sergeant swiped his lips with his tongue and blew out a breath before answering. "He's still at Camp Pendleton. He has a couple more weeks of basic."

"He doing okay?" Eric asked, sensing a problem.

"He's scared."

"Can't say that I blame him. But we can't have him going over there scared, can we? Cautious yes, but scared, he'll get himself... Have you talked to him?" Eric asked, changing the direction of his statement.

"I'm so scared for him myself that I'm having a hard time. I know I need to build him up, give him confidence, but he's my son."

"Want me to talk to him?"

"Are you up to it?"

Eric was aware of what he was being asked. "I'm a marine, I'm up for it."

"You okay, Lieutenant?"

"That's the second time you've asked me that."

"That's the second time you didn't answer."

Eric laughed. If it weren't for the particular assignment he'd be content to remain here. He got along with the sergeant. "My marriage is going down the tubes and it's my fault. My wife isn't talking to me."

"Marriages go through rough patches. If you love each other you'll make it work."

"She's been trying so damn hard, as hard as I've been trying to wreck things. I have to tell you, we are the couple that this should have never happened to. She's all I ever wanted since I was seventeen years old. It took me so many years to get up the nerve to tell her how I felt about her…and now…"

"The clubbing. Is that what got you in hot water?"

"No, the war, the clubbing was just the last straw."

"Did you know that I've never seen action, not in Desert Storm, not in Bosnia, not now? I volunteered three times to go, but I was never sent over. My blood pressure is so damn high that I'm thankful I haven't been kicked out all together,

"You feel guilty for not going?" Eric asked.

"Yes." The men looked at each other before turning to stare at opposite walls. Then the sergeant turned to Eric. "And you feel guilty for coming home."

"Yeah."

"You sure you're going to be able to talk to my son? I mean, I want him safe and I want him to come home without guilt."

"Don't worry, I won't drop any of my personal crap on the kid when I call him. He's made his decision and I'll let him know it was a good one and that he should be proud of it." Eric pulled in a deep breath. "I'm still proud of being a marine. I have doubts about things, but basically I feel proud. I'm really hoping things work out for your son."

"Yeah, me too."

Eric decided to end the conversation before it went any farther. He wasn't ready to talk to the sergeant about the possibility of his son not coming home. And he sure as heck wasn't ready to admit that it wasn't that Gabi was just not talking to him, that she'd asked for a divorce and meant it.

Eric swallowed, still unable to believe he'd actually received papers stating for all the world to see that Gabi no longer wanted to be married to him. He was refusing to move out of the house, hoping she'd come to her senses, realize her mistake, that they were soul mates who couldn't get divorced.

He'd screwed up big time and now he was serving time waiting for Gabi to forgive him. She'd been almost to that point before finding the panties and condom in the car. Eric had a good idea who'd probably put them there, Jamilla, but he hadn't sought her out to ask.

Eric didn't want to give her ammunition to use against his wife. Asking Jamilla would mean it bothered Gabi. Eric had tried pointing that out to Gabi, but the look she'd given him for even having Jamilla in his car was reason enough not to pursue it. Besides, he had a feeling Jamilla would lie if asked and say things happened that hadn't.

It seemed good sense always came a little too late. He'd stopped going clubbing and now Gabi had started. He'd attempted conversations, but she'd looked daggers through him, not answering. He'd even offered to go with her, to no avail. Something about the club she was going to preyed on Eric's mind. He'd heard the name before but didn't know where.

Finding out more about the club where Gabi was going came to be all that he cared about. Finally, Eric typed the name, *The Orgasmic Stallion*, in the search engine of his work computer. Using the computer for personal things was frowned on and this was the first time Eric had ever done it. At the moment he didn't care. He got lucky on the first try.

Male exotic dancers strutted on the computer screen. Eric couldn't believe it. His wife was going to a strip club. He should have guessed that from the name of the place. He was surprised to see how big the place was, amazed at the number of employees. Then he clicked on pictures, saw the wait staff, the bartenders, and swore out loud when he saw the face of Gabi's old boyfriend Reggie. "Damn, I don't believe it."

"Anything wrong, Lieutenant?"

Eric turned off the computer. So that was where his wife was spending her nights. Hell no, no way.

The hours for his shift didn't end soon enough. Eric couldn't wait to get home to confront his wife. And she was still his wife. He had no intention of letting her spend her nights in a strip club and definitely not one where her old boyfriend worked.

Eric tried to calm down as he thought of all the matches that had recently appeared around their home. He smiled. It was Gabi's way of getting even. He thought maybe he should let her get it out of her system, but the very thought that getting it out of her system might mean her going to bed with Reggie made him crazy. He couldn't just sit around and wait for that to happen.

Eric had hoped that he could talk to Gabi but the moment he walked up the stairs he could smell the faint hint of the vanilla perfume Gabi used. Eric sucked in a breath. That scent mixed with Gabi always brought him to his knees. Now was no different. He stared through the bedroom door watching her dress. He made noise but she refused to even turn in his direction. He sighed loudly. Still nothing. He walked slowly toward her.

Gabi applied an extra coat of lipstick, doing her best to ignore Eric. He was staring at her, trying to make her turn. She was nervous enough already, dressed as she was. She looked like anybody's slut. She took a deep breath, trying to give herself courage to leave the house and go out in public in the getup she had on.

When Eric started walking toward her, she almost lost it. Even now, as angry as she was, she couldn't not appreciate his walk. He was slow, graceful, sensual, even when he wasn't trying. He had always reminded her of a sleek black panther with his beautiful brown eyes. She felt herself weakening and moistness collecting in her center. Habit, she scolded herself, just habit, but nevertheless she felt a tremor in her chest.

Gabi had spent a good portion of her life loving this man. She couldn't think about that now. She'd given him a year of chances, and he'd done the unthinkable. Now it was her turn to make him feel what she'd felt every day for months. He was worried, she knew that. He deserved to worry, she thought, and applied yet another coat of lipstick, ignoring the fact that her hand shook as she was doing it.

"Where are you going, Gabi?"

Eric walked up to her and looked her up and down. The tight top that was more like a scarf barely covered her breasts and showed ample cleavage and most of her abdomen. He frowned at the tight black leather pants she had on. Eric walked slowly around his wife, looking at her and making his displeasure at her appearance known. He narrowed his eyes and stared at her new hairdo.

Then Eric came to stand directly in front of Gabi. She was going over the top, he thought, just to prove a point. He looked at the makeup on her face, a ton in his estimation, way more than he was used to her wearing.

"Where are you going, Gabi? You're dressed like a hoochie."

"You didn't seem to mind it when Jamilla wore an outfit way more revealing."

"Jamilla is a hoochie, you're my wife. Now don't make me ask you again. Where are you going?"

"I'm going to a movie."

"A movie?" He narrowed his glare. "Dressed like that?"

"Why not?"

"Mind if I come along?"

"I don't think you'll like the picture. It's a chick flick, a love story."

"I like love stories."

"It's a girls' night out."

"Sounds like you don't want me to come." He watched while a flash of annoyance crossed her face.

"Look, Eric," she began, "we're technically separated. You live your life and I live mine. I've filed already for divorce, you have your papers. There is no reason for you to question me about my comings and goings."

"You're still my wife."

"Yeah, right, and that means a hell of a lot, doesn't it? If you had thought about the fact that you were my husband, maybe none of this would have happened."

Her voice had turned sharp. She was more than a bit annoyed; it was no longer an act.

"Listen, Eric, why don't you go back to doing what you were doing for months. Just go back to staying out and don't come back."

Eric swallowed around the lump in his throat. "Are you doing what you think I've done?"

She glared at him. Annoyed was no longer how she was feeling; she was downright furious. "Why are you so worried about what I'm doing? I'm divorcing you. What I do is no longer your concern."

"You're still my wife," Eric growled.

"Not for long." Gabi turned slowly, her voice calm, icy cold. "The appraiser's coming tomorrow."

"We're not selling the house."

"Then buy me out." Gabi was glaring. She was hurting and she wanted to stop. It had been much too long. Electric currents were running through her body. There was a slight buzzing sound near her right ear. She swiped at it with her hand, not in the mood to listen to voices telling her to have faith. She'd had enough of that. "Why are you still here? Why can't you just leave?"

"I can't."

"You can." Gabbie glared at him.

"I'm not going to stand by and watch you become a tramp."

"Now, isn't that the pot calling the kettle black? You thought nothing of it when you were doing it."

"You're my wife," Eric repeated helplessly, knowing that his words carried little power.

"And this is my body. I'll tell you this much, Eric. If I am sleeping with anyone it's because I want to. If I sleep with them twice it's because they're getting the job done." Gabi turned and walked out the door, allowing the anger to take control. How dare he think he could now play the enraged, jealous husband? For a minute she wished Reggie did it for her. If he so much as stirred desire within her, even a little bit, she'd give him some. Too bad for Gabi, she didn't want Reggie.

Eric couldn't believe the way Gabi sashayed out the house as if he didn't even exist. He thought of her with Reggie, and the fury burned in his brain. Yeah right, she was going to a movie dressed the way she was.

She'd better hope and pray he didn't find her at the club. Regardless of what Gabi thought, they were still married. And if he had anything to do about it he intended they stay that way.

It didn't matter that it had taken this long for the fog to clear. Now that it had, he was beyond thinking he wanted his wife to find someone else. That was a lie, and had always been a lie. He didn't want Gabi with anyone but him.

Eric changed from his uniform, pushing to the back of his mind the thought that he had been the one to start them on this path. But he was doing as he'd said. He was going to counseling. It didn't matter that he'd only been once in the past month. That was all the time he had.

The pounding music was giving Gabrielle a headache. Clubbing had never been her thing and having to fight Reggie off while at the same time keeping him close enough to use for her plans was wearing her out.

"Girl, you sho 'nuff know you're fine. Marriage ain't took nothing from you." Reggie eyed her up and down. "You could stand to gain about ten pounds though."

For the first time in a month Gabi laughed and meant it. She'd tried to lose those pounds for years and now that she finally had, wasn't it just like a man to tell her she needed to regain them? She grinned at Reggie. "Thanks."

It did feel good to have him looking at her as though she were a tasty treat but that was all it was, a compliment, nothing more. Gabi didn't feel the tightening in the pit of her stomach. She didn't feel her juices flow. She didn't feel the love.

"Ladies, get your hands together for Chocolate Pudding."

Reggie touched her shoulder. "I'll see you as soon as I'm done."

Done? Gabi's mouth dropped. Reggie was a stripper? She hadn't known. He'd never danced the other times she'd been there. The only thing Reggie had done was serve drinks. This was a new twist. An evil thought took hold. Gabbie turned toward the stage, positioning her chair for a good view, hoping that Eric came while she was watching the floor show.

Reggie gyrated across the stage and Gabi appraised him, very good body, prerequisite six pack and muscles out to yonder. He dropped to the floor and simulated sex acts. Oh Lord, Gabi thought, does this fool think he's turning me on? It was obvious he was performing for her. Reggie's eyes were fixed on her as he started crawling across the floor toward her, his tongue making it obvious what he was insinuating. Now she was hoping Eric didn't walk in at that moment. She wanted to make her husband jealous, not have him commit murder.

Reggie stood and reached his hand out, pulling Gabi's chair closer to the base of the stage, grinning at her the entire time. He was in front of Gabi presenting quite a view from his vantage point on the stage with her sitting directly beneath him, his package swollen and as far as she could tell, hard. He reached out his hand to touch her and it was all Gabi could do not to move away. She needed him. If she rebuffed him now, he might not be as willing.

When he came so close to her face that she could smell the musk from between his thighs and see the tiny spot of secretion, Gabi moved slowly back and Reggie laughed, making the women go wild and wave dollar bills in the air. Gabi wondered what would make Reggie back off. She fished in her purse for a bill, but he shook his head no very slowly. Then before Gabi could stop him, he was off the stage and grinding his nearly naked butt against any part of her he could get to.

Gabi looked over her shoulder quickly, heaving a sigh of relief when she didn't spot Eric. She wondered if she would be having fun if she weren't so miserable. No, she didn't think she would. She was embarrassed. Mercifully when she finally had the nerve to look in Reggie's eyes, he got the message, chucked her under the chin and hopped back on the stage, then shimmed his butt for the audience and stood there while they screamed and stuffed money down his G string, all the while rubbing his chest, touching him.

She heard his throaty laugh and Gabi couldn't help laughing also. Reggie was made for this life. He'd been heading toward it when they were teens. It suited him. Gabi had to admit he had the body and the looks. But she would have given him the moniker 'Caramel Candy' instead of 'Chocolate Pudding.' His skin was a rich caramel color and his dreads made him look like God's gift to women. Put that with everything else and almost any woman would be happy.

Almost. But Gabi didn't want Reggie. She'd always wanted Eric, even when Eric hadn't wanted her. Now it seemed they were back to that. Her heart sank. It didn't look as though her husband cared enough to follow her after all. Ten minutes later she was still feeling a bit morose.

When Reggie sauntered from the dressing room, Gabi gawked, wondering why it had taken him ten minutes to come back out dressed in nothing more than the G string he'd left the stage in.

"Reggie, I thought you were changing." Gabi moved away; she didn't want to stand this close to him, not the way he was dressed, or rather undressed.

"I was going to change," Reggie leered at her, "but I'll probably do better like this for awhile."

She glanced around the club. "You're working the room for more tips?"

"No," Reggie grinned. "I'm only working you."

"You don't have to work me."

"I suspect that I do. Don't forget we have history together. I know you, baby. I think I have to bring my A game for you, make you see what I'm working with these days." He ran his hand over his chest and down his abdomen, then reached for hers and placed it on his chest. "How does that feel?" Reggie asked.

Like a sweaty, hairy chest, she wanted to say but didn't. Instead Gabi asked, "Can we slow down for a second, let a sister breathe?" It was time to forget her plan and take her butt home.

"Where's Eric? I can't believe he lets you come here knowing I work here."

"First off," Gabi backed away pretending to pout, making sure to wet her lips, watching him as he gazed at her, tracing them with her tongue, "Eric doesn't *let* me do anything, he's my husband, not my daddy."

"Sho, you right," Reggie answered. "So tell me, baby, you're thinking about stepping out on him or what? He ain't hitting it like he should?"

Gabi closed her eyes to the vulgar question. She wanted to slug Reggie but to answer his question, no, Eric wasn't hitting it right. He wasn't hitting it at all. Still, to have another man talk about her personal business made her want to smack the taste out of his mouth. She swallowed the anger and took another step back. "Why don't you go behind the bar and get me a bottled water and we can talk about it." *Yeah, right,* she thought.

Why wasn't Eric following her as she'd done him? The hoochie mamma clothes she was wearing had brought fire to his eyes. Now if only he'd do what came naturally and follow her. She knew he was curious.

She glanced up, saw Reggie coming toward her with the bottle of water and a glass in his hand and at the same time she saw Eric. Damn, this wasn't the way she wanted it. She wanted Eric to know how it felt to find your spouse all hugged up and touching someone else.

At practically breakneck speed Gabi ran toward Reggie, pummeling into him and pushing him against the bar. He sprawled over a stool.

"Damn, baby, you must really be thirsty."

She laughed, going between his open legs but not taking the water from him. She didn't want his hands on her so keeping them full was a good thing. Her heart was pounding. She could feel her husband's anger like bullets hitting her in the back. Gabi could hear the still quiet voice within caution her that she was heading for trouble but she ignored it. This was her life and she was going through with it.

"Oh, oh, baby, I think we've got company," Reggie said a moment before she felt pressure on her arm and was pulled away.

Eric glanced around the club, the absence of any male customer sending warning bells through him. He paused, listened to the screaming women and his eyes flew to the stage and the gyrating male stripper. A damn strip club. He hadn't believed it when he'd seen the matches nor when he'd found the information on the Internet and he didn't believe it now that he was here.

Gabi was at a strip club. When he found her he was going to take her home kicking and screaming if he had to. She was not going to stay in a club filled with a bunch of naked men.

Commotion from across the room at the bar caught his attention. Eric blinked, recognizing Reggie under all the long hair. When his vision completely adjusted to the dim lighting, his heart sank. That couldn't be Gabi between Reggie's legs. His confusion turned to blind rage and propelled Eric across the room. His only thought was to get Gabi away from Reggie. He grabbed her arm. "Gabrielle, what the hell do you think you're doing?"

"Eric," Gabi said as though in shock, making her eyes go big and round. She pulled on her top as though to straighten it out. She ran a hand down the front of her tight leather pants and looked down as though checking to see if she was buttoned up. Both men followed the path of her gaze. Eric was glaring, fit to be tied. Gabi covered her mouth with one of her palms and widened her eyes even more, trying to fill them with shock.

Reggie glanced at her and smirked, his eyes telling her that he was aware of what she was doing. She shot him a look, pleading with him not to give her away.

"Eric, long time, no see, man." Reggie leaned forward to shake Eric's hand and Eric shoved him backwards. Reggie shot Gabi another look, one that said, I-owe-you-that-one-Gabi-but-no-more.

"Don't long time, no see me," Eric growled between clenched teeth and this time gave Reggie a solid shove with the palms of both hands right in the center of Reggie's bare chest.

Before anything could jump off, Gabi positioned herself between her husband and Reggie. "Stop that," she ordered Eric. "You have no reason to do that. His hands weren't on me. He's holding a glass with one and a bottle of water with the other."

"You're coming home with me."

Of course she was going home with him; that had been her plan. "I'm not ready to go," she said instead.

"Gabi, I'm warning you. I will physically pick you up and carry you out of here if I have to." He glared over her head toward Reggie. "I wouldn't advise your getting in this. It isn't your business and I don't need any excuse to kick your ass. I just plain damn don't like you. And to find you dressed like that pushing up on my wife. It wouldn't take but a word to make me kick your ass, just on G.P." Eric glared at Reggie before turning toward Gabi. "Now come on, Gabi, get your stuff and let's go."

"No," Gabi answered defiantly and was genuinely surprised when the grip tightened on her arm and her husband swooped her up into his arms and carried her out of the club. He stopped, looked around, spotted her car and headed for it. Eric didn't say a word until he opened the door and nearly shoved her inside.

"You have no right to do this," Gaby hissed, mildly offended yet at the same time excited that he'd come. She glanced up at him and saw the fire in his eyes. Their gazes held for a moment and she shivered in spite of her plans. She had to shake away the thought, but her husband was still the one who did it for her. She could feel her emotions churning, the lust building in her nether regions. She could feel the pool of liquid desire being released.

"I have every right," Eric answered. "Now drive and I mean home, Gabi."

Good, Gabi thought and drove away checking her mirror, wanting to tell Eric to back up off her car. The fool might end up ramming her, he was so angry. But anger wasn't what she was going for. Anger could be gotten over. She was going for the jugular. She was going for gut wrenching pain. She wanted to make him hurt as badly as she did. And she knew exactly how to do it.

Chapter Sixteen

For thirty minutes Eric sat glaring at his wife while she behaved as though nothing was wrong. He was waiting for her to apologize, anything. And that damn smile on her lips was beginning to get on his nerves. When he could take it no longer, he got up and began marching from one end of the room to the other.

"I don't believe it, you were stepping out on me." Eric was pacing back and forth. He was so angry that he was unable to be still. He'd halt for a moment and glare at Gabrielle, then he'd return to his pacing. He wanted to strangle her for behaving like that. What the hell was she trying to prove? And with Reggie, of all people. "I can't believe you were with Reggie."

"No, I was at a club."

"I saw you, Gabi, dressed like that and standing between his legs with him having nothing on but a damn G string. He might as well have been naked, Gabi!" He took her hand. "Come on," he said, "I want you to see what I see." He tightened his grip as though he thought she might resist and didn't release her until she stood in their bathroom in front of the mirror.

"Look at yourself, you look cheap. You put on even more paint than you had on when you left here. You're my wife," he roared. "You won't embarrass me or yourself like that ever again. Do you hear?"

Gabi sat on the edge of the tub and stared at him, not answering, allowing him to rant and rave. Okay, his anger was justified in a way. When he finally took a breath she swallowed. "You keep forgetting, we're getting a divorce."

"Hell no!" Eric shouted. "I told you we're not getting a divorce, you're my wife and it's going to stay like that. I love you, Gabi, and you love me. Okay, you got even with me. I know you set this up. Now we're even, we can forget this nonsense and stop acting crazy. We're not kids and we're not getting a divorce. Now wipe that crap off your face so we can talk."

Evil filled her. For the first time in Gabi's life she wasn't thinking of the consequences, the right or wrong of what she was doing, only that it felt good for once not to be the one hurting. "I like what I have on-"

Before Gabi could finish her sentence, Eric was scrubbing her face with a wet towel, and then he scooped her up in his arms and carried her kicking and screaming toward the bed.

"What do you think you're doing?" Gabi screamed.

"I'm going to make love to you and make you remember us. I'm going to drum all of this other nonsense out of your head."

"You can't just make love to me."

"Like I keep telling you, you're my wife."

"So damn what? We're getting a divorce."

"We're not going out like that, Gabi." Eric started pulling off his clothes, throwing an arm over Gabi as she attempted to move.

"Do you plan on raping me?" she asked.

"I plan on making love to you."

"Without my consent."

He shrugged.

"That's rape, Eric."

"Then I suggest you consent because it's going to happen."

"Why, because I was with Reggie?"

"No, because I love you, damn it, and you've been so damn stubborn. You're going tit for tat and it isn't going to happen like that. Now give me permission," he demanded, pushing her back and pulling her leather pants from her body.

For a moment Gabi thought of stopping what she was going to do. As much as she'd been telling herself she no longer had feelings for her husband she'd known all along it was a lie. He stared at her for a nanosecond and the love in his eyes touched her core. Eric was right, she loved him, but right now she didn't want to.

"Okay, you have permission," she said as his fingers hooked on the side of her silk panties and pulled them down her hips. His fingertips brushing her skin sent liquid fire coursing through her. This was the feeling that Reggie could never produce in her. Her body reacted this way only for Eric. Though lust raged inside her, she didn't want to be so easy.

She couldn't speak to him; her voice had already trembled, letting Eric know that she wanted him. Good Lord, that was the one thing she couldn't fake. She did want Eric to make love to her. She closed her eyes, trying to will the feeling away, but it wouldn't leave. Not when his lean brown body was poised over her and his lips were so close to hers. How the heck could she resist him? She never had before.

"Can't we stop fighting?" Eric moaned and entered her quickly.

Her traitorous legs wrapped around him. It had been a long time, she acknowledged as her arms held him close. He felt so good, his strong brown body covering her, his face pressed close, his lips trailing kisses all over her body.

Gabi trembled inwardly. If only, she thought. The scent of the burnt panties returned to her. He wanted her because he believed she wanted another man. The thought was summarily knocked out of her mind when Eric worked his magic. The feeling of ecstasy he produced was all that she was aware of. She could feel her eyes roll back in her head, and her moans were for real, nothing fake about them. She trembled with her approaching release.

He should have done this weeks ago, Eric thought. He should have just marched his ass back into their bedroom and taken charge, not allowing Gabi to throw a hissy fit. He knew he wasn't guilty of sleeping with anyone. In fact, the very thought of doing it had vanished the moment his wife thought he'd done the deed.

He'd missed her so much, he thought as he thrust repeatedly into her heat. Her initial fight had made him so hot, so hard. Her scent permeated the room, wrapped around him and drove him home. With each thrust, Eric thought he would come but he held off, waited until he knew his wife was plunging over the edge. It was always so good when they came together.

"Hurry," Gabi urged her husband. "I can't wait much longer."

"I know, baby," he moaned. "I want us to come together."

His soft whisper was like a cold bucket of ice water being dumped on her, waking her up. Eric was so damn smug. He knew her body so well. He thought this was all it took to make her get over her hurt. Yes, she loved him. With everything that was in her, Gabi loved him. And he had no right to desecrate that love.

Don't do it, the voices were shouting at her. One voice became ten and ten a thousand. She was going to ignore the voices. She had to do this for herself. She had to know that Eric loved her enough to bleed as she'd done.

He heard her moan. Now was the time. He growled as he felt his release nearing.

Gabi loved when they came together and now was no different, except this time when she felt them crest she opened her mouth and screamed, "Reggie."

What the hell?

"Reggie!" Gabi screamed.

"Reggie?"

Oh no she didn't! Eric couldn't stop the release, couldn't hold it back. Damn. Eric shook with the force of his release, feeling a strange energy surrounding him and Gabi, feeling a difference when his fluids entered Gabi's wetness. He groaned and fell on Gabi for about the space of ten seconds. Then as his breathing returned to normal he lifted off her and looked down at her smiling face. "Hell no!" he roared. "You didn't just call me by another man's name."

"But I didn't," she said innocently. "Did I?"

Oh, that was her game. Eric was so angry at her that he wanted to do as she'd done when she'd caught him with Jamilla. He wanted to throw something, namely her.

"This wasn't fair, Gabi. That was evil. You waited until I was right there and did something like that. Why don't you just get a knife and stick it in my heart?"

"I just did."

"I thought it was an accident."

"It was," she said and started to cry, covering her eyes. "Reggie just made me feel wanted, loved."

She wailed as though that was supposed to make him feel better. He glared down at her. Yes, he'd started it but still, damn, it hurt.

He dropped to his knees on the side of the bed, pulling her with him. "We're going to stop this."

"You started it."

"Tit for tat, baby?"

"Tit for tat. How does it feel?"

"Look, you wanted to hurt me, and you did. We're even. It's over. Now we're going to stop this nonsense and start acting like we're married." He looked straight into her eyes. "We both know you did this to get back at me. And I'll admit your using Reggie was the best way to pound some sense into me."

"I didn't use Reggie."

Eric glared at her and pulled her closer. He could feel her warm breath on his face, smell the scent of sex mixed with the sugar cookie smell. "Reggie might not know you were using him but you were. Now come on, admit it. You never did anything with him, right?" He saw the gentle smile that curved her lips. "You're evil. You're not going to say, are you?"

"Honey, why would you think my being with an old boyfriend...oops, I mean talking to an old boyfriend, was any reason to worry?" She cocked her head a little to the right, her gaze sweeping him up and down. "Don't you remember? I still had my panties on."

"Gabi?"

"Don't Gabi me, I did have them on."

"I don't know whose panties were in the car."

"I do. I'm sure they were Jamilla's."

"Have you asked her?"

"Do you think I'd give either of you the satisfaction?"

"Gabi, I don't need this right now. I'm hanging on by a thread here. Do you have any idea how rough my new assignment is on me right now?"

Gabi pushed away. "How would I know? You don't talk to me, remember?"

When she was far enough away she shoved out her foot, hitting Eric squarely in the chest. "You do what you damn please for months, then when you think you have something to worry about you want to blame it on the marines. I'm not blaming the marines for your actions and I'm not blaming the war. I'm blaming you. And if I did sleep with Reggie, at least I waited until we were separated to do it."

Eric roared so loudly that Gabi found herself moving farther back in bed. She'd struck a nerve. He was ticked.

"Tell me the truth now!" Eric growled, his eyes bulging and his hands clenched at his sides.

"I was tempted," she replied softly, knowing that her quiet demeanor was doing a heck of a lot more to her husband than shouting it out.

"Don't do this, Gabi."

"I'm not doing anything."

"Tit for tat, baby. I know what you're doing."

"Good." She smiled. "Since you know I'm only doing this for revenge, you should stop worrying about it."

"You're not going to bait me, I know you love me."

"Of course I love you…just like I knew you loved me when you were tempted, when you were out dancing with every hoochie you could find. I knew you loved me when you kept pushing me away, refusing to talk to me. I knew you loved me when I caught you practically having sex with Jamilla in public. I knew you loved me when you talked to me like I was nothing and treated me like crap, when you refused to make love to me, when you pulled out as though I was stupid. And I knew you loved me when I found the used condom and panties in our car."

"Did you do anything, Gabi?"

"No more than you did." She leaned back on the pillows and closed her eyes. "Maybe a little more, maybe a little less." She sighed. "Reggie does look good, though, doesn't he? I think he's been working out. He dances at the club." She hunched her shoulders. "I don't blame him if that's what he wants to do. He told me he makes very good money."

"He's a stripper?" Eric's eyes narrowed. "Reggie is a stripper? Did you sit there and watch him strip down to that damn G string? Is that why you were standing between his legs?"

"Exotic dancer." Gabi laughed. "I don't think he'd like being called a stripper, but hey, go for it. In answer to your question, yes, I watched him dance. He's very good. He kinda dedicated his dance to me." She ran her tongue across her lips. "His stage name is Chocolate Pudding. It should be something like Caramel Candy, or Brown Sugar." She laughed harder. "Can you believe it, Brown sugar?" She allowed her eyes to close slowly and wrapped her arms around her body.

"In about two seconds I'm going to strangle you." Eric glared at her and took a step toward her.

"You're into wife beating now?"

"I'm not going to beat you, just strangle you."

Gabi laughed and rolled over to her side of the bed. "Brown Sugar," she whispered softly in a seductive voice. "I want me some Brown Sugar." She laughed harder and pulled the covers over her head. Good, she thought, let him stew.

"I know you didn't sleep with Reggie."

But he didn't know it. He was stomping around the room trying to reassure himself, plopping down on the bed. "Gabi, don't do this to me, I can't take it. I know I've been treating you like crap, pushing you away. I thought I wanted you to leave me. Baby, I can't take it. Come on, please tell me the truth, tell me you haven't been sleeping around with Reggie."

He was begging, begging her. He'd never begged for anything. If he had he would have begged her at seventeen to be his. His voice was hoarse. He swallowed, pulling her closer. "Baby, please tell me you didn't do it." He was about to give up when finally Gabi turned back to face him.

"I didn't sleep with Reggie. I didn't sleep with anyone. I love you…you're my husband. Don't you know that I would never cheat on you?"

A tremor started in Eric's soul and traveled through-out his body at the deadpan voice Gabi was using. She was saying the right words but she was saying them in that stupid monotone voice just to piss him off. He hissed and threw a pillow at her and headed for the shower.

"I know you, Gabi, you wouldn't cheat on me. You're just trying to hurt me, make me crazy. I know you."

"Maybe you don't know me as well as you think," she taunted.

Eric didn't even bother to turn back to glare at her. She was just torturing him. She wouldn't sleep with Reggie just like he wouldn't sleep with anyone else. But he'd been tempted, he'd wanted to, he'd thought about it more than once. And he knew his wife. If she thought he'd done it, and she did, she would do anything to get back at him. He scrubbed his bald head. Then again, she would also set it up so that it would look like she had, just to get revenge. He pounded his fist against the shower stall, wishing he knew the truth. Payback is a mother, he thought.

It was positive, there was no doubt about it, Gabi was pregnant. She'd doubted the urine test strip, but the blood test was irrefutable evidence. But how? Her husband was sterile. Now how the heck was she supposed to tell him this news? She could hear him now after all the fighting they'd been doing for the past weeks over Reggie.

"Whose is it, Gabi?"

"It's yours."

"Right."

Gabi couldn't blame Eric. If she didn't know she'd not slept with another soul other than him, she would wonder also. But she knew she hadn't, despite what Eric would think. *And what you led him to believe,* the little voice nagged. God, how stupid could she be? That was the last thing a woman should ever do to her man.

But she'd busted him dancing with that skank and feeling her up and she'd retaliated in the way she knew would hurt him the most—by finding an old boyfriend and making sure her husband saw her with him. It hadn't taken much encouragement to make Reggie think he was getting into her panties. He'd been licking his lips and giving her sly glances, even after her husband had snatched her arm and shoved Reggie. Who wouldn't think that she'd been screwing around?

And don't forget you called out Reggie's name and pretended it was an accident. Her apology and the crocodile tears, swearing nothing had happened, had made Eric believe otherwise. Now this. Damn.

Gabi groaned. It all made so much sense now, the tender breasts, the vomiting, the raging hormones, the unusual bloating. A wave of nausea rose so quickly that had she not already been in the bathroom she wouldn't have made it.

A couple of minutes later she spat out the toothpaste and allowed the tears to fill her eyes. This was a mess, a for real mess and she didn't know how she was gong to handle it.

"Gabi, are you going to stay in that bathroom forever?" Eric yelled.

Why wait? It was now or never. Gabi pushed the door open and squared her shoulders for a moment. Her husband with his deep pecan brown skin that was smoother than a baby's bottom, took her breath away. She looked at his nicely shaped bald head and a shiver traveled from her womb to her heart. She closed her eyes for a second, loving this man more in this moment than she ever had. He'd given her the one gift she didn't think they would ever have. And telling him would rip their tattered marriage to shreds. She watched as he narrowed his gaze and looked at her.

"What's wrong with you, girl? You look like you're sick or something."

She heard the concern coating his words and swayed as his brown arm reached to steady her. As it did, darkness claimed her.

190

"Gabi, Gabi, baby, what's wrong?" This time the worry had elevated into full scale alarm.

Gabi moaned and forced her eyes open to look into the worried eyes of her husband. She was surprised to find she was on the bed. Eric hovered over her, his right hand holding a cold towel on her forehead.

"I'm sorry we've been fighting so much, baby. It's stressing you out, I know. Damn, it's stressing me out as well. I love you, baby. Nothing happened with Jamilla, nothing happened with anyone, I promise you that. Let's start over, baby." He leaned down, placed his lips lightly on hers, and kissed her.

Oh God, for just a moment let us be the two people we used to be before we started fighting, before we stopped trusting each other. Tears ran down her cheeks and Gabi succumbed to her husband's embrace. Her head pressed against his broad shoulder, she listened to the beating of his heart and held on tighter.

"Don't cry, baby, I love you," Eric said softly, his arms going around her, holding her close.

"I love you too," she admitted, hoping that it wasn't too late.

"Then stop crying, okay?"

"I'm pregnant."

The words burst out of her before she could reel them in, before she could prepare her husband.

"You're what!"

She couldn't say it again. Gabi could only look at him as he moved away. Betrayal quickly filled his eyes and disbelief ravaged his features. Tears replaced the look of betrayal in his eyes and he moved across the room, wrapping his long arms around his body. He stared at her, shaking his head, unable to talk.

"It's yours," Gabi whispered softly. "I swear it is." The look that came into her husband's eyes made her want to die. She'd killed something in him. A chill pierced her core and snaked its way slowly over her spine. She had what she'd wanted; she'd killed his soul as surely as he'd killed hers. But now that it was too late she was aware that she had never intended to heap this kind of pain on her husband.

"Eric, it's yours. I swear I've never cheated on you."

She moved backwards on the bed as his glare cut a hole through her.

"Is that what our fighting has been about for the last months? I couldn't give you a baby so you found someone who could? What about me, Gabi? What about us?" His voice broke. "I can't look at you right now." Gabi started to speak and he held up his hand to stop her, then pointed a finger in her direction, his arm shaking with fury. "Don't speak, not now."

He couldn't look at her, not now, not knowing she carried another man's baby in her belly. He had to get away, had to leave her before he hurt her and if he hurt her he'd never be able to live with himself. Nothing had ever hurt him like this. Actual pains were shooting through his body.

As he drove around aimlessly, Eric thought of the time he'd spent in Iraq, the knowledge that he could be killed at any moment never leaving him, the sounds of gunfire, the wounded, the dead and dying. None of it had ever given him the feeling he had now.

In all of it he'd known he would come out of it alive. He had a wife to get home to, a wife he loved with everything that was in him. He'd promised her they would start a family when he returned home.

He pulled into the lot of the supermarket and parked at the back, away from any cars. His chest was tightening up and he felt as though he couldn't breathe. The sobs tore lose from his throat and there was nothing he could do. He shook his head, trying to make himself stop. He'd not cried like this when his best friend went down in battle beside him, or when he'd held his bloodied body and looked into Bo's eyes begging him not to die. Sure he'd cried, but not like this.

In one moment he'd lost all that he'd ever wanted and with that loss the will to live was slowly seeping from his pores. If there were a way for him to erase the last hour from his memory he would. But there was no such magical elixir. Eric breathed in hard as the images flooded him. He saw his wife's face with the tears falling non-stop and he shuddered, sobbing harder. This wasn't supposed to happen, not to them. He'd loved Gabi since she was fifteen and he'd seen her with a group of friends in the park. She'd been licking an ice cream and had stopped for a second and smiled at him. In that instant she'd claimed his heart and his soul.

Eric could still see her smiling at him. He remembered all their firsts. Damn, this was the only first that hurt like hell, *the first time one of them cheated on the other. Or was it the first?* he wondered. He'd come so close to doing it himself when he first came home from Iraq and he'd almost done it again once they were given the news that they could not ever have the babies they'd planned for, waited for. "Oh Gabi," Eric moaned aloud. "Gabi, how could you let this happen? How could you sleep with someone else? How could you be having another man's baby?"

If she could die right here, right now, she would. Gabi touched her stomach and looked down. She was going to have a baby. She couldn't die. This was what she'd wanted for the last seven years of her marriage. If only she could go back to six months ago, if only the one guy she'd chosen to make her husband jealous had not been Reggie. If only, if only… But it was too late now. They'd been fighting for weeks over an affair she'd never had and she'd only pretended because she'd thought he'd cheated on her. God, what a mess.

Chapter Seventeen

W hose baby is it, Gabi?"

"It's yours."

"Right."

The conversation was going as she'd anticipated, word for word. Eric's voice was ice cold, all traces of feeling removed from his voice or his features. Should she beg, plead?

"There's a simple way to prove it." Gabi watched while his head tilted just slightly and a glimmer of hope lit his eyes and died out.

"DNA, once the baby is born." She looked down. "Or you could go back to the doctor. He must have made a mistake. I don't know. I only know I haven't been with anyone."

"I don't believe you."

"I know you don't but it's true."

Eric's fists closed and his eyes followed. "I'm not a fool. I want to believe you more than I've ever wanted anything in my life."

"Then believe me."

For a moment they stared at each other until she heard the groan from across the room that told her he couldn't do it. He couldn't believe something so crazy.

"Please, just go to the doctor and get another test, you'll see. It's only an hour out of your life. That's all I ask, just have him repeat the test." She saw him swallow as he stared at her and read every thought she was having. That part was easy because they were having the same ones. "I'll call and set up the appointment for you."

Eric stared at his wife, the love of his life. He wanted so much to believe her, to believe the doctors had made a mistake. He went to the drawer and pulled out the sheets of paper that had destroyed their lives and their marriage. The papers said he was sterile, not a low sperm count, sterile. How was that going to change? He watched Gabi move toward the phone and a sound issued from his throat. He shook his head. "Not your office. I'll find my own doctor and make my own appointment."

"You think our lab would lie because I work there? Are you crazy?"

"No, I'm not crazy. That's the reason I'll find my own doctor. There are enough of them listed. I'm not stupid."

"I didn't think you were. Until you go to the doctor what are we going to do? Are we going to talk about this?"

"There isn't really anything for us to talk about…not until we know."

"There's a baby involved now, not just the two of us. We have to stop this silly squabbling."

Before he could stop himself he was across the room and standing an inch from her. Gabi had pushed his last button. She knew how much he loved her, had always loved her, had once wanted a dozen babies with her. He could feel the rage boiling upwards. He took a deep breath, a mistake, he realized, as soon as her scent hit his nostrils. She always smelled like fresh baked sugar cookies, always good enough to eat.

"I haven't done anything wrong."

He held up the papers he was still clutching. "Was it through osmosis or maybe wishing? Is that it, you wanted a baby so badly that you wished it into being?"

"I didn't want just any baby, I wanted our baby, yours and mine and this is what we have, our baby." Gabi couldn't help cringing as her husband's eyes flashed fire. She blinked, suddenly afraid. She didn't even sense the pain, just his anger. She took a step back cautiously, wondering if her husband would hit her. He never had and she'd always sworn that if he ever did she would pick up whatever was handy and do her best to lay him out in spite of his being six-three. She was far too old to take a butt whipping. Uhh uhh, wasn't going to happen, not to her.

"Stop looking at me like that." She tried to say the words firmly but they came out as a mere whisper and she cursed herself for it.

"What are you going to do if I don't?"

"Move."

"Move?" Eric planted his massive body more squarely, blocking his wife's path deliberately.

"I'm not kidding," Gabi hissed.

"Neither am I."

So what did she do now? Gabi drew back her hand and swung it forward only to have Eric catch it in his viselike grip. "You're hurting me," she said, attempting to use her other hand to pry loose from him.

"I hurt you? Just what do you think you've done to me? You've killed me. I'm still breathing, but I'm dead. How could you do this, Gabi? How could you?" He loosened his grip.

How she wanted to shout at him that he'd killed her also. She wanted to remind him of Jamilla, of the panties and the condom, but she wanted him to believe her more. They'd been given a miracle and she wanted to make him see that. "I...I'm not going to keep pleading with you. If you don't believe me then there is nothing I can do. Just be careful you don't destroy what little we have left. You're going to feel like a fool when the doctor tells you you can father a child, aren't you?"

Gabi shoved past Eric, wanting and needing more space. Her breath lodged in her throat. If she heard his footsteps behind her she swore she was going to run like hell.

Eric sank into the thick mattress and wished he were dead, that he'd died in Iraq. At least he would have died believing his wife loved him, that they could fix any problem they had between them.

Well, this was one problem that he didn't think they could fix so easily. No, this one would require a test result showing he was not sterile. Even then, Eric didn't think he would believe it.

He could demand DNA of the baby and Gabi, and even from Reggie. He shuddered hard. This had happened to a lot of his friends when they'd been so far from home, fighting. Their wives and girlfriends had deserted them, cheated on them, had babies. But he'd never worried, not about Gabi. He could count on her, come hell or high water. She loved him. Again, a hard shudder. Eric rolled out of the bed and went to the medicine cabinet. He had to take something to dull the pain, anything.

He rummaged in the cabinets, not finding anything that looked as if it would cure what ailed him until he spotted the bottle of over the counter sleeping pills. For now he needed them. He wanted to lie in bed and sleep for a thousand hours. Hopefully when he woke he would find that this had only been a nightmare. If he were lucky, the whole last year of his marriage would have only been a nightmare.

Tears filled his eyes. He'd made it home alive and whole. After an entire year from his wife, what a cruel joke fate had played on them. Sure, he'd wanted to fight for his country, but he'd had no idea what the hell they were even fighting for. For twelve months he had not seen his wife, not kissed her thighs, not tasted the sweet nectar that was Gabi, not made love to her. Hell, if he'd thought it out, he would have never enlisted in the first damn place.

Then again, he hadn't really enlisted. He'd sort of been forced into it from having gone to college and allowing Uncle Sam to pay for it. Man, payback was a real rip-roaring bitch. Just because he'd done the ROTC thing and been promised a commission, he'd gone for it, anything to impress his wife, a woman he should have never had to impress after they were married. But Eric had always felt a little out of his league with her, like anytime he stepped out of line there would be someone there to take his place.

Eric growled. Reggie had always been the fly in the ointment, the one who'd dated Gabi because Eric had lacked the nerve to ask, the one to take her to her first prom, the one who'd broken her heart when she'd caught him kissing another girl at the prom.

It was at the prom where Eric had found Gabi crying and comforted her. He'd always wondered and believed she'd dated him out of gratitude and at the time it hadn't mattered. He'd loved her so much that he was ready to take her any way he could get her, gratitude not withstanding.

Pain radiated through Eric, but there was one thing he could do, one person he could force to tell him the truth. He glanced over at the closet, the thought of what he was about to do weighing heavily. He was only going to scare Reggie, not kill him. He gazed at his trembling hands, not knowing if his thoughts were the truth or a lie. Either way, he was going to do it. He returned the pills to the medicine cabinet. Sleep could wait. Right now he had more important matters to attend to.

Eric walked to the closet, reached up and brought the locked steel box down. He ran his hand across the cold metal, swallowing as he did so. What ifs ran though his mind. If he shot Reggie, what then? Did he come back and kill Gabi, then himself? Because if he killed Gabi there was no way in hell he could live with that.

He laid the box on the desk and went to his drawer across the room to retrieve the key, telling himself the entire time that he was just going to use the gun to force Reggie to tell the truth.

A few minutes passed and he was almost done. He should have moved quicker, done less thinking, but no matter, he was still going through with it. He heard the door open, heard Gabi's gasp of surprise. He pulled the brush from the barrel of his 9mm and continued doing what he was doing. "Eric."

He ignored Gabi calling his name. Picking up the magazine he loaded the bullets. One by one he felt the tips of the smooth projectiles. He'd had so much guilt over the killings he'd done. None of it had been personal, this was.

"Eric, what are you doing?" Gabi asked, standing directly in front of him.

"What does it look like I'm doing?"

"Are you planning on killing me?"

"I don't know yet."

"You're crazy, you know that?" Gabi splayed her hands on her hips and glared at Eric.

"Should you talk that way to a man with a gun?"

"Not to any man, to my husband. We've both made mistakes, we've hurt each other."

"That's true," Eric agreed as he dropped another bullet into the magazine. "But I didn't make a baby with anyone. I didn't sleep with anyone."

"You did make a baby, Eric, you made a baby with me."

He sighed, glared at her and looked at the gun in his hand. "I was willing to try and forgive you, but you don't want that. You want me to pretend that a miracle happened. Sorry, Gabi, I can't do that."

Eric finished what he was doing, put his gun in his pocket and replaced the case in the closet. "You can still stop this, Gabi. Tell me the truth. I have to know the truth. You tell me that you slept with Reggie, that it's his baby, and I'll find a way to forgive you."

"I'm not going to tell you that, it's not true." She was shivering. Though diamonds sparkled in her eyes, the tears didn't fall.

"You don't care if I kill Reggie?" he asked.

"Of course I care," Gabi said slowly. "I care because I lied to you and had you thinking I was sleeping with him. I wanted revenge. That never works out, does it? Eric, baby, you've got to believe me. Reggie didn't even know what I was doing."

"You telling me he didn't want you?"

"He wanted me, and he thought he had a chance of getting me. But he never had a chance and he doesn't deserve to die for just wanting me."

"What does he deserve to die for?"

"It's not his baby."

"Then tell me whose baby it is."

"I've told you."

"Not good enough, Gabi, but I give you credit, you're playing it real cool." Eric tilted his head a tiny bit and smiled half-heartedly at her. "You don't believe I can kill?"

"I don't believe you can kill an innocent man and not in cold blood."

"But I have, Gabi, I've killed an innocent man in cold blood." Eric laughed again as her mouth widened in surprise. "What the hell did you think I was doing in Iraq?"

"You're not there anymore. You're home. This is not a war zone, and you don't get to shoot people. You'll go to jail."

"And I'll get out. Depressed marine officer, combat fatigue, unable to cope. My behavior since I've been home will be the proof to set me free. I'm a soldier, Gabi, I've been trained to kill. Do you think it's easy to turn it off?" He watched as Gabi narrowed her eyes.

"You've thought about this?" she asked.

"Some."

"You can't do this." Gabi was trying to keep the fear from her voice but it was impossible. She was afraid, afraid for Reggie and herself, but most of all afraid for Eric. Too late she wished she'd listened to the voice. She'd had a choice, and now her choice had led her here.

"I believe you," she said. "I don't think you slept with Jamilla."

Eric stared at her. "Your belief is a little late, baby." He moved slowly toward the door, turned and stared. "Tell me the truth."

"I have," Gabi pleaded, wishing she could go back in time. If only she had listened. "God," she moaned. "Eric, baby, don't do anything crazy, please."

The pressure in his chest was excruciating. Eric took a breath and released it. "I can't just let this go."

"Why not? I did. I didn't talk to Jamilla," Gabi said, willing to try anything.

"And you're not a man."

"But I wanted to kick that heifer's behind." Gabi glared at him, remembering the feelings she'd had that night she'd caught Jamilla with her hands all over Eric's body. She still wanted to kick her behind, but she hadn't.

"So you understand my feelings?"

"I understand but there's no need. Like you told me, keep your dignity, baby. It's not like you to fight over a woman." He was staring at her and she wasn't sure if he even heard her.

"You think that's what this is about, me playing macho? You think my pride is wounded and now I have to revenge my honor? This is about so much more, Gabi. This is about who we are. You are my life. You own my soul, I can't live without that."

"You don't have to," Gabi pleaded.

"I'm talking about knowing the truth."

Gabi sighed. "You're going to destroy our lives."

He walked back to her, tilted her chin, kissed her lips, and patted her abdomen. "You already took care of that."

Mixed emotions washed through Eric. He'd driven to the club on automatic pilot. Too much thinking and he'd end up in trouble. He kept Reggie's face in his mind, wondering what he would do if Reggie maintained that he wasn't the father of Gabi's baby. What would he do then? He didn't know.

"I want to see Reggie Washington," Eric said pleasantly to the bartender. "I owe him something."

"Sorry, he's not working tonight."

"He's not here?" Eric asked, surprised, wondering if somehow Reggie had been warned. Gabi, he thought. Of course Gabi would have called to warn him.

Eric worried his top lip with the tip of his tongue, trying to think of a way to get around the suspicious bartender. "Reggie told me to come by tonight, that he would be here. Are you sure you don't have it wrong, that Reggie might be coming in later?"

"Not tonight."

"Does he sometimes just drop in?" Eric was aware the bartender was eyeing him suspiciously. "I really need to see him."

"If you have something to give him you can leave it with me."

"No, I don't think so," Eric answered, "this I have to give to him in person. It's too important and too personal to leave with anyone. I have to make sure he gets it. You wouldn't happen to know where he lives, would you?" Now the bartender looked definitely suspicious.

"What's wrong?" the bartender asked. "Did Reggie come on to your old lady? Listen, the dancers don't have to do anything, the women come after them. I keep telling you guys, don't blame the dancers. Put your woman in check."

For a moment Eric wondered if he pulled the automatic from his pocket if the man would continue talking. "It's not like that," Eric said instead. "We're old friends. We've just lost touch."

"Then leave your name," the bartender said, his eyes narrowed into suspicious little slits. "I'll see he gets it." He shoved paper and pen toward Eric. "Here."

Call me, Reggie, Eric wrote. *I need to talk to you.* He glanced up at the bartender and knew the man was watching him closely, probably with his finger on the panic button. He'd told the man he had something to give Reggie.

He looked back at the note and added, *I have something to give you that you might be happy about.* He shrugged, signed his name and handed it over. It was then he realized that Reggie might not want the baby or Gabi on a permanent basis. He hadn't wanted her before and he didn't seem like he'd settled down much in the years since Eric had seen him.

A flutter began in his chest, a fragile sign of hope. Maybe he and Gabi still had a future. Reggie wasn't big on commitments and Gabi knew that. Eric turned and left the club.

For over an hour Gabi sat numb, not knowing how to put her degenerating marriage back on track. She'd called the club to warn Reggie, and was relieved when she was told he was not scheduled for work. At least that would prevent Eric from doing something stupid. She trembled, wondering how far gone he really was.

She couldn't imagine her husband killing her, but then of course she could never have imagined him hitting the clubs and disrespecting her the way he had. She didn't know how the condom and panties had gotten into their car if Eric wasn't involved. He maintained that he hadn't had sex in the car or anyplace. If she was asking him to believe that he was sterile and had given her a baby, she'd have to try and believe the story he'd woven.

Gabi yelled for her guardian angel. He'd been absent now for weeks. The quiet she'd always thought she wanted proved now to be not so good. Gabi trembled, wondering if her guardian angel was watching over Eric. She wondered for a moment which of the two of them needed an angel more. After all, Eric had the gun.

"Have faith."

A smile formed on her lips and Gabi gave a prayer of thanks. *I've never known why you've been telling me to have faith. Now I think I do. If I'm wrong and Eric kills me we're going to have to have a talk on the other side.* She laughed nervously.

"Eric, baby, I hope you can hear me. I didn't cheat on you," Gabrielle said softly. "Why would I? I've always loved you, you and only you." She fell back against the sofa pillows, remembering when they'd first met.

She'd been in love with Eric since she was fifteen. She'd given him every indication that she liked him, but he'd done nothing about it for years and she'd been forced to forget him. That was the way it was done. In her circle of friends, girls did not under any circumstances chase after boys. Lucky for Gabi, when her foster homes changed, her school and friends didn't. She was still able to adore Eric from afar.

Gabi groaned aloud. That was childhood, this was real life, her life, and she was an adult. She'd played silly games with her husband trying to one up him for his flirting, for the horrors she'd imagined.

And she'd done it with the one man her husband considered a threat and hated. Didn't he have the sense God gave a billy goat? Didn't he know that she would never let Reggie touch her, not in that way? She hadn't when she was dating him and she sure as heck wouldn't let him make love to her when she was married. She'd only flirted with Reggie to show her husband how it felt.

Gabi had wanted to hurt Eric the same as she was hurt. His denial that he was not intending to sleep with Jamilla had given her little comfort. His hands shouldn't have been all over her. Gabi had seen that

203

with her own eyes. The knowing looks of pity she'd received from her friends since then hadn't helped one little bit.

Eric was surprised to see his wife's car in the drive. The way he'd acted before he left he'd thought for sure she's have the police at the house. He hadn't expected Gabi to wait for him. He wondered again if she'd had anything to do with Reggie not being at the club. It didn't matter, he thought, and opened the door.

"You called the club?" he asked Gabi.

"Yes, Reggie wasn't there."

"Why did you call?"

"I didn't want you to shoot him."

At that Eric smiled.

Gabrielle held his gaze. "It wasn't Reggie I was worried about, Eric. I didn't want you in trouble."

Eric's hand slid in his pocket and he brought out the gun, looked at it, then at Gabi. He pressed the release button, holding out his left palm to catch the magazine. He handed it over to Gabi. Then he checked the chamber as per his usual habit. He was nothing if not disciplined.

After making sure the gun was empty, he handed it over to Gabi. "I need to sleep," he said and walked up the stairs. Eric headed straight for the medicine cabinet and retrieved the bottle of sleeping pills. He dumped several in his hand and smiled, thinking of Gabi before he put most of them back into the bottle and swallowed only three.

As Eric felt the pills working, his mind traveled backward to the moment they'd begun fighting, when he was first trying to protect her, when she found him with Jamilla. Then he thought about finding his wife hugged up with Reggie, of all people, with Reggie's eyes telling them both what he wanted.

The man hadn't even had the decency to get upset when he saw Eric. And he'd done nothing to protect himself when Eric shoved him, just laughed. That alone had pissed Eric off royally.

But the crowning point had been when Gabi called Reggie's name out when Eric was making love to her. Mistake, she'd said.

How the hell did one confuse Eric with Reggie? It had to have been deliberate, that much he knew, and they'd been fighting about it ever since.

Eric couldn't help thinking that in spite of the fact that they'd been working on their marriage, putting the divorce on hold, Gabi had still been going out. The matches from *The Orgasmic Stallion* he kept finding around the house proved that. Now he wondered if what he thought was an act had been the real thing. Eric groaned. He was as confused as hell as to whether it had been an act or the real thing.

Eric's last thought as he gave in to sleep was that it wasn't all his wife's fault, some of it was his. But the larger portion he blamed on the powers that be. Maybe it was Gabi's God. Eric wasn't sure who to blame, but he knew whoever had made him had apparently forgotten to give him what he needed to give his wife babies and it was his own bruised ego that had almost led him astray. Almost.

Tears of relief rolled down Gabi's cheeks and she mouthed a silent prayer. The weight of the gun in her hand was not nearly as heavy as the weight on her heart. She wondered about the things Eric had said, that he'd killed innocent, unarmed men.

A tremor started in her body and she shook uncontrollably. She'd badgered Eric for months to tell her what had happened. Now that she knew why he hadn't, she didn't think she could take it.

This time Gabi didn't need her angel to tell her to have faith. She had her own common sense. Whatever had happened to her husband was eating him up alive and now this. She rubbed her belly, wondering if he wanted her to go against all that she cared about and abort. She wouldn't do it, not even for Eric. She would not harm the baby they'd created. True, it might not have been created in perfect love, considering it probably happened the night they were fighting, the night he'd found her with Reggie, but it was loved nonetheless, at least by her.

Gabi blinked several times and dried her remaining tears with the palm of her hand. It was awfully quiet in the house. She thought of Eric's eyes when he'd said he was going to sleep. She remembered the cursed bottle of pills. He wouldn't, she thought, but she didn't know at this moment what her husband was capable of.

She walked slowly up the stairs to her bedroom, the sound of her feet lost in the plush carpet. She couldn't allow them to continue like this; they had to talk. Her body was shivering, her teeth chattering. So many things had gone wrong so quickly. Who would have ever thought Eric would go after anyone with a gun? Once again she thought of the look in her husband's eyes when he'd said he wanted to sleep. Trying to push the feeling aside wasn't working for Gabi.

Panic propelled her up the stairs faster, and a hitch in her chest pushed her into the room. Revenge wasn't worth all of this drama. It was too late to take back what she'd done, too late for her husband to have faith in her. The sight of Eric sprawled across the bed tore at her. She observed him for a long moment, taking in a breath before walking over to awake him.

"Eric," she called softly at first, then more urgently, pushing on his shoulder, getting worried that he wasn't answering her. He never slept this soundly except the time he'd taken the pills, she thought. Drawn as if by a magnet, her vision zeroed in on the over the counter sleeping pills beside the bed and her breath caught in her throat.

Gabi tried to calm herself, mindful of the last time she'd thought Eric was trying a little too hard to forget his pain. She glanced down at him and rational thinking flew out the window. Would her husband do something so crazy?

Not unless he thought he had nothing to live for. Terror seized her as she picked the bottle up and peered inside. Gabi had no way of knowing how many had been in there or how many he'd taken.

For a second she stood there frozen, hoping that like the last time, he'd only taken a couple. She attempted to force her mind to believe that, but the sight of her husband lying there so still pushed her into an area where she didn't want to go.

"Eric," Gabi screamed, hitting him as the tears ran down her cheeks. "Wake up, baby, wake up."

Eric heard the fear in her voice, the worry, and he blinked awake. Gabi was hitting him. He grabbed for her hands. "What's up?" he said, sitting up and pulling her into the bed.

"How many pills did you take?"

He frowned.

"Don't play with me. How many sleeping pills did you take?"

Eric frowned again and looked at his wife as though she were losing her mind. "What the hell are you talking about? You woke me up for this? Damn."

"The pills," Gabi said angrily, shoving the bottle into his face. "How many did you take?"

As understanding dawned Eric laughed. *Did she think he was that big a punk?* "I took three. I know it said two, but I wanted to sleep. Is that okay? Damn, baby, after the day I've had I need to sleep." He glared. "I wasn't trying to kill myself, like I wasn't trying to kill myself with antidepressants. Every time you find me asleep are you going to assume that I'm not a man, that I'm taking the coward's way out?"

He felt the shudder as it passed through his wife's body, saw the relief in her eyes and then her body sagged against him and she began to cry. Surprised, Eric held her. This wasn't an act, she'd been worried.

Awareness stole over him. This was what had pushed Gabi away, had made her seek out Reggie, his talking to her that way. What the hell had happened to make him do that? He felt his resolve cracking. He tried to order himself to be a soldier, to not give in to the pain, not to cry like a baby, or a little girl, but he could feel the push of hot tears.

"Baby, I…I'm sorry I made you worry. I'm so damn sorry for so many things." He held her tighter. "Gabi, I knew how disappointed you were, so was I. If I could give you a baby I would. Do you even know what it did to me not being able to?" He felt the tears fill his eyes and run into her hair.

"But you did, Eric."

He shushed her, not wanting to hear her lies, not now. Right now he only wanted to hold her close to his heart to believe again. "I love you, baby. No matter what's happened my love remains true. We've both done things to hurt our marriage and each other. But I don't want to go on without you, Gabi. I guess we'll have to find a way to make this work."

"Eric, I know it was a mistake. Have the test done again. I promise you the results will be different. Have faith in us, baby, have faith in me."

More tears fell. "I'll try," he whispered. "For us I'll give it my best shot." And he would try. Even if the baby came out the spitting image of Reggie, Eric would do his damnest to make the marriage work.

Chapter Eighteen

If Eric had thought he knew pain when Gabi announced she was pregnant, he was wrong. He sat in front of the newest doctor listening to the results, all hope that Dr. Samson had been wrong now crushed. Eric's mouth was dry, his hands clenched at his side in fists.

"How sure are you?" Eric asked.

For a moment there was silence before the doctor shuffled the papers. Then his gaze connected with Eric. "The tests are pretty accurate."

"No one has ever made a mistake?" Eric sighed and asked quietly.

"Of course. There are mistakes in everything and for something like this we routinely send the specimen out to two different labs." He shrugged his shoulders. "That's the reason the price of the labs is so high and why you'll see the charge on your bill twice." He held his breath. "If it happened to me I would want to be certain."

Eric stared at the man. "Are you absolutely certain that there is no way, not even once, that things could have changed, that I could…that I could give my wife a baby?"

The silence was killing him. Eric was holding onto his sanity by a thread. For more than three weeks, he'd walked a thin line, praying that the baby his wife carried was his, and that by some fluke, some miracle, things had changed, that maybe the first doctor made a mistake.

"Mr. Jackson, you're married?"

"Yeah…I am." Eric dragged his gaze to stare directly at the man.

"There are many babies that need homes. You have the option of adopting or artificial insemination."

Eric blinked. *Artificial insemination.* He thought of the gentle swell of Gabi's belly. There had been nothing artificial about how the seed was planted in her womb. He stood, a little shaky, almost falling back into the chair. He'd better get the hell out of there before he lost it.

He took the papers the doctor offered him and ignored the outstretched hand. How could he possibly shake the hand of the man who'd delivered the death blow to his hope. The pity that rapidly filled the doctor's eyes made Eric's hand go out to return the quick press of flesh, the male bonding ritual. Eric didn't want the man's pity. Pity would not fix what was wrong in his world.

He'd promised his wife he'd call her the moment he knew, but changed his mind. He'd tell Gabi when he got home. He didn't want her making up more lies before he could return home. He wanted to look into her eyes when he gave her the news, when he busted her.

A second before he reached his car a loud noise pierced the air and Eric went down into a crouch. *Gunfire*. He breathed heavily, reaching for a weapon that wasn't there. Then he leaned against the door of his car trembling, knowing the noise he'd heard had not been gunfire but merely a car backfiring.

He'd been home a year and had not had many flashbacks. He'd had dreams while asleep and could almost accept that but not this, not while he was awake. Now it seemed almost on a daily basis he was reliving the twelve long months he'd spent in Iraq. Eric shook his head, untwisting his long frame and coming up to his full height.

As strange as it seemed, Eric could understand it. He was in a different war and in danger of losing everything he held dear. His body was just in danger mode. He shook it off, opened the door and drove home.

Gabi tried not to look at the clock, but still her eyes sought it out. Eric should have gotten the results by now. She'd been praying for almost a month now for a miracle. She was a nurse, this just didn't happen.

She'd talked to several fertility specialists and they'd agreed. A sterile man cannot make a baby.

And this was a baby she carried. She'd even hoped it was a tumor. God forbid, Gabi had wished the worst thing possible in order to prove to her husband that she had not cheated on him.

"Please, God," she prayed aloud, "please let the test result be changed. You know I didn't cheat on Eric and I know it but no one else will ever believe me. He's going to leave me, God." *If he doesn't kill me first*, she thought, remembering the strangeness of her husband's behavior since she'd told him.

Eric was fast heading for a mental breakdown. It was as though they were sitting on ammo and the result of his test would light the fuse. She loved her husband. Why couldn't they be granted a miracle? Her situation wasn't much different from the bible story of Zacharias she'd read in St Luke. Because they were old and Elisabeth's womb was barren Zacharias had prayed for a miracle, that his wife would bear him a son. Her womb was made ripe and she conceived. Gabi's eyes closed. If Zacharias were alive today and something like that happened, he would no doubt run his wife to a doctor demanding a DNA test. Back then he'd had no choice but to accept that his wife had not been unfaithful.

Gabi blinked. But Zacharias hadn't fully accepted the miracle even though the angel Gabriel had prepared him for it. And wasn't he made mute because of his disbelief? For a moment she smiled, wishing the same thing would happen to Eric.

A scream filled the air. Surprised, Gabi realized that it was from her. She'd not intended to scream but the problem warranted it. She heard the click of the lock and her body tensed.

"Eric," she called, walking to the door to meet him. The dead look in his eyes was her answer.

God, no miracle, then how about letting the floor open up and swallow me?

"Eric," she whispered, "I swear-"

"Do you love me?"

"I love you," Gabi answered her husband.

"I love you too and I'll find a way to forgive you." He pulled her into his arms but she pushed away.

"Eric, do you remember what you told me about being a martyr? The tables have turned and now I don't want you playing the martyr. I'm not guilty. I didn't ask for forgiveness on this."

"Then maybe you should." Eric pulled the balled paper from his pocket and extended it.

"I don't need lab results to tell me what I did or didn't do. I didn't cheat on you, Eric, and it seems you're faced with a decision, either to believe me or not. That's your choice."

"Believe you, or believe the irrefutable proof that I can't give you babies? Damn it, Gabi, I've been lying to myself for the past three weeks hoping against hope that maybe, just maybe, your God had performed a miracle. But it looks like He's not in the miracle business, at least where we're concerned."

"You don't believe me?"

"No, I don't believe you, and you know something else, Gabi, it pisses me off that you didn't have the decency to use a condom. If you had, none of this would have happened. You didn't even worry about picking up a disease and transmitting it to me.

"You and I both know how many women Reggie has slept with. He always did. Even when you were dating him, baby." Eric stopped and glared. "I thought you must have truly loved him to let it go."

"I was never in love with Reggie. And yes, I knew he was sleeping around. It meant he didn't pester me to sleep with him."

"Then why were you crying when you found him kissing another girl?"

"Because he did it in my face. He'd never done that before. It was my prom. If I hadn't invited him, he wouldn't have been there. I was crying because I felt like a fool. Reggie was in college like you. He didn't belong at a high school prom and neither did you."

"What if Reggie has AIDS? You could have handed me a death sentence. Now I not only have to worry that my wife is a lying cheat who thinks I'm crazy, but that I might have something medicine can't cure.

So forgive me if I'm unsympathetic to your lie, but I'm the injured party here, not you. You should be on your knees kissing my ass that I'm not leaving you."

Her eyes narrowed and a breeze stole over her, cooling her body until it was ice cold. "I should be grateful, Eric? For what, that you don't believe me?"

They were squared off. "Did you believe me about Jamilla?" he asked.

"I saw you with Jamilla. There's a difference."

"I saw you between Reggie's legs. There is no difference."

"He didn't have his hands all over me, not like Jamilla's were on you or the way you had your hands all over her body."

"From where I stood, he did."

For a long moment Gabi just stared at Eric, shaking her head in frustration. "What are you going to do, ask Reggie if this is his baby?"

Gabi's hands flanked her hips and she hissed through clenched teeth, "I have been in love with you since I was fifteen years old. I didn't cheat on you, Eric."

Pain filled him and suddenly all of the fight began to leave his body. Eric no longer knew what to do. Damn, if only he didn't love her so much. He wanted to fight with her, force her to tell him who she'd slept with, but the fire in her eyes, the anger, the righteous indignation… Gabi believed she was telling the truth. Damn. What was he going to do?

Eric walked toward Gabi, saw the fury mount in her and reached for her, pulling her to him, kissing her hard, ignoring her hands attempting to push him away. They were not going out like that, not without a fight. He struggled against her anger, felt the sob in the base of her throat and drew on her tongue, pulling her pain into his body.

I love you, Eric repeated over and over in his mind, needing those words as his mantra, her love for his shield. Maybe he could believe despite all the evidence to the contrary that they had a miracle that couldn't be proven. Eric took a hard breath. Wasn't that the meaning of a miracle, something that couldn't be proven? At least they had a few months. They'd make the best of them and deal with everything else later.

Gabi's arms wound around him and he pulled her even tighter. If this was all there was to being married they could pull it off without a hitch. But this wasn't the real world and they would still have to deal with that when the kisses stopped. He shuddered and braced as he adjusted his stance with his wife's weight in his arms.

"This isn't going to solve anything."

"Maybe not," Eric groaned, "but I need to make love to you so badly right now, that if I don't, I'll go crazy for real."

Gabi's head eased back to his shoulder and she sighed. "Baby, we've made love more in the past month than we have in all the time since you've returned. It's like we're chasing ghosts."

"Stop talking, Gabi, please. Just for once, stop analyzing me and make love to me. I need now more than ever to feel like a man, your man. Can you give that to me?"

Her silence was his answer but she was right. Since he'd returned home things had changed. That was a puzzle to him. He'd wanted so much to make love to his wife for the entire year he was gone and when he'd returned home he'd found himself insatiable, finally able to hold her, trembling in relief that he was home, that she'd waited for him, that she loved him.

It had taken a month before he'd come up for air. Eric knew exactly when the change occurred. The day he stepped foot on the Great Lakes base, the day he'd seen Linda's grandson dressed for war. That had been the beginning of Eric's constant conflict. It had been the first time he'd ever had problems making love to his wife.

That had also been the first time in his marriage that the thought had ever come to him to make love to someone other than Gabi. But it seemed all of that was just practice for the real test. Overcoming his initial objections and coming on board to start a family had made the slow changes in his marriage go full steam ahead.

He wondered if he had never agreed to have a baby if any of this would have happened. He'd felt so emasculated, so horrible that he was unable to give his wife his baby, that he'd almost made a mistake. Before he could do it he'd come to his senses.

Every day of every month since he'd been home replayed in his mind. Eric thought about the doctor who'd told him it was probably nothing more than combat fatigue or post traumatic stress. Whatever the hell it was, Eric had wanted a remedy. He wanted to make love to his wife, he needed to. And when he finally took the pills and was able to perform like a man, he'd cried like a baby and Gabi had held him, allowing him the safety of her arms to shed his tears, not judging, not thinking him less than a man. Or so he'd thought at the time. Now?

"Eric, baby, what's wrong?"

He'd have to let it go. He undressed her slowly. "I wish to hell I'd told you the first time I saw you how much I wanted to be with you."

"I wish you had too."

"Then maybe none of this would have happened. You would have never dated Reggie."

"I was never in love with Reggie."

Eric moved down his wife's body, pulling her brown nipple into his mouth, biting down gently, feeling her squirm. "I'm not going to hurt you, baby. I'll never hurt you again."

He traced her breast with his tongue, coating it with his saliva, claiming each inch of her as his own. She was his. Eric would not give her up, not to Reggie, not to anyone. His tongue found her earlobe and swirled inside the delicate shell and found the air hot. He blew his breath inside and whispered, "I love you."

He ran his hand over her hips, her belly, between her thighs. Pushing in one finger at a time, he found her dry. Determined to change that, he pulled on her breast, felt the liquid leave her body and pool on his finger. "That's better," he moaned when she arched upward wanting more of what he was doing to her. He'd oblige, he'd wipe any thought of Reggie... Eric shuddered. Not now, he thought, now was for them.

Three hundred and sixty-five days he'd missed her and three hundred and sixty-five days he'd been home. He wanted his wife more than ever. She was his lifeline to sanity. Maybe if they pulled through this he'd tell her why he'd done all the crazy things that he had. Maybe he'd even answer some of the questions she'd asked. And just maybe he'd release some of the horrors.

Gabi shivered in his arms and moaned softly. Her sugar cookie scent wrapped around him, begging him to take her and he would, only he'd do it slowly, have her begging him to enter her. He'd brand her so she would know no matter who she'd been with, he would be the one her body cried out for.

Kissing every inch of her, Eric began again in earnest, moving slowly downward, tasting her sweetness, trembling himself at the ache in his groin. Gabi's nails were digging into his skin and her cries were becoming more fevered and pronounced. She wanted him, that much was obvious. When he was sure he was the only one she wanted, he'd take her. He'd drive away thoughts of anyone but him.

He and he alone would own the key to her secrets. Her wetness was spilling out of her, covering her thighs, his fingers, his cheek, his tongue and Eric smiled amidst the warmth of it all and pushed her legs farther apart.

"Tell me what you need, Gabi," he said on a husky breath.

"You," Gabi mumbled, "I need you."

"And who else?"

A shiver came out of him and he pulled on her nether lips, biting lightly. A contraction came from Gabi's womb and she shuddered with the pleasure he was giving her. Eric held her close, suckling her. His fingers replaced his lips momentarily as he pulled away to ask, "Is there anyone else for you, Gabi?"

"Don't do this, baby," Gabi whimpered, "not now. There has never been anyone but you."

"Tell me who else you want, Gabi."

"No one," Gabi whispered softly, giving in to what her husband wanted. A tear slid from her eyes and ran down the side of her face. She couldn't blame Eric for doubting her. If she could take back the things she'd done she would, gladly. If she ever gave advice it would be to tell people that revenge didn't pay, far from it. Revenge destroyed.

"I love you, baby," Gabi said, and closed her eyes, running her hand across his head, the need to touch her husband enveloping and overwhelming her. *God, please*, she prayed inwardly. These stupid tests are going to destroy my marriage. They're going to do what my seeking revenge couldn't do. The test results trump my divorce papers. I don't want a divorce. I never did, but especially not now. Please, God, help us.

"Have faith."

Again the disembodied voice whispering in her ear. More tears slid beneath Gabi's lids. Her guardian angel was back but this time Gabi had no answer for the whispered words. She had tried having faith and her husband had drifted away. She'd tried having faith and she'd plotted revenge. She'd tried having faith and was now pregnant with a baby she'd prayed for. She'd tried having faith and knew in her heart she was slowly losing her husband.

Gabi opened her eyes and looked at the ceiling, wondering if her guardian angel was hovering over them. I'll try to have faith, she said silently. And she would, but it would make it so much easier if she only knew when the fighting and doubts would be over.

Gabi closed her eyes again. She would do her best to have faith, to fight for them until the baby was born. to hold onto her husband and her marriage.

As hard as she tried to shove it away, doubt crept in. *What if after the baby is born the DNA says it isn't his?* Gabi groaned low and sighed, hoping Eric would think it was lust that was bringing out the sounds she'd made.

Eric's senses were tuned to every movement Gabi made, every sound, every moan, every sigh of pleasure. She was tight with tension. He sensed the anxiety and when she moaned Eric was aware it was not with pleasure.

Gabi was lying to him with her body. The thought stuck like a knife in his chest. What had happened to cause this? Even when they were fighting they'd always had this. In making love they were honest with their feelings. They were always so open with each other. Neither had to doubt if the other was receiving pleasure. Even for the few weeks he'd pulled out of her to prevent her becoming pregnant, he hadn't done so before she had an orgasm. Eric had always known he'd pleased Gabi and she'd known that he was satisfied. But now, now this wasn't them. There were too many doubts.

Eric reached his hand up to touch the tiny bulge of her belly. The tightening in his chest increased. All she'd wanted was a baby, the one thing he couldn't give her. He rubbed his hand back and forth across her abdomen. It was then he nearly lost it.

He burrowed into her heat, tasting her, determined to make her forget, to make himself forget. For now he would concentrate on giving the both of them pleasure. He would lose himself in her body.

On the crest of Gabi's orgasm Eric made his way back up and entered her, plunging hard and deep, making her feel him, wanting her to never want another man.

Eric's eyes were closed because they didn't have to be open to see the tears in Gabi's eyes. He was a man, and he didn't want his wife to see the ones in his own.

Over and over he thrust, giving no mercy, not a second for either of them to think. Now was for them and they needed it as much as they needed each other. They were coming on some hard times and Eric didn't know if they'd make it through.

Chapter Nineteen

Lieutenant, you only have a few minutes left. Isn't there something you want to talk about?"

Eric turned from the window where he'd been gazing out for the past forty-five minutes. "No," he answered.

"That's always your answer."

Eric waited, not responding.

"Why do you keep coming here?"

"Because I promised my wife that I would."

"Have you thought of bringing your wife to the sessions?"

"No," Eric answered quickly. He heard the therapist sigh. She didn't know what to make of him. For months he'd been coming to her and he had yet to speak to her of his problems. It wasn't her business.

"You're wasting your money and your time, not to mention mine, Lieutenant."

Eric glared. "You're getting paid either way. Why do you care?"

"I want to help you."

"You can't." Eric's eyes closed and he thought of Gabi and the baby. He thought of the call from Reggie wanting to know what Eric had wanted to give him. Gabi had been watching Eric when the call came.

Her eyes had been big and round. The expression on her face begged Eric to believe her. He knew one thing for sure: Gabi didn't want Reggie as the father of her baby. He'd looked at her and had known that.

Maybe Gabi had wanted in her own way to find a way to make them a family. He couldn't hate her for that. When Reggie had asked him again what he had for him, Eric had told him an apology.

The smile on Gabi's face had been worth it. The conversation had been the way for both of them to close the door on whatever had happened with Reggie. He was no longer important.

The knot in Eric's gut increased as he thought of it. Reggie would never be completely gone, though. Once the baby was born, he'd be a living, breathing reminder of his wife's infidelity.

Eric had to learn to suck it up, to pretend to Gabi that it didn't matter. He'd have to pretend to the baby that it didn't matter and he'd have to learn to pray because something told him that it was going to require a lot more discipline than even a marine had. It was going to require the faith that Gabi kept telling him to have, that the voice kept whispering to him about.

Eric had thought more than once of trying things Gabi's way. Hell, his sure wasn't working. Eric needed something to believe in. He'd tried everything else, and now he might just be forced to give Gabi's God a try. He remembered his promise to fall to his knees in worship if he could be granted a miracle and could give Gabi a baby. This wasn't how he'd meant for it to happen. This wasn't a baby he'd given her. But his pledge still stood. After the birth of this baby he would still like to find he'd done the impossible. That he'd been the first sterile man in history to give his wife a baby.

"Lieutenant, how do you know I can't help you unless you talk?"

Eric stared at the woman for a second. He'd been so lost in thought that he'd forgotten her and forgotten where he was. He smiled at the woman who wanted to fix him. "I thought about killing a man a few months ago." He saw the shock that came over her face and smiled. "I loaded my gun and went after him." He stopped.

"What happened?" the therapist asked.

"I didn't kill him."

"You changed your mind?"

"No, I couldn't find him."

"Are you going to try again?" the therapist asked.

Eric glanced at the wall clock, then at his watch. "My time's up. I'll call for another appointment."

Dyanne Davis

With that he left the office not knowing why he felt good for shocking the therapist, but he did. It was the first sign of lightness he'd had in way over a month. He and Gabi were both trying so damn hard, being polite, sleeping in the same bed, making love. And in the morning it took them so much time to look at each other that they'd stopped. One of them would shower and leave for work while the other was in bed. It was not a spoken agreement but somehow they'd found themselves in that pattern. One day they would have to be up in the light of day at the same time.

This was the first time since Gabrielle had met Terry and Ongela Jackson that she'd ever felt dread before entering their home. She loved them almost as much as she loved Eric and telling them what they'd come to tell them was not going to be easy. She could just imagine their disbelief. The one thing besides losing her husband that she didn't want to lose in her life was Eric's parents. She hesitated as they began to walk up the walkway. "What are you going to tell them?" she asked Eric.

"The same thing you told me," Eric answered.

"Are you going to try and make me look bad?"

Eric sighed. "I won't tell them anything, I'll let you tell them." He waited.

"Are you going to be for or against me?"

"I'll never be against you, baby."

Gabi heaved, taking in a deep breath. "You know what I mean. Are we in this together, or are you going to throw me to the wolves?"

"What is it you want from me, Gabi? Do you want me to tell my parents a lie, that I know for a fact the baby is mine?" He saw a flicker of pain. "I won't say anything. How's that?"

"That's just as bad as your saying you don't believe me. If you're with me then you have to…" She stopped. "Never mind, Eric. Let's get this

221

over with." She made her body into a rod of steel and walked inside, ignoring the look of concern on the faces of her in-laws.

When they were all seated Gabi licked her lips. "We want to tell you something." She glanced at Eric and he sighed and moved closer to her, putting his arm around her shoulder. He didn't want to but he was offering her solidarity. She would have felt better if he believed in her but for now it was nice to have it at least not three against one. It wasn't exactly two and two but she had at least this much support from him.

She blew her breath out. "I'm pregnant." She'd planned to say, 'Eric and I are having a baby,' but somehow she couldn't quite force those words out.

"Pregnant?" Ongela almost smiled, then stopped and looked at Terry. "Gabi, did Eric have another test? Did they prove that he's…" The woman stopped, glanced at her son and couldn't continue.

"Was there a mistake?" Terry asked.

"No," Eric said.

"Yes," Gabi answered.

"Which is it?" Ongela asked. "It can't be both. Is Eric sterile?"

"He can't be sterile," Gabi bristled. "I'm pregnant." Eric groaned beside her and she turned toward him. "It's our baby. I haven't been with anyone else." She held her husband's gaze. He was trying. "Baby, I'm telling the truth."

Eric's eyes closed and he got up. "I need a drink." He walked into the kitchen and Gabi sat before his parents alone. They were staring at her.

"Gabi, did Eric's test change?" Ongela's voice was stern as she stared at Gabi.

"No," she answered, "but I'm telling the truth. It's his baby."

"Gabi," Ongela moaned and walked out the room. Gabi was left with Terry. If Ongela, her main support had left the room, she hated the thought of what her father-in-law would think. "I didn't cheat on Eric, Dad. I never have."

Terry was sucking air through his teeth, trying hard to find a way to believe her. "You tell me, Gabi, you're the professional here. If his tests didn't change, how could he be the father? Gabi, we know how much you want a baby, honey. We can forgive you, but don't ask us to believe you. This is nonsense. You're our daughter, pure and simple. We love you and we always will."

Gabi's voice was small now and she felt lost. The three most important people in her life, and none of them believed her.

"I'm not getting rid of it," she muttered.

"No one would want you to do that, honey. We can accept your child into our family."

Gabi bit her lips. "It's your grandchild."

"It will be our grandchild. We'll accept it, just as we accepted you into our family and into our hearts."

Gabi looked around. Eric wasn't coming back. She went into the kitchen after him. She stared at his back. His long arms were wrapped around his torso and his head was bent. He was moving back and forth rocking his body. She called his name softly. "Eric." He turned toward her and she could tell he'd been crying. He was still rocking.

"Not now, Gabi, not now. I'm trying, just give me a little time. I've wanted to give my parents this announcement for years, but not like this. Just give me a few minutes and I'll come back out."

Eric turned away and Gabi walked back out of the kitchen and up the stairs to find Ongela. Her mother-in-law had always trusted her, always taken her side. She knocked on the closed bedroom door.

"Mom, can I come in for a second?" At first she didn't get an answer, then a muffled voice came, followed by movement behind the closed door. At last Gabi heard the words she wanted.

"Come in, Gabi."

Gabi walked in and stopped when she saw the reddened eyes of her mother-in-law. She wrapped her arms around her body in the same fashion Eric had. "I'm not lying," Gabi pleaded.

"Gabi, you told me you were going to have an affair. Eric told us that you've been going to a strip club. He told us that even after he told you not to, you still went back and that he'd found you there with your old boyfriend. I was on your side. I figured he'd hurt you and you wanted to make him jealous. I never thought in a million years you would do something like this."

Ongela turned away and it broke Gabi's heart as she saw the woman trying to hide her emotions. The tears were streaming down her face. Gabi couldn't hold back on her own tears. The only mother she'd ever known was turning her back on her.

I shouldn't have lied, Gabi thought. *I shouldn't have told her I was going to make Eric pay. I shouldn't have been out for revenge.*

More tears came. There were a lot of things Gabi shouldn't have done and she knew it. She should have listened to her mother-in-law and her guardian angel telling her not to seek revenge.

She'd known she'd crossed the line when she'd screamed Reggie's name when her husband was making love to her. *God,* Gabi prayed silently. *I'm so sorry for hurting Eric, but please don't take my entire family from me, please don't.*

She took in a deep breath. It wasn't time for her tears; she was the one who'd inflicted pain on her family. She would have to deal with the consequences. When Ongela turned back to her, Gabi wiped her eyes. She had to listen regardless what was said.

"Gabi, I have always loved you," Ongela began. "I've wanted those grandbabies you kept promising me. And in time I will love your baby and I will play grandmother to it. But don't ask me to believe this. I'm not going to lie to you, Gabi. I don't believe you."

Gabi stood in the middle of the floor, tears running down her cheeks. "Please," she begged.

"Gabi, go on back downstairs. I want to be alone. I just don't feel like talking to you about this now. I'm so disappointed in you. I never expected you to hurt me like this. I've always gone to bat for you, always taken your side, but on this, no, Gabi. I can't take your side on this. Now you'd better go on back down. Eric's probably looking for you."

Gabi left the room. Eric wasn't looking for her, no one was. She walked back down the stairs with a heavy heart. This was a hell of a lot harder than she'd expected. She'd known they would have doubts, but she'd never expected the entire family to be in tears, never in a million years, and definitely not because she'd just told them they were going to be grandparents.

"You okay, Son?" Terry had walked into the kitchen as Gabi went up the stairs.

Eric was miserable. "No, Dad, I'm not okay. How can she expect me to believe something so wild?" His eyes were brimming but the sight of his father's tear-filled eyes stopped Eric's tears. One of them had to be strong.

"What are you going to do?" his father asked.

"Just get through it. I love her, what else can I do?"

"Do you want her to get rid of it?"

"She'd never agree."

"That wasn't my question."

Eric exhaled noisily. "You know how badly she wants a baby."

"That still doesn't answer my question."

Eric lifted his eyes. "I wanted so badly to give her a baby. She has never asked me for anything. You know she's never been the kind of woman to demand jewels, trips or anything. She just wanted a baby." His voice was hoarse and filled with pain. "And I couldn't give it to her," he continued. "Do you know I prayed?" he asked his father. "I prayed to be able to give her a baby. And this, I guess, is my answer. She's going to have a baby. So in answer to your question, do I want her to get rid of it? No. Do I believe it's mine?" Eric closed his eyes and shook his head. "How can I? I've taken a semen analysis three times. I've talked to the doctors. Gabi even talked to the specialists. They all say I can't give her babies."

"What are you two going to do?"

"We're trying so hard to work it out. The entire time that I've been home has been really messed up. First one thing, then another. This is killing me, it is, but when I weigh my options, my not being with Gabi, I'll take this any day."

The kitchen door opened and Eric looked over his father's shoulders at Gabi. He stared at her stricken look and wondered how much she had heard. She turned and walked back out but he didn't go after her and neither did his father.

Gabrielle had never felt so alone. It had never felt like this even when she was a kid and without warning she was forced to move from one foster home to the next. She'd always expected people to turn their backs on her, to put her out, but not here in this house. These people were her family; they claimed to love her.

"God, please help me," she said under her breath, going to the closet and looking in Eric's coat, taking out the car keys. She couldn't stay there, not with everyone against her, looking at her with the accusing stares. But the tears were worse, the disappointment. She had been use to being alone at one time in her life and if that was what she had to go back to she might as well start getting use to it again. Gabi was at the car, her hand on the ignition, when Eric slid in on the passenger side.

"Were you going to leave me here?" he asked.

"I can't go back in there."

"You knew it was going to be rough."

Yes, she'd known. She turned to face him. "Your parents and you are the only family I've ever had." Gabi swallowed, she didn't want Eric's sympathy, just his love and his belief in her. "I've been alone before, Eric. I don't want to be, but I can do it again. It's just a little more than I can take right now, my entire family all gone from me at the same time."

"They want you to come back in, Gabi."

"I can't." She lay back against the seat. "I want to go home." She turned on the ignition. "It's my fault for attempting to get revenge on you. If I hadn't, maybe you'd believe me."

Gabi stared at the look in her husband's eyes. "Well, maybe it wouldn't be quite this bad." She sighed in frustration, knowing he would have never believed her anyway. Still, revenge always blew up in your face. She wished again she had listened to all of the warnings. She'd refused to listen because of her own pain. So some of this pain she deserved, but not all of it.

She took in several cleansing breaths and halted her tears. She wasn't going to drive and cry, she had a baby to think about. The baby had done nothing wrong and Gabi wasn't going to go off half cocked. She glanced across the seat at Eric. "Why don't you go back in. They're your family, you can stay."

"You're my family too, Gabi, and where you go I go." He opened the car door. "Come on, let's change places. I'll drive."

She hesitated, her hand on the door handle. "Eric, get back in. I think I'm in better condition that you are." When he climbed back in and leaned against the leather cushion, Gabi knew what had to be done.

Eric carried the cartons of Chinese food into the house, not having bothered to call and ask Gabi if she was cooking. He was trying to be nice, thoughtful. He hoped she appreciated it.

He didn't smell food and was glad that he'd stopped. He found Gabi sitting quietly in the kitchen. Something else was wrong. Now what? he wondered.

"What's up?" he said, going to her.

"I've packed your bags and I got a room for you for a week at the motel down the street. Maybe you can go stay with your parents or something until everything is settled."

"Until what's settled?" he asked, setting the greasy bags on the table. "Gabi, talk to me. What's going on, baby? We're doing okay, we're working this out."

"No, we're not working this out. We're going through the motions, pretending. We can't even look at each other, Eric. I think it's best if we go ahead with the divorce. You're keeping everything bottled up inside and one day you're going to explode. I love you, baby, but I have to think about our child now. I can't have you around the baby like this."

"I'm going to therapy," Eric said, not looking at her.

"I know you are, but it doesn't seem to be helping. I don't want you to start to hate me, or to hate the baby. It still scares me that you went after Reggie with a gun."

"But I gave you the gun when I came back."

"I know, but you never should have gone after him with a gun in the first place. What happens when the baby's born, or when it's older and you take it into your head that the child has disrespected you? I can't take that chance."

"Gabi, I love you."

"I know, baby. I love you too. That's what's making this whole thing so hard. This is the last thing I want to do, but I just can't take a chance."

"Are you still giving tit for tat? Is it because of what you heard me say at my parents' home?"

"No, that's not it. No more playing, no more revenge. I'm having a baby and the baby has to come first."

"You're being stubborn. I think we can make it."

"Tell me what happened in Iraq, what changed you?"

Eric's eyes clouded over. "Gabi, you don't want to know what happened in Iraq, you only think you do."

"I want to know what changed you, what changed us. I need to know what brought us here to this point."

He sucked in a deep breathe and blew it out hard. "If I told you all the things you think you want to know it might be the one thing that would make you stop loving me. I don't want that to happen. There are lots of mistakes that brought us to this crossroad. Yes, a lot of it has to do with Iraq, some of it has to do with my not talking. But I would if I could, Gabi. I've admitted I started it. I'll even admit you were right. I wanted you to leave me, to divorce me, to have a full life."

"But why, Eric? Don't you think I deserve to know the reason why we're getting a divorce?

"You went to a lawyer and filled the papers."

"Eric, this isn't a joke. Talk to me, please. I want to help you. I've always wanted to help you. Maybe if you try taking some of the burden from your shoulders and putting it on mine you'll start to heal."

His fingers brushed her shoulders and he leaned down and kissed them. There was a raw ache inside him. If he could tell anyone of the things he'd done it would be Gabi. But she was the one person he didn't want to know. "Baby, your shoulders are much too pretty to carry my burden." He felt her bristle and straightened to gaze into her eyes. "Let it go, Gabi, please."

"You told your father. That I can understand. You're telling a therapist. I know I should understand that also and I'm grateful that you're getting it out. Still, it hurts that as much as we have always loved each other you can't tell me what has made you push me away repeatedly."

He sighed, wishing that he could do as Gabi asked. Sure he'd talked with his father but it had all been general. His father had understood his need to keep the horrors inside. The guilt he'd returned home with had only been intensified by all the things he'd done to Gabi. He saw the flicker of hope that had been in her eyes fade and then die completely. "We could keep trying, Gabi."

"Why? We're not going to change anything until we learn to trust each other completely again. And we can't do that just yet. So I think it's better if we both try to get on with our lives."

"But, Gabi, I don't know if I can have a life without you."

"I'll be here if you need me but I can't live with you. You've got your family and I've got our baby. This stress won't be good…" Gabi looked down and worried her top her lip with her tongue. She saw the pain in her husband's eyes. He still didn't believe.

"The stress won't be good for my baby." She pushed the words out. The baby was still hers whether he wanted a part in it or not.

"I brought dinner." Eric stared at her with tears in his eyes. "You feel like eating?"

"Not really, but I have to. I'll do everything I'm supposed to do to make sure nothing goes wrong with this pregnancy." She got plates from the cabinet and was putting them on the table when Eric slid his arms around her.

"We're not ending up in bed tonight," she said, winding her arms around him, sucking in her breath. She had to be strong enough for the three of them.

"Gabi."

"I know," she crooned to him. "If you could believe me you would. I can't say that I blame you. It's a lot to ask. For me to want you to have faith, it's too much to ask," Gabi said, holding him to her for a long moment before pulling away. "Let's eat dinner so we can stop prolonging it," Gabi said and started dishing out the food.

How either of them managed to eat without the rice sticking in their throats was a miracle. Then again, it was no more a miracle than the baby growing in her womb, or the fact that she could stand there and watch Eric lift his bags into the trunk of his car and drive away, out of her life. This time he'd not tried to fight with her about leaving. He'd also known it was time.

Gabi closed the door and lay against it for a long time, feeling the wood, envying the sturdiness of it. And she cried for them, for a war that had separated them. She cried for her guardian angel, as he'd failed to listen to her. And Gabi cried for the hurt and disappointment they'd both endured. Then she cried for their unborn child who might not ever have a father.

But our baby will have a mother, she thought, drying her tears, and I will love it enough for the both of us. With that thought Gabi went into the kitchen to clean up the remnants of the dinner, the final traces that this was a home shared by more than one. From now on there would be one plate, one glass. But she would survive. She was carrying a baby, she had no choice.

This couldn't be happening but it was. Eric stood under the prickly shower, the cold water stinging his skin, trying to feel, wanting something, anything, to make him come alive. "What happened?" he asked the question out loud.

"*Have faith.*"

Eric heard the voice loud and clear. "What am I supposed to have faith in? Tell me how in the hell I can have faith in something that isn't possible? Tell me that." Wrapping himself in a huge towel he turned off the water, headed for his room and sank on the bed, groaning with the weight of the crumbling of his world.

Chapter Twenty

With nothing much to look forward to, Eric had begun weighing his options. He sat across from Sergeant Ross, deciding to break his news to him before he tried it out on Gabi. "I'm thinking about asking for another tour in Iraq," Eric said quietly. The sergeant looked at him, his face ashen.

"Why? I thought you were coming out," the sergeant replied.

"I think I may have changed my mind."

"Everything okay, Lieutenant?"

"Sergeant, we've been working together long enough now, it's just the two of us. We're in this together. Just call me Eric and ask what you will."

"Everything okay with you and your...your wife?"

"No," Eric said and reached for his cap. "It isn't. We're having a very rough time right now. I don't know if we'll make it. Come on, let's go see if we can round up any new recruits."

For the second time in a week Eric was standing in the therapist's office looking out the window. This time the therapist didn't bother asking him to talk. Eric heard the ding of the clock signaling the end of his session and turned to the woman.

"My wife and I have separated," he said and walked out the door. He had not said those words to anyone and only to the therapist when it was time to leave, when she wouldn't have an opportunity to ask him questions.

He lifted his eyes skyward and wondered if anyone was paying attention. He wondered if he could call on the voice that had been whispering to him since right before he'd felt the hand in the small of his back pushing him to safety, the hand that had saved his life in Iraq.

This was killing him, this not knowing. All this time and he still didn't know who'd saved him or why. Those mysterious words to have faith that were whispered on occasion weren't enough. Eric needed more. He needed answers. He needed to know what to have faith in.

He thought about Gabi and wondered if it was easier for her. He wanted to tell her his decision, that he was going to go back to the only life left for him now. He wanted to return to Iraq. He no longer had anything to lose.

He flipped his cell open and called Gabi, surprised when she said he could come by. When he arrived he rang the bell of his home, feeling like a stranger.

"I have something to tell you," he murmured hoarsely a second after Gabi let him in.

She was waiting, her gaze expectant. He knew what she was looking for, a confession, an unburdening of his soul. It wasn't going to happen. He still didn't want her to know the things he'd done, the things he was capable of.

"I'm thinking of asking to be sent back to Iraq." He waited, she said nothing. "Gabi, did you hear me?"

"Yes, I heard you."

"Don't you have anything to say?"

Gabi was fuming. She couldn't believe this was what Eric had come to tell her, not of the pain he'd been holding inside but some idiotic nonsense about going back into a war he was now out of. She was so angry with him that she couldn't stand the sight of him. Damn him. They were expecting a baby. What did he think he was doing?"

He reached out a hand, touched her gently, and she smacked his hand away. "What do you assume this is, a game? I can't believe you. You've lost your damn mind. Do you believe I'm going to give you my blessing, say prayers for you, for your safety? Are you crazy, Eric? I need you here. Do you understand me? I'm having a baby by a man who doesn't believe it's his. I'm holding on to my sanity by sheer will. This is the last thing I need to hear. Is this tit for tat, or do you just have a death wish? You can't talk to me about what happened the last time and you've been home over a year. What do you imagine is going to happen to you if you go back and are lucky enough to come home a fourth time?"

Gabi was shaking so hard that she reached her hand out and held on to the chair in front of her to steady herself. "If you go back I will never forgive you."

"But you're divorcing me."

"That's not a good enough reason for you to do this, Eric. I need you here."

"Not being with you, I don't have much reason to not go," he said and looked at her.

"You're not going to use me as a crutch, Eric. You talk to me and tell me what the hell's going on."

He smiled at her. "Nothing." He lifted one shoulder. "I was just thinking of doing it. I haven't done it yet."

"Are you so anxious to die?" she asked. "Are you that afraid of death that you're rushing to challenge it?"

Gabi's reaction was not what he'd expected. She was disgusted with him, not begging him not to do it, not crying, just yelling at him. "I didn't say I was going to go back for sure," Eric said defensively, not liking that she wasn't begging him not to go.

"Look, I just wanted to run this by you. I have to go and look at an apartment. I'll talk to you later," he said, escaping out the door, not able to bear the blazing anger in her eyes. She was scoring him where he stood.

Again Eric found himself standing in the therapist's office. At least he was going on a regular basis now. "Women, you're all alike,' Eric said softly. "You all want a man to talk. Why can't you understand men don't need to talk?"

"Maybe you men don't need to talk, but maybe women need to hear you."

"It's my right not to talk. It doesn't mean anything."

"It doesn't mean anything to me, Lieutenant. Like you keep telling me, I get paid either way. But if I were the woman in your life and you behaved in this stern military manner at home, I think I'd kick you out also."

Eric glared at the woman. She refused to look at him, staring instead at the pad in her hand, making notes, notes about him.

"You think you know me well enough that you can sit in judgment on me?"

"Of course I don't know you," the therapist answered. "You've being coming here for months and you haven't said more than a dozen words in all that time. No, Lieutenant, I don't know you. And I wonder if anyone does."

Eric clenched his fists in frustration. This woman was irritating. He hated having people ask him personal questions, he always had.

"Your time's up, Lieutenant, but I'm sure you know that. You never bother to talk until it's time for you to leave."

Eric glared at the therapist for the breath of a moment and he sucked in his breath. This wasn't going to help his marriage. This woman wasn't the one he should be talking to. No way was he going to confide things to her that Gabi had begged him to tell her. No way. "I'm not coming back," Eric said without a roar or without glaring. "Thanks," the therapist muttered and returned to her pad.

"Lieutenant, would you like to go out after work and get a drink?"

Eric laughed but without amusement. "No, I don't think so."

The sergeant shrugged. "I just heard today my son will be heading off to Iraq in two weeks." He waited.

Eric sucked in a breath of air before answering, knowing what his friend was going through. "Sure, I think we could both use a drink tonight."

"Not you, Lieutenant, if you don't mind. Tonight I think I'm going to need a designated driver."

"You've got it," Eric answered. Heaven knew the man had been his designated partner for more times than he cared to remember.

It was a funny thing now that Eric thought of it. He hadn't been back to a club since Gabi had first mentioned the 'D' word. Not even after she'd stopped going out had he had any desire to do it. It was strange.

Two hours later Eric had to include other strange things in the same category. Before he'd been determined to push Gabi away, tempted to cheat with other women, to get caught. When he was free to do what he pleased, he no longer had the urge. Now all he wanted was what he'd wanted when he first got on a plane and went to Iraq. He wanted his wife. He wanted his happy life back. He no longer cared if he was addicted to loving Gabi. He wanted to be addicted to loving her and he wanted her to feel the same way about him.

"Hey, Eric, you've sort of gotten lost in the last couple of months."

Eric looked into Jamilla's eyes. "Hi," he said.

"Want to dance?" she asked.

"Nope."

"Come on, Eric, you're a great dancer."

"Thanks, but no."

"Why not?"

Air filled his lungs and left in one gigantic hiss. "I have a wife, Jamilla."

She came back with, "I heard you two were separated."

"We are, but it doesn't stop the fact I still have a wife." It was time. He'd allowed this woman to hurt Gabi almost as much as he had. That would be rectified tonight.

"It didn't work, Jamilla, that's not the reason we separated."

"What are you talking about?"

Eric watched the way Jamilla's eyes darted about. He'd always known she'd planted the panties and condom in his car. "The panties and the condom. Gabrielle laughed about it. She thought you were so obvious...so cheap," he said and smiled, wanting the woman to feel a tiny bit of the humiliation she'd heaped on his wife.

"It was a joke," Jamilla said defensively.

"Good," Eric answered, "that's what we thought."

"Do you want to dance?" Jamilla asked again. "That last time, I thought we were good together, that we could be very good together." Her eyes narrowed and she rolled her booty in a suggestive manner, leaving nothing to the imagination.

Still Eric wanted to make her say it. "Are you asking me to have sex with you?"

"Dang, Eric, you don't have to be so cold, but yeah, I want you to make love to me."

"I can't make love to you if I don't love you."

"Well then, let's have sex. Let's bang some boots, tear the house down. You rock my world and I'll rock yours."

"Do you really think I'd sleep with you?" Eric asked softly. "You can't rock my world, no matter what you do. Only Gabi can rock my world."

Eric saw the instant Jamilla became angry. She did the neck roll thing and stood back as though she were going to swing on him.

"Well, that wasn't the feeling I got when you were all up on me in the club that last time."

"That last time I'd been drinking. Maybe I had considered having sex with you for a minute or two, but it would have been only that, sex. I didn't have feelings for you then and I don't now. I've never wanted but one woman, Jamilla, and that's Gabi."

"But she's divorcing your ass."

"And you think that stops me from wanting her?" He laughed. "Even if the divorce goes through it won't stop me wanting or loving her. And it won't change the fact that if you strip butt naked and flipped it up in my face that I wouldn't take it. You're nasty for being my wife's friend and trying to sleep with me. And I'm nasty for having encouraged you."

Eric turned back to the bar and lifted his Coke to his lips. He saw Tracie sitting at a table over from them. He hadn't noticed her before but now he saw her smile. He gave a semi nod of recognition. At least Gabi didn't have to worry that Tracie was also trying to knife her in the back.

Suddenly with clarity he hadn't had in almost a year Eric knew without a doubt what he had to do. He had to talk to Gabrielle, something that was proving harder and harder to do. She'd changed the locks and her cell number. She didn't want to talk to him since he'd told her he was thinking of asking to be sent back to the war. Still, he had a feeling she'd want to hear what he had to say.

Chapter Twenty-One

Gabi," Eric said as they both headed for the courtroom with their lawyers. "Can we talk?"

She stopped for a moment and he could feel her struggling with the answer. Her voice came out in breathy little wisps. She was trying hard not to cry, that he could tell because he was having the same problem.

"Can we talk, Gabrielle?"

"When this is over, Eric, we can talk, not now. It's not going to do any good. You're not going to change, and there is nothing for us to talk about. But after the divorce maybe we can try to be friends. I'd like that."

She walked away leaving a hole in the center of his chest. Eric didn't want to be just her friend. He wanted to be her husband.

"Come on," his attorney urged. "We have to go in now." Eric walked woodenly through the heavy doors, glanced at Gabi and her attorney, then took a seat alongside his own attorney. This was killing him. He couldn't let this happen but Gabi was ignoring him, not giving him a chance to talk.

"Gabi," he called out to her. She glanced at him, then turned away.

Maybe he would have to let this happen; he didn't seem to have a choice. He listened as the attorneys got up and spoke their piece. All the time Eric felt a tightening in his chest. Then magically the pressure of a hand on his spine pushed him forward. "*Have faith*," the now familiar voice whispered.

"I killed a man, Gabi." All eyes snapped on him but Eric was focusing only on Gabrielle. "In Iraq, there was a truck heading for us. We ordered the driver to stop, he didn't." Eric stood. "I stopped him. I killed him." Gabi's gaze was fastened on his.

"He didn't have explosives, the brakes had failed on his truck. I killed an unarmed civilian because he had a bad truck and I got a medal for it." A tremor ripped through Eric.

"Four months later another truck came, identical situation, only this truck was going faster. Again the driver wouldn't stop. This time I hesitated." He snapped his fingers. "Only a tenth of a second but hesitation is hesitation." He noticed that the courtroom had become quiet. Not even the judge was trying to stop him.

"I heard your voice in my head telling me to be careful. I heard another voice telling me to have faith. Right before the truck came barreling toward us I had been thinking of you, how much I loved you, how much I wanted to come home to you. When I spotted the truck and heard your voice, your warning, I knew this truck was the real deal. A split second hesitation, then I fired. I killed the driver. This truck had explosives." Eric took in several deep breaths before continuing. "It exploded, killing several of my men. Something saved me, and I've felt guilty about it ever since, Gabi. I've wondered if my hesitation cost my men their lives, if my thinking of you did it.

"I love you so much. I did then and I do now. I'm sorry that I didn't talk to you. I couldn't tell you all of this." He shook his head. "You asked if I were trying to die. Maybe so. I'm not afraid of dying; I'm afraid of living without you in my life."

He was walking toward his wife when he saw the tears streaming down her cheeks. The look in her eyes nearly stopped his heart. She hadn't stopped loving him. "Can we talk, Gabrielle? We're going to have a baby."

"You sure picked a fine time to want to talk," Gabi answered.

Her knees were weak. She'd heard every word Eric had said and understood the meaning behind them. This was the first time he'd said, 'We're having a baby.' She didn't know if it meant he believed her, but she knew it meant he was willing to try.

Her poor husband was saddled with so much guilt. She wondered if he'd told his therapist. Gabi wanted to thank the person, whoever it was, who'd gotten Eric to open up. She tilted her head a bit, wondering if the voice would tell her also to have faith. It wasn't necessary. This time she'd use love.

"Well, Gabi, can we talk? Is it too late?"

"It's never too late," Gabi said, rounding the end of the table. He lifted her into the air so quickly that it took her breath away. Then he sat her down and his hands circled her face and held it between his strong brown hands. "Baby, I love you," he said softly. His lips landed lightly on hers and her eyes closed. She heard clapping and looked behind her at her attorney. She was clapping, tears in her eyes. "Thanks," Gabrielle whispered, walking with Eric out of the courtroom.

"You sure know how to make a stand on a grand scale, don't you?" Gabi smiled through her tears.

"I'm a marine, Gabi. When we do something, we do it big and we do it right." He pulled her tighter. "Can I come home?"

"Yes, but we're going to talk."

"And then make love." Eric nuzzled her neck with his lips, his nose, dismissing the people staring at them with disapproving looks in the hall of the courtroom and in the elevator.

Gabi's head leaned back into his kisses of its own accord. "Did you mean what you said, that we're having a baby?"

"Yes," Eric whispered into her ear, feathering the hair at the nape of her neck, sending sweet shivers through her.

"We're going to talk a long time, Eric, and I'm going to ask a lot of questions, mainly why you wouldn't talk to me. I want to know why you've been pushing me away. Even with what you've said it's not enough of a reason for us to be here at this point." She felt his arms slipping away. "When we get home," she said, bringing his arms back around her.

Another Man's Baby

Once home Gabi threw all of the pillows from the sofa onto the floor. Positioning herself for comfort she looked up at Eric grinning down at her. "Come on," she said, "this is going to take a long time."

"I've told you everything," Eric said, dropping down beside her.

"No, baby, I know better than that. What you told me was the tip of it. Why did you treat me the way you did for the past year?" He looked away. "This isn't going to work if you don't say it, Eric."

"I don't want you to know."

"That much is obvious." Gabi reached her hand over to touch his cheeks. "Tell me, baby. What else do we have to lose?"

Eric worried his lips with his tongue, then slid his teeth over them, trying to find a way to tell her what he had to say without hurting her more. He sighed, then stared at her, trying to pull enough air into his lungs to tell the horrible truth. "I blamed you."

Gabi scooted back, trying to get away from him, her eyes wide in surprise. "You blamed me!" She barely stopped the words 'that's crazy' from coming from her lips.

"I know it's crazy," Eric said softly, trying his best not to make eye contact with her.

"Did you feel that way when you first came home?" Gabi couldn't help asking.

"No, when I first came home I didn't want to soil you." He stopped and grinned. "Well, at least after that first month." He shook his head. "I know, baby, I know. You don't have to say it or look at me like that. I knew it didn't make a damn bit of sense but it was the way I was feeling. Actually it was more of my blaming the hold you have on me, the way you own my very soul that had me pissed off. I felt like such a punk—a punk who'd put his men at risk."

Eric reached for her hand and rubbed her hands between his, daring now to look at her. "I couldn't wait to get home. I couldn't wait to see you, to touch you, to make love to you." He kissed her gently on the forehead. "I loved you so damn much that it was a physical ache in my gut not to be home with you. The last tour was the hardest for me to get through. I don't know why, just that it was."

"Eric, you're trying to avoid the hardest part of this. I heard what you said in the courtroom. You said something saved you."

He fidgeted, wondering if she'd want to have him locked up. It was crazy, just like the voice he'd been hearing. When he didn't answer Gabi immediately, he saw her wall going back up. There was no room for compromise. He had to tell his wife all of it if he wanted to keep her. He took in a breath and blew it out.

"A hand, Gabi, there was a hand on my spine. I felt it. It shoved me out of the way of the blast. I thought I was dying. I heard your voice. I felt your lips underneath mine. I could smell you, baby, I swear I could. That's when I knew for sure I had to be dying, but I wasn't."

"Maybe one of your men pushed you out of the way."

"No one pushed me. I asked, and they said no one was behind me, but there was a hand, Gabi. I didn't imagine it."

"I believe you." Gabi took a deep breath and smiled, shaking her head. "I wish you had told me this sooner, like when it first happened. I believe you."

Eric stopped stroking his wife and stared at her, trying to determine if she were merely placating him. He shivered. "Are you serious?"

"Yes."

"Why? How could you believe this?"

"I knew when it happened about four or five months before you came home."

Gabi watched Eric's eyes lift. "I saw it happen. I thought at first I was just dreaming, but I saw it all. I woke up and still I saw it."

Tears formed in Gabi's eyes and she clutched Eric's hands in hers. "I begged God to save you, to put out His hand and spare you. I thought you were going to die. I wrapped my arms around you in my mind. I kissed you and I whispered to you and begged my guardian angel to take care of you. At first I felt in my heart that you were dead."

A shudder began in Gabrielle and she lost her voice. "Baby, I thought you were dead and all I wanted was to die myself. Then this calm, this peace flooded my body and I knew you were alive. Eric, I could feel your lips on mine also. You were kissing me back. Then this tremendous feeling of stillness came over me and I heard a voice whispering to me to have faith. I knew for sure you were not going to die. Two days later you called me and we both started to cry."

"I didn't cry."

"We both started to cry, I remember that. You told me you wanted to hear my voice." Gabi's voice broke and she moved even closer to Eric as her arms opened and her husband kissed each hand before taking her in his arms. "I didn't know you'd heard me, or that you'd felt me."

"I did and I told you to stop, or you were going to get me and my men killed." Eric laughed. "I can close my eyes and still feel you there in Iraq with me."

"Eric?"

"I couldn't figure out why I'd been spared." He looked at her in wonder. "You were praying for me, you saw it?"

"Yes."

"Why not the others? Why didn't you pray for all of us?"

She just looked at him. It sounded as if he were now blaming her for praying. "Eric, I've been praying every day for the troops. I'm still praying. I didn't stop, not even then. When I saw the truck I asked my guardian angel to protect you. It was a reflex. Are you going to blame me for not having time to phrase it better?" She pulled away, some of his residual guilt filling her. "I'm so sorry about what happened. If I could go back and redo it, I would pray a different prayer."

For a moment they looked at each other, neither speaking. Eric had not meant to make Gabi feel bad about praying for his safety. That was selfish of him. It was also one of the reasons he'd not wanted to unburden himself in the first place. He smiled finally. "I always knew our love was powerful. I never knew just how much." At first Gabi didn't respond, but then she smiled.

"I always knew, Eric," Gabi whispered.

"I should have known too, baby."

"Is that why you blamed me? But you never knew of my prayer until now." She blinked. "What's the real reason?"

He groaned. "It was my loving you that was the problem. All I could think about was you, coming home to you. I wanted to be able to fall asleep every night with you in my arms. After what happened, I doubted myself, doubted if I'd done the best for my men. A tenth of a second, Gabi, I swear that's all it was."

"Do you think it was your thinking about me or the...the...you know, the other incident." She stopped as Eric flinched.

He closed his eyes and pulled her close. A tremor began in his body and he couldn't stop it. "I know that it was considered justified, but I keep seeing it over and over. I keep wondering about the guy's family, his kids, his parents, his wife. Maybe the guy had a wife he loved as much as I love you. Maybe he wanted to return home to her as badly as I did to you. What right did I have to come home alive when he didn't? What right did I have to come home alive and just continue life the same as before when some of my men didn't make it back, when some of my friends didn't?"

Sobs raced through Eric and he tried to stop them, tried to mentally order them to return to the deep recesses from which they'd come. Damn it, he was a marine.

Buy it was as though a damn had broken. He sobbed until there was nothing left. Eric was holding onto Gabi so tightly that he knew he had to be hurting her. But he couldn't let her go. She was his lifeline and he'd almost lost her. He unburdened all the horrors that he'd seen and done, telling her finally of the babies, holding her so tightly in his arms that she moaned in pain.

"Baby, Eric, I'm so sorry you had to go through that, that I've added to your pain by demanding you tell me. I didn't know. I'd read some of the stories in the papers but...to have seen it. I can understand why you didn't want me to get pregnant," she said softly.

"But I had wanted babies with you, I was dreaming of our having babies when the truck came."

"It makes sense, Eric, even blaming yourself and blaming me. I can see why you hesitated about our starting a family."

Eric pulled back to gaze into Gabi's eyes in disbelief. She understood. He couldn't believe it. Every horror that he'd seen came to his mind and he told his wife everything, leaving nothing out, not trying to make the things he'd done better or worse, just telling her what had happened. And all the time he stared into her eyes and found no condemnation, just love and understanding. "I'm sorry I unloaded all of this on you."

"And I'm sorry you didn't do it sooner. I was a little jealous that you were talking to your father and the therapist and not me…but now…now I'm so glad you had someone to talk to."

"I didn't." Eric hesitated. "I never really talked to my father about the things that happened. Some he guessed because of having been in Vietnam. We dealt with some of the same things. We never had long conversations about any of it. But I never told the therapist. I wouldn't do that to you. I wouldn't give someone else what I wasn't giving you." He kissed her shoulders repeatedly. "I didn't want to give you this horror, but I see your shoulders are big enough. I wish I had told you sooner."

"So do I, baby, so do I. We've always worked well as a team. You should have never had to shoulder this pain alone." She closed her eyes tightly. "I feel such sorrow for you, the troops and the Iraqi people. I can't begin to imagine the pain involved in sacrificing an innocent baby." Her hand slid down to her abdomen in a protective manner and tears slid down her cheeks. "I can't…the grief the parents must have felt. I can't begin to tell you that I understand what you went through, but it makes me more grateful than ever that you came home to me, that God saw fit to save you for some greater purpose."

"Why, Gabi? I don't pray. I don't even know if I believe. Why me? Even you, Gabi, you don't go to church and you're not always on your knees. Why us, what's so special about us? It can't just be our love, baby."

"I don't care what it is," Gabi answered, smoothing her hand over his bald head. "I'm just thankful you came back alive." Her own sobs hitched in her throat. "When you were…when I thought you were cheating, when I found the panties and the condom I wished…." She licked her lips.

"Yeah, you don't have to say it. I wished it too. I wished I had died there when you put me out. I don't know how the hell I could have hurt you like that."

Gabi was once again pulling away and Eric knew why. He held her, shaking his head. "Gabi, that wasn't a confession, that's not what I meant. I didn't sleep with Jamilla. I promise you I didn't. And it was Jamilla's panties. I saw her a couple of nights ago at the club. She wanted to take up where she thought we left off," he said quietly. "I got her to admit the panties were hers, that she'd put them in the car. She said it was a joke."

"A joke," Gabi muttered between clenched teeth. "Destroying our marriage was a joke to her?" She pulled back from Eric with renewed anger for the incident in her eyes.

"We're talking, baby. Remember, this is the forgiving part. Will you forgive me for hurting you?"

A sigh fell from Gabi's lips. "If you can give me a good reason. I don't understand, even with the guilt. I don't understand why you would risk us. I don't know why you would start chasing other women. I don't get it." Her shoulders came up. "It's going to be really hard for us to trust each other again." She watched as his eyes fell to her abdomen. "Did you really mean our 'baby'?"

"Yeah, the baby is ours." He hesitated. "Can you accept that from me, for now, without asking for more?"

"Meaning can I accept that even though you don't believe it's yours, can I accept that you're willing to claim it?"

Eric looked down. "Yes, that's what I mean."

"Why do you think the voice keeps whispering to both of us to have faith?" Gabi stared at her husband and smiled slightly. He didn't answer and she was aware she was pushing him to believe more than he could at the moment. She would take what he was offering. After all, Gabi didn't have a doubt in the world that she would be able to prove the baby was Eric's. "Okay. I can handle that for now. But, Eric, you still didn't answer. Why all the whoring around?"

Eric stared at her, taken aback. Okay, he wanted back in his wife's good graces. Matter of fact, he wanted to ensure she remained his wife. He'd take whatever she was dishing out.

"Whoring around is a bit strong, but I knew what I was doing, so I won't fight you over your word choice." He pulled her close. "I don't know, baby. I have no idea what got into me. It was like I was playing this role, trying so hard to find the right fit. Nothing was working for me. I hated having to see troops leave, to give them a pep talk. And the enlistments center…" He shuddered. "You have no idea of the hellish job that is. There are millions of Americans that support the war. And they all support the troops, but when you go to their homes and ask to take their sons and daughters…" Eric sawed his lips with his teeth and shook his head.

"For over a year now I've been so damn conflicted and afraid to say so. To say so means I'm unpatriotic or a coward." He swallowed. "But it's getting harder and harder to see more Americans go off to fight. I'm having a hard time believing in the rightness of this war. I know people on all sides die. I know that, Gabi, but I also know the Iraqi people have lost many innocent lives. Even the ones that weren't innocent, they had families."

He pulled her even closer, wanting to crawl into her skin if he could. "I killed a man, Gabi, an innocent man and nothing anyone says can make that right in my book."

"You didn't know."

"No, I didn't know, but it doesn't do a damn thing for the hurt in my belly. It doesn't make it go away."

Gabi was feeling some of the agony her husband had gone through. She wanted to help him. She touched his heart with the tip of her finger. "Did you ask for forgiveness?"

"You mean him? Did I ask the man I killed for forgiveness?" Truly, Gabi had no idea what she was saying. Eric was trying to be patient with her. "How was I going to ask a man I killed to forgive me?"

He frowned at her. "Did you think I was going to go and ask his family? Damn, baby, that scene played out as duty. You dig? I gave an order, he disobeyed. It was duty, baby, I'm a soldier."

"If that's true, why are you still carrying the guilt?"

"Because underneath the soldier was a man with frailties and weaknesses. I can't forget."

"You don't have to forget, but you can be forgiven."

"Gabi."

"Will you forgive me for hurting you, for using Reggie to make you crazy, for pushing you over the edge? I didn't know what you were dealing with. Will you forgive me for giving tit for tat?"

"I know what you're doing, Gabi. It's not that easy for me to be forgiven for what I did."

"But it's the first step." She clasped Eric's hand. "Ask," she said.

"I can't."

"You don't have to do it out loud, but do it, baby." She held his gaze. "Do it for me, for us. Do it so we can have a fresh start and this won't come between us again."

Eric groaned and let out a breath. He closed his eyes and held Gabi in his arms as the words 'please forgive me' raced through his mind. He didn't direct the words toward anyone, just allowed them to be thought. "I don't feel any different," he said when he opened his eyes.

"Forgiveness doesn't happen that quickly. It takes wanting it." Gabi shook her head. "It takes thinking you deserve it, it takes lots of hard work. Baby, you did a heck of a lot more good over there than you did bad. Just you remember that. You went there to fight for freedom for the Iraqi people. It doesn't matter if you no longer believe that. When you went, you believed it. Even with the kids you're ordered to recruit, you can't tell me that you're not proud to be in the military. You're not trying to get these kids to give up their lives, you're trying to get them to share in your passion, your commitment. You believed once in what you were doing and if you don't believe now that's okay."

"But that makes me a hypocrite."

"It makes you human."

"But look at you, baby. You believed in something and you took a stand. When you didn't fill out those papers for that patient's abortion you weren't a hypocrite, you stood by the power of your conviction."

"I also am not a soldier. No one can order me to do something. Besides, there are other people in my office that see it as their job. Eric, if you and I were divorced and I was raising our baby alone," she said, emphasizing the our, "who knows what I would do if I were told to. If it meant I couldn't feed our child, who knows? No one ever knows what they can or can't do. We can't say until it comes to us. Just like the war, Eric, we can say we support it until we have to give up our babies. Life is hard. Like that old saying, 'Don't judge until you've walked a mile in another man's moccasins.'" He grinned and so did she. "Even if you didn't tell her about the things that happened in Iraq, that therapist really got you to open up."

"It wasn't the therapist." Eric gazed at his wife, looking at her lips, wondering when she would think they'd talked enough, wanting badly to kiss her, to suckle her breasts, to bury his head between her thighs, to plunge his fast growing erection into her wet heat.

Startled, Gabi's mouth opened with a small gasp. "No? Then who?"

"You, baby. I couldn't just let you walk out of my life without trying everything. You wanted me to tell you what had happened, and I had to try. I worried that you might hate me for it, but still I had to try."

"Hate you, baby? I want to kiss you and every other soldier who protects our country. You're all true heroes in my book."

He was still staring at her lips. But he knew there was so much more they needed to say, so much more Gabi needed to hear.

"Eric, I didn't sleep with Reggie."

Eric sucked in a breath, his eyes lowering as he pulled his lip between his teeth and sawed it gently back and forth.

"I didn't sleep with anyone, baby, but I'm not going to ask you to go on blind faith. This one will be an easy one to prove." Gabi held his gaze. "In four months I can prove that to you."

"I'm not asking for proof, not any more."

"But I'm going give it to you. This is not going to be between us. This won't be one of the things you will have to forgive me for."

He played with his hands. "What about Jamilla? Do you believe me? Are you willing to forgive me?"

"If I weren't I wouldn't be sitting here with you right now."

"You don't have to worry about Tracie though. She was at the club, she saw me turn Jamilla down. She smiled her approval at me. What the hell was I thinking?" Eric covered his head with his hands.

"Yeah, what were you thinking?" Gabi hit him several times over the head, then moved in closer and gave in to the look in her husband's eyes. Why shouldn't she? She wanted to kiss him also. They would be alright. It would take time but thank God their marriage would survive.

Chapter Twenty-Two

Eric lay next to Gabi in their big bed. She'd finally drifted off to sleep but he was unable to. He was running everything through his mind, all the confessions, all the doubts, everything. His body still burned from their passion. They'd made love nice and slow, taking the time to get lost in each other the way they always had, not going for the release but the soul connection, and they'd found it.

Now Eric lay just looking at Gabi and the round mound in the center of her body. An electrical energy emanated from Gabi and touched him. He put out his hand, feeling it and was awed by the power.

"Have faith."

"I'm learning," Eric whispered.

"The baby is yours."

Yes, Eric thought, the baby would be his. Regardless of the biological father, the baby would be his.

"You don't understand, Eric. The seed is yours. Have faith."

Just like that, the voice was gone as well as most of the strange, powerful energy. Eric stared around the darkened room. This was getting to be a bit spooky. He wasn't insane, had never been prone to imagine things. He smiled. It was the first time the voice had called him by name. It was also the first time the voice had actually had a conversation with him telling him more than to have faith.

Eric had wondered for over a year who the voice belonged to. Now he knew. It had to be Gabrielle's guardian angel. For a moment he wondered if hearing the voice just then had been wishful thinking. What the voice had said was impossible. He was still sterile.

Eric kissed Gabi's forehead, then bent lower and planted a kiss on her abdomen. The electrical energy returned and appeared to be centered right there in Gabi's womb. In that energy there was a knowing.

It started slowly. Something worked its way from the soles of his feet, and inch by inch traveled through his body and rested in the crown of his head before it made the downward journey. Eric blinked, a smile breaking out on his face. In that instant he felt a connection to the fetus in his wife's womb. His eyelids fluttered and a pounding began in his chest, rapid and prolonged.

Damn. This was his baby. He wasn't just saying the words anymore for Gabi's benefit. He didn't know how, but it was his. Eric spooned his body around Gabi and laid his hand gently on her abdomen as the energy radiated through his palm and throughout his body. "You're mine," he whispered as he fell asleep.

Three months later Eric made his decision: He was leaving the military. He had a teaching degree and he'd try to influence the minds of children for better. He looked at Gabi's swollen belly. There had to be a better way and he had to have something more to give to his son or daughter.

"Why are you looking at me like that?"

Eric grinned at Gabi. "It's been so long in coming I never thought it would ever happened but today I woke up and for the first time I didn't feel guilty. I didn't dream last night about Iraq."

"Did you dream?"

"Yeah, about you and our baby, about all the other kids we'll have." He watched Gabi's face, saw the tears and shook his head at her. "Don't cry, baby, not this time, not about this."

"Am I hearing you right?" Gabrielle asked, her voice almost a whisper, the hope shining from her voice.

"Hell, yes. I should have known all along. You know something, Gabi," he said, going to her, lifting her and seating her on his lap. "I kept thinking the words 'have faith' meant something else. I didn't know what. But I think I finally have a glimmer of the meaning."

He put his forehead to hers. "This is our baby, Gabi. I know that. I don't mean that it's a baby I'm laying claim to because it's yours. I know that it's mine, my flesh and blood.

"And I know we're going to have more. It's not that I'm being macho, thinking that I wasn't shooting blanks. I wasn't. I've thought about it. I know the moment we made that baby. I felt it, there was something different in our lovemaking."

Eric tapped Gabi's forehead. "Aside from your calling out another man's name there was more. There was a life forming. I felt this electrical energy leave my body and enter yours. I didn't know it was a baby at the time but I do now. And your guardian angel only confirmed it for me."

"What about all the reports?"

"I don't have the answer to that, but they're wrong. I know that as surely as I know I love you."

"You believe me."

"Yeah, baby, I believe you."

Gabi closed her eyes and leaned into her husband's chest. He'd just given her the second greatest gift of their married life, his belief in her in spite of everything he'd been told. This was what she had been waiting for, this moment. They were back. Nothing else mattered.

The first pain hit low in her back and Gabi moaned. Since she was already a week overdue, it didn't take much figuring to know this was the real deal. Still, first babies took a long time. "Umm," she moaned as another pain hit her and she bent over.

"Is it time?" Eric was at her side before the pain left.

She squeezed his hand as slight fear invaded her and she pushed it away. She knew this baby was her husband's. She didn't care what any tests said. But how would she dispute DNA? What if it still said the baby wasn't Eric's? Sure, he believed now, but would he believe then?

One pain came rapidly after another and Gabi knew it was time to go. This baby was rushing to be born, to put an end to the questions.

"I'm going to call my parents," Eric said, reaching for the phone. "Their grandchild is about to be born and I don't want them to miss it."

"Eric, are you sure they'll want to come?"

"You're about to give birth to our first child, their grandchild." He kissed her as another pain hit and she clenched her teeth in pain. "I want my entire family here...but if you don't want them—"

"Call your parents," Gabi mumbled, squeezing his hand.

This was it. Eric paced outside the room waiting for his parents. What if it isn't? No, damn it. He pushed the voice away. This is my baby. I do have faith; this is my son. He saw his parents coming and rushed up to them. "The nurse will show you where to scrub up and you can come in. Gabi wants the entire family there. It's your first grandchild."

Ongela and Terry Jackson glanced at each other and Eric shook his head. "It's mine," he whispered softly. "This is your grandchild, your blood. I promise. Now come on and let's watch my son come into the world."

During labor Eric gave words of encouragement to Gabi, telling her how much he loved her, how much he loved their child. She wasn't screaming out as much now, just holding onto him, wanting to look at him it seemed, and he knew why. She was a bit scared but it didn't matter. Eric had no plans on getting a DNA test, or another damn test. He didn't need anyone to tell him this was his child.

"Eric?"

"Baby, don't even think it. This is my son," he whispered on her lips. "It's mine, Gabi. It's mine." He kissed her. He couldn't help grinning in spite of her pain. "I'm going to be a father, Gabi." Tears rolled down his cheeks. "I'm really going to be a father."

Eric glanced toward his parents. They were crying. He didn't know if they were crying because they thought he was deceiving himself or because they wanted a grandchild so baldly. Either way it didn't matter. The two most important people knew this baby was his, he and Gabi. Convincing anyone else wasn't necessary.

"Push," the doctor ordered.

And with a big push and a scream Gabi pushed his son out into the world.

A few minutes later the baby was placed in his arms. Eric could swear the baby was already smiling at him and holding on. Eric's heart filled to overflowing. And gratitude for all the powers that be flooded him. True, he hadn't been a big believer before, especially not in miracles, but this tiny, warm, brown body that he held in his arms was a miracle he and Gabi had created together.

"Let me see him," Gabi asked and he smiled and laid the baby on her chest. Eric watched as she stroked the baby with her fingers. When Gabi held out a hand for his, Eric's heart melted with love. If he thought he'd been whipped before, there was no hope for him now. He clasped Gabi's hand in one of his and with the other he stroked his son just as Gabi was doing. Their eyes met and they smiled. They were a family. This was the reason he'd been saved.

The muffled cries from across the room eventually registered. Eric looked at Gabi, then his parents, and lifted his son back into his arms, cradling him gently, holding his tiny head in the palm of his hand. He carried the baby to his parents and placed him in his grandmother's arms. Then he walked back to Gabi.

He bent to kiss Gabi lightly on the lips. Noticing her attention was averted, he glanced at her and saw the fear in her eyes as she watched his parents with their son. Eric straightened up slowly. He watched as his parents exchanged private glances.

"It doesn't matter what they think." He looked down at Gabi. "That's my son." Eric's breath was coming in shallow puffs. He couldn't believe his parents would be so insensitive to Gabi's feelings. He stood beside Gabi, staring across the room at his parents who looked down at the baby, then back at Eric. Shock was clearly written on their faces. If Eric had known that would be their reaction, he would have never invited them to witness the miracle of the birth of his son. He squeezed Gabi's fingers harder, trying to tell her with his touch that they didn't matter.

Eric couldn't believe it. His parents' reaction was getting worse instead of better. They were looking at him so strangely that he had to fight the unwanted doubt. He refused to allow them to sway his own knowing.

He heard a moan from Gabi and glared at his parents. "No," he shook his head at Gabi. "This is my son. I don't have to believe or have faith. I know it!"

Tears were welling up in Gabi's eyes. "Baby," Eric said, "you need to have faith in me. I'm not lying to you. This is our son. Ours, Gabi, yours and mine."

As soon as he could, Eric left the room, anger at his parents for hurting Gabi crushing him. He pointed his finger in their direction and motioned. He marched all the way to another wing before stopping.

"How could you have done that to her?" he asked. "You love her. How could you stand there and stare at my son with such disbelief in your eyes. That's my son," Eric said, wiping at the tear that had unexpectedly slipped down his cheek. "That's my son in there, and you just ripped Gabi's heart out."

"Son," his father laid a hand on his shoulder.

Eric took a step away from his father. "Dad, I can't believe you. It doesn't matter what the two of you think. I know he's my son. And just like you're the guardian of Mon's heart, I'm the guardian of Gabi's. I'm not going to let anyone hurt her again, not even me."

"Eric, stop glaring at us. We know it's your son." His father laughed and hugged him and his mother joined in.

Eric pulled away and looked at both of them in disbelief. He shook his head. "I saw you, saw the way you looked at the baby. Gabi saw it too."

"Yes, we were looking at him in disbelief because frankly, as much as I love Gabi, I didn't believe that cock and bull story she's been telling.

She told me out of her own mouth that she was going to make you hurt. We discussed it. I knew she planned on having an affair."

Ongela stopped at the look of pain on her son's face. "What could I have done to stop her, Eric? She's a woman and she'd been hurt by you. I just never expected she'd end up pregnant and then claim the baby was yours and have the nerve to stick to what had to be a lie."

Eric backed, away his eyes narrowing. "She's not lying," he snapped.

"I know that now," Ongela repeated. "Your dad and I both knew it the moment you put the baby in my arms. He opened his eyes and it took me back thirty years. It was your face I was looking at, yours. I've felt like this only twice in my life, once when you were born and a few minutes ago when you placed my grandson in my arms. That baby is yours, Eric. You don't need DNA or semen analysis or any other test to tell you that."

"I wasn't planning on it," Eric said quietly, awed that his parents believed, wondering if they were telling the truth.

"I have no idea how," Ongela began. "Are you sure you're sterile? Maybe the labs screwed up. What am I talking about, maybe? They had to have gotten the tests wrong. You should have them repeated."

"I took the test three times."

"Then maybe it's a miracle. I don't know, Son, but that baby is yours! I felt it, I saw it. He's yours, he's ours!" Ongela cried. "He's ours!"

Terry Jackson looked at his wife and son. "It's not a miracle. The miracle is that Eric and Gabi got through this mess. But that baby in there, his being yours, there is a logical explanation. I know there is. But like your mom, I saw it too. He's the spitting image of you. That little guy looked at me. Babies don't even open their eyes a few minutes after birth. But it was like he wanted there to be no doubt about who he was. There's something about this baby, some energy. I can't explain it but he's my grandson." Terry looked at his wife. "Our grandson."

Eric stood there trembling before his parents. "Are you serious, you're not just saying that?" He wanted to bawl like a baby, something his brand new son hadn't even done, but that's what Eric wanted.

"About something this important I'd never lie to you, Eric, not about this."

Eric held his father's gaze. He worked his mouth but no words came out.

Terry smiled. "Just like I know when you're lying, don't you know me well enough to know I would not lie to you about this?"

Eric held his parents' gazes for a long moment before he broke down. His father's arms came around him and then his mother's. This time Eric did not pull away; he held on to them and he cried and they joined in.

"I…I…I don't know how it happened. I don't care how it happened. I didn't want you thinking I was deluding myself. I know that's what you've been thinking, I know that, but I knew he was mine. Somehow the baby let me know it. I felt the connection one night while Gabi was sleeping. It was just me and my son, just the two of us, and I knew."

Eric held his parents tighter. "I believe her," he said, "I believe Gabi, not just about the baby. I believe she never cheated on me."

He lifted his head and stared directly into his mother's eyes. "Mom, I never cheated on Gabi. I came damn close but I never crossed that final line. And I found out how the condom and the panties got in the car."

"Gabi believes you?"

"Yes," Eric answered.

"Then none of the rest of it's important. Explaining those things your wife found in the car is a lot easier than the four of us knowing our flesh and blood. Doctors have been wrong before and they're wrong now." Ongela wrapped her arms around her son. "Thank you for making us grandparents."

A weight lifted off Eric's chest. His parents believed him. He'd have to go back and tell Gabi. He turned and smiled at his parents before running down the hall. "I have a son," he said and ran back down the hall to be with his wife and son. The guardian angel had been right all along. They'd needed faith.

Another Man's Baby

Six weeks after Baby Terry was born, the proof Gabi had insisted on came. They took the envelope and the baby to Calumet, to his parents, and as a family they opened it together. Each of them smiled when the result was read. The baby was clearly Eric's.

"You want to do another semen analysis?" Gabi asked.

"I don't need that, baby. It's only numbers on paper. I didn't need the DNA, that was you insisting on proof. We're not taking any more tests or anyone else's word for things this important to us."

"Not when we have this living proof in our arms." Ongela kissed the baby's pudgy cheeks. Then she flipped through page after page of baby pictures. In the six weeks since his birth, little Terry looked more and more like Eric every day.

Eric grinned at his parents, then at his wife. "As soon as we get home, maybe we'll start working on that granddaughter you want, Mom."

Gabi and Eric decided to put all their ghosts to rest. Her co-workers had asked repeatedly for her to bring the baby in. At first Gabi resisted. She'd learned a lesson about bragging about her happiness. Perhaps if she hadn't bragged about what a great husband Eric was Jamilla wouldn't have gone after him so relentlessly. Then again, who knew why she'd done it? Gabi had her family intact. She wasn't going to allow bitterness over Jamilla to ruin it. Besides, Eric wanted to introduce the world to his son, so she'd given in.

The moment they stepped inside the door of the clinic, Tracie ran up to them, and it wasn't to see the baby. Something big had happened.

"Jamilla was fired," Tracie spat out before they could ask. "Mrs. Rivers called that TV show, *Spouses Cheating*, and they had her husband followed. He was found in a hotel room with Jamilla. She was butt naked in bed. Mrs. Rivers got the motel to give her the key. She opened the door and went in and the cameras followed."

Gabi could feel Eric's eyes on her. She turned to face him. "I didn't have anything to do with it," she said, puzzled. "I promise I didn't, baby. When did all of this happen?" Gabi asked, bringing her attention back to Tracie.

"Last night, and don't worry, Eric, I did it," Tracie said. "I was sick and tired of watching Jamilla come on to the patients' husbands. When I saw what she'd done to you and Eric that was the last straw. You remember telling me about the show, Gabi?"

Gabi nodded her head in the affirmative.

"It just so happened that one day Mrs. Rivers came in wanting pills for depression. We got to talking and she confessed that she thought her husband was cheating. I told her to call the TV show and they would have a private detective follow him for free.

"When it came out, Mrs. Rivers came up here and told on Jamilla. She had the tape and everything. She was looking to kick Jamilla's behind. Doctor Tom held her back. He had to call the cops and everything. Then when things died down, he fired Jamilla right on the spot."

"Why didn't you call me?"

"You didn't need to hear any of that mess. You and Eric are finally getting your life back together. My husband and I didn't make it, but I've been rooting for the two of you."

Tracie finally stopped and peeked at the baby. "And now look what you have, a beautiful new baby." She held out her hands to hold Baby Terry.

Gabi looked at Eric. "I'm trying so hard not to gloat," she told him quietly. "Karma is a mother, and I don't want to have to pay for gloating."

Eight months had passed since Eric had promised to work on the granddaughter and Gabi was pregnant. It wasn't a fluke. He called his parents to tell them the news, but they were screaming at him, not allowing him to tell them his reason for calling.

"Turn the television on CNN," Ongela was screaming with a sense of urgency in her voice.

"But, Mom."

"Turn it on, Eric," she screamed. "Now! Hurry up, this is important. Call Gabi."

Eric hung up without even saying goodbye. He shook his head, changed the channel and yelled for Gabi. He held little Terry while Gabi sat beside him playing with the baby's fingers.

"Darnell Washington has been taken into custody. CNN has learned that for the past two years Mr. Washington, a laboratory technician whose specialty is checking for sterility using semen analysis, has been falsifying results. He has been falsely reporting on the tests ordered by doctors. It's not known how many men have been affected by this or what repercussions may follow, as Mr. Washington worked for the two largest medical laboratories in Illinois and specimens are sent there from all over the country. When questioned, Mr. Washington simply stated it was karma. He is sterile and his wife cheated on him and attempted to pass the baby off as his.

When asked if he felt possibly ruining the lives of others justified his actions, he reportedly said, 'Someone ruined mine.' We'll have more on this story as it unfolds."

Eric looked at Gabi and they laughed. This time there were no tears. The phone rang. When Eric answered, his father shouted, "I told you there was a reasonable explanation for all of this mess. I knew it. Oh, God, Eric, I'm so happy for you, Son. You have your proof."

"I had my proof months ago, Dad. By the way," Eric laughed, "tell Mom Gabi's pregnant. This time we think it's going to be a girl. Tell her to just have faith in that."

Laughing harder, Eric turned from the phone. He hugged Gabi to him as they held their son between them and they both laughed. Then Eric saw Gabi mouth 'Thank You,' as she looked skyward. He might not have been a big believer before but he was beginning to be. He laughed again and said, "Thank You," out loud, looking at Gabi and holding her hand. They'd made it in spite of the obstacles. And maybe it was someone's faith that had enabled it, he didn't know. He only knew he was truly fulfilled. Remembering his promise, Eric handed his son over to Gabi. He fell to his knees and thanked God for giving him the ability to give his wife babies. Then he added, "Most of all, God, thank you for the miracle of life itself."

"Amen," Gabi softly murmured.

Eric rose to his feet and hugged his wife and son to him as if he would never let them go.

About the Author

Award winning author, Dyanne Davis lives in a Chicago suburb with her husband Bill, and their son Bill Jr. She retired from nursing several years ago to pursue her lifelong dream of becoming a published author.

An avid reader, Dyanne began reading at the age of four. Her love of the written word turned into a desire to write. Her first novel, *The Color of Trouble*, was released July of 2003. The novel was received with high praise and several awards. Dyanne won an Emma for Favorite New Author of the year.

Her second novel, *The Wedding Gown* was released in February 2004 and has also received much praise. The book was chosen by Blackexpressions, a subsidiary of Doubleday Book Club as a monthly club pick. The book was an Emma finalist in March 2005 for Steamiest Romance, and for Book of the Year. *The Wedding Gown* was also a finalist for *Affaire de Coeur* Reader's poll.

Dyanne's *Misty Blue* is a sequel to *The Wedding Gown*. It received a four star rating from *Romantic Times*. In December of 06 *Let's Get It On* also received a four star rating from *Romantic Times*. In February 07 *Misty Blue* was a finalist for best cover and best romance sequel. Dyanne was a finalist for author of the year. *Misty Blue* garnered an Emma win for best book cover. *Two Sides to Every Story* and *Forever and a Day* were also released in 07.

Dyanne has been a presenter of numerous workshops. She has presented several workshops for teens at Chicago and Suburban high schools. She has a local cable show in her hometown to give writing tips to aspiring writers. She has guests from all genres to provide information and entertainment to the audience. She has hosted such notables as *USA Today* Best Selling erotica author, Robin Schone and acclaimed numerologist, and Rekki Master, Philip Clark. The queen of the vampire huntress series L.A. Banks was a guest on the show in July 07.

Dyanne's first book for Parker Publishing was *Forever and a Day*, a story about new love taking places while trying to survive Hurricane Katrina hit the shelf Feb. of 2007. Dyanne will for the first time be writing under a pseudonym for Parker Publishing. Her first vampire novel, *In the Beginning* was released June of 2007 under the name of F. D. Davis.

When not writing you can find Dyanne with a book in her hands, her greatest passion next to spending time with her husband Bill and son Bill Jr. Whenever possible she loves getting together with friends and family.

A member of Romance Writers of America, Dyanne is now serving her second term as Chapter President for Windy City. Dyanne loves to hear feedback from her readers. You can reach her at her website. www.dyannedavis.com She also has an on-line blog where readers can post questions and photos. http://dyannedavis.blogspot.com and http://www.authorsden.com/dyanne-davis You can find her blogging on http://www.Amazon.com She's also started a romance reader and writers on line book club with more than a dozen authors, and would love to have you join them. http://bookmarked.Target.com. The group is called, Romancing the Book. Any problems getting in, send Dyanne an email and she will send you a personal invitation.

Parker Publishing, LLC

*Celebrating Black
Love Life Literature*

Mail or fax orders to:

12523 Limonite Avenue
Suite #440-438
Mira Loma, CA 91752
(866) 205-7902
(951) 685-8036 fax

or order from our Web site:

www.parker-publishing.com
orders@parker-publishing.com

Ship to:

Name: _____

Address: _____

_____

_____

City: _____

State: _____ Zip:_____

Phone: _____

Qty	Title	Price	Total

Shipping and handling is $3.50, Priority Mail shipping is $6.00
FREE standard shipping for orders over $30   Add S&H

Alaska, Hawaii, and international orders – call for rates   CA residents add
7.75% sales tax

See Website for special discounts and promotions   Total

Payment methods: We accept Visa, MasterCard, Discovery, or money orders. NO PERSONAL CHECKS.

Payment Method: (circle one):   VISA   MC   DISC   Money Order

Name on Card: _____

Card Number: _____ Exp Date: _____

Billing Address: _____

_____

City: _____

State: _____ Zip:_____